Jackie LaRue would rather
her friends doing normal t
miles offshore, helping her
Coast Guard light station into an adventure bed and
breakfast. A mysterious legend has resurfaced about the
light station, prompting a local crime boss into action. Using
their powerful mob influence, they recruit a person from
Jackie's past to use any means necessary to undermine the
restoration and get the property. As she and her
grandfather continue to renovate the structure, Jackie
learns firsthand that the legend is real. An improbable
underwater encounter leads to information that her family
is not the only one in the fight against those trying to steal
the property, and that forces will soon clash on the
structure. She must either give in to youth and innocence
or grow up quickly and join the all-out struggle to save
the light station and her family.

Praise for Sandy Harris' new novel East of Nowhere

"A captivating family saga set on the North Carolina coast
with more than enough twists and turns to keep you up
late reading until the end."—*AG Riddle, author of The
Atlantis Gene and The Origin Mystery trilogy*

"Sandy Harris has a keen eye for detail -- for setting,
pacing, characters, and action. EAST OF NOWHERE is a
Southern thriller that rarely slows down, and keeps readers
engaged and wanting more."—*Johnny D. Boggs, award
winning author*

"Filled with vivid, exhilarating descriptions of the world of
the sea, *East of Nowhere* captures the love of a teenage
girl for her grandfather and the dangers they encounter
turning a light station in the middle of the ocean into an
adventure bed and breakfast. Treacherous enemies, looming
death, courage, and heroism all combine in this
unforgettable novel."—*Vicki Salloum, Author of Waiting
For You At Midnight*

Commander Thompson turned, facing the spring-loaded target holders installed on the rusty old Coast Guard light station, and fired his Colt Model 1911 .45 pistol. The paper rippled as a large hole appeared just inches from the center X. At the pistol's report, Lieutenant Brooks stepped on the second button, and the second target creaked upward. It squealed like fingernails across a chalkboard and ground to a stop, resting at a forty-five degree angle. The men shuddered, and Thompson cursed under his breath. Brooks, trying not to look worried, pressed the button again, then again, but nothing happened. Ensigns Rogers and Corbin, without being told, both ran to the target frame and pulled and snatched, trying to loosen the rust. It took a couple of minutes, but someone finally produced a hammer and a can of WD-40, and Rogers sprayed oil and wailed on the bolted hinge at the deck while Corbin heaved and pulled. Three big swings had it free, and the metal supports sheared rusty flakes of metal as the target mechanically jerked upright.

The Commander, who had been reprimanding one of the men for not having his shirt tail tucked neatly, heard the target move. He turned, raised his Colt, and just as Lieutenant Brooks yelled no, the big-bored pistol bucked in his hand. Thompson had not seen the two men behind the target frame still gathering their tools, and the heavy bullet tore through the paper target just under the bullseye, then straight through Ensign Corbin's neck. Blood sprayed, as the man staggered backwards, mouth unhinged, gurgling, and before Rogers could catch him, toppled over the rail into the churning sea below.

EAST OF NOWHERE

Sandy Harris

Moonshine Cove Publishing, LLC
Abbeville, South Carolina U.S.A.
First Moonshine Cove edition April 2020

This book is a work of fiction. Names, characters, places and incidents are products of the author's imagination or are used fictitiously. Any resemblance to actual events, locales or persons, living or dead, is entirely coincidental.

ISBN: 978-1-945181-1801
Library of Congress PCN: 202004744
© Copyright 2020 by Sandy Harris

Cover images courtesy of Mr. Sam Blount, Jr., cover and interior design by Moonshine Cove staff

About the Author

Sandy Harris grew up on a farm in eastern North Carolina. There, he spent untold hours in a boat, in the woods, or in the field, cultivating a deep love for all aspects of the great outdoors. After receiving degrees in Wildlife Biology from NC State, and Forestry from Auburn University, he has spent time as a farmer, Sunday School teacher, biologist, forester, environmental scientist, and freelance writer.

Sandy has authored numerous outdoor magazine articles with topics ranging from wildlife management techniques to 'how-to' pieces about making and hunting with Native American style bows and arrows. He enjoys all genres, but has always had a soft spot in his heart for a good mystery. Sandy's first novel, *At First Light,* intertwines his love for the natural world with those gritty crime mystery television series he grew up watching as a kid. His second novel, *East of Nowhere,* still holds a hint of mystery, but captivates young and old alike, with a tale of a young teen navigating her way through an adventure of a lifetime.

Sandy resides in Wetumpka, AL with his wife, Kristy, and two sons, Ethan and Eli.

https://sandyharrisauthor.com

EAST OF NOWHERE

July 12, 1982

Lieutenant Commander Edwin Thompson strolled across the flat roof of the Frying Pan Shoals Light Station. He didn't have to see the gray waves below to know they were still big and still bullying the four main pilings that held the structure seventy feet above the sea. The steel flexed almost constantly (it was only dead still when the sea was like glass) but the storm that just passed had upped the ante . . . it had actually scared him. The metal spoke to everyone a little differently, but there was no mistaking what it was saying to anyone who was listening now. The howls, creaks, and moans escaping from the rivets and bolts holding it all together made his skin crawl.

A cigarette appeared in his hand. Damp from humidity, it somehow still lit, and through a plume of smoke, the Commander's hawk-like eyes scanned the endless eastern horizon. He longed for something to be out there. A passing battleship, a breaching submarine, a cargo freighter, even a worn-out fishing trawler would do, but every day it was the same. Nothing was out there except the sea. The sky was the only thing that seemed to change, and this morning it didn't disappoint. Light lavenders and teasing pinks slowly gave way to a deep blood red close to the water. However brilliant, the colors were all partly masked by scattered, dark, menacing clouds that gave the horizon a hint of the macabre. While he gazed across the ocean, a silver streak of lightning surged from the dark cloud bank. The metal seemed to tingle through his boots, and long seconds passed before a slow roll of thunder fought its way across the miles.

Stepping over a shallow pool of rainwater, he glanced at his watch. Five-oh-one. "Humph," he grunted and reluctantly sipped the steaming black coffee. There might have been nothing out on the water to look at, but lowering the cup, he easily spotted an incorrectly pressed pleat on the sleeve of his uniform shirt. He muttered something about personally seeing to it that Ensign Floyd, the worst Coastie he'd seen in twenty years, understood the proper regulations and procedure for pressing duty attire. Thompson had only been in command for two months, but the middle-aged hardliner had made an instant impression. Regrettably, there wasn't much to work with, but he'd still made great strides, whipping his junior officer and the ten enlisted men into far better shape than even he'd expected. He had said proudly at his first staff meeting that before his time there as Commander was done, he'd have everyone ready for full Naval battle, should the Navy have the need. He was making good on that promise.

Despite the progress, the men all hated him, and he knew it. Thompson assumed correctly that his predecessor had been lax, allowing privileges that were not by the book. Snap inspections uncovered fishing rods leaning in every corner and nudie magazines in plain sight. He understood the temptation to be a nice guy, but being a nice guy wasn't what he was there for. Twenty years prior, while the ensign insignia graced his own uniform, he'd pulled every kind of crap-duty imaginable—and it was performed without so much as a whimper. It was just how things were done. Although he'd never been assigned to an offshore light station, regulations were still regulations, and orders were still orders. If no one else did, Thompson understood the proprieties must be followed . . . to the 'T.'

The Commander's graying hair fluttered in a gust. He wiped the salty mist from his eyes and glanced at his watch again. Five-oh-four. A warm rage began building in his gut when a light hiss poured from the loudspeaker mounted on the tower. Irritating pops and clicks were soon followed by a heavy belch of static, then reveille began to play. On the west side of the platform, at the base of the tower leading to the navigational light, a door opened. Thompson's second in command, a young Lieutenant named Brian Brooks, appeared on the platform.

Thompson said, "Good morning, Lieutenant. Glad to see you up and at 'em so early this morning."

Brooks returned something that resembled a salute and said, "Yes, sir. We've been hard at it all night making sure the light stayed operational."

"Any progress on the glitch?"

"No, sir. We've run the wiring three times. We can't find anything wrong with it."

Thompson gazed thoughtfully again at the horizon. The pinks and lavenders were being chased away by a bright orange glow exploding from the water. "Well, something's wrong with it, and we are going to fix it. Today. Understand Lieutenant? I will not have a ship run aground on the shoals on my watch. I don't care if all of you have to take turns flashing a coal oil lantern up there."

Brooks grimaced, unable to hide his disgust.

Thompson cut an eye across the open water. The storm was now just a thin line of dark clouds on the faraway horizon. He sipped from his cup and a hint of concern slipped into his voice. "Did you feel this thing swaying in that squall? For a minute there, I thought we were going over."

Brooks nodded. "It was a pretty good licking, but this old lady has been out here a while, and there hasn't been a storm or hurricane yet to dent her. I hear the support pilings were sunk thirty feet deep."

"Well, let's check everything just to make sure nothing popped or separated. Repair as needed, Lieutenant."

Brooks nodded.

"Speaking of repairs, where are we on the targets?"

"They worked yesterday evening, sir. Still a little sticky at times, but they do work."

Thompson ran his fingers through his hair, silently recalling the briefing about the targets before his transfer aboard. During the scuffle in Vietnam, when it was uncertain who might be cruising the Eastern Seaboard looking for easy targets, the Department of Defense deemed it a good idea for personnel manning all offshore Coast Guard stations to be armed and proficient with sidearms. Plans were drawn, and a contract was developed to install ten automatic light arms target holders on the rig and others like it. In less than eight months from when the Vice Admiral stamped the authorizing paperwork, the Frying Pan Shoals Light Station was fitted with new pop-up target holders. The men were issued Colt 1911 pistols with a monthly ration of two hundred rounds each. Weekly target practice was required, and for years, the men who were counting the seconds until they could retire or transfer off the hulk enjoyed the opportunity at what everyone jokingly called recoil therapy. It was the only thing they looked forward to, and the only thing that eased the boredom from their everyday chores of sweeping, mopping, sanding, and painting. Morale soared, but in 1976 the single stroke of a pen from a well-meaning penny pincher somewhere at the Pentagon decommissioned the need for sidearms, and simultaneously put an end to the fun. But just prior to Thompson's reign on the light station, fearing the possibility of hostile Soviet submarine traffic, the high brass in Washington reinstated the small arms directive.

Years of neglected maintenance in a perpetual salt mist environment had the automatic target holders stymied, and one of Thompson's first orders was to have them refurbished into good working condition. In three days, the men had them scraped and painted and oiled. Brooks hadn't lied to his commanding officer. The target holders did work most of the time, however slow and squeaky they were.

Thompson raised and lowered the cup, smacked his lips, and glanced at the target holders. "Good, Lieutenant. Brief the men after calisthenics. Now that we have them working, I would like to see where we stand with marksmanship. They're all first-class slobs and unfit to serve, but perhaps they can competently operate a sidearm."

After thirty minutes of toe-touches, push-ups, and jumping jacks, the men were ordered to get their weapons and assemble again topside, and for the first time since the Lieutenant Commander set foot on the structure, everyone was where they were supposed to be ahead of schedule. Thompson inspected the line of smiling men, then started the speech he had rehearsed the evening before. "Men, we have orders direct from Washington to maintain a certain level of proficiency with sidearms. Apparently, President Reagan's verbal jousting with the Soviet Union has everyone on edge, and we, being on this damned metal island way out here off the coast, are feared to be the first units that would most likely encounter the enemy. I'm not sure anyone would be interested in us, and even if they were, I'm fairly certain we'll be greeted with torpedoes instead of boarding parties. But my job is not to make policies or question them, my job is to make sure orders are carried out. So, until further notice, every Monday morning after calisthenics you will participate in sidearm training and target practice."

After the Commander quickly reviewed the finer points of correctly field-stripping, cleaning, and operating the Colts, he walked them through the expected practice routine. Each man was to shoot at different distances for score, but Thompson quickly described a supplemental hybrid practice session he'd developed. One at a time, each man would stand exactly ten yards in front of the middle target, and fire from left to right in rapid succession. After the first shot, the range officer would press the corresponding button, swinging the next target into position. The second report would trigger the third target to rise, and so on until they had shot all ten targets. The 1911s only held seven rounds in the clip and one in the chamber. By design, the men would have to drop the spent clip and load another on the fly to quickly finish shooting the last two targets, effectively meshing two separate training scenarios into one.

Pleased at his own brilliance, the Commander turned, facing the spring-loaded target holders folded down neatly against the platform. He nodded at Brooks, and the junior officer pressed a button with his boot on a control panel welded flush with the platform. The leftmost target swung upright revealing a black paper target with concentric numbered white-lined ovals. With all the flair of a western gunfighter, Thompson drew and fired. The paper rippled as a large hole appeared just inches from the center X. At the pistol's report, Brooks stepped on the second button, and the second target creaked upward. It squealed like fingernails across a chalkboard and ground to a stop, resting at a forty-five degree angle. The men shuddered, and Thompson cursed under his breath. Brooks, trying not to look worried, pressed the button again, then again, but nothing happened. Ensigns Rogers and Corbin, without being told, both ran to the target frame and pulled and snatched, trying to loosen the rust. Someone finally produced a hammer and a can of WD-40, and Rogers sprayed oil and wailed on the bolted hinge at the deck while Corbin heaved and pulled. Three big swings had it free, and the metal supports sheared rusty flakes of metal as the target mechanically jerked upright. The Commander, who had been reprimanding one of the men for not having his shirt tail tucked neatly, heard it move. He turned, raised his Colt, and just as Lieutenant Brooks yelled no, the big-bored pistol bucked in his hand. Thompson had not seen the two men behind the target frame still gathering their tools, and the heavy bullet tore through the paper target just under the bullseye, then straight through Ensign Corbin's neck. Rogers screamed as his uniform instantly turned red—a gaping hole now taking the place of his friend's Adam's apple. Blood continued to spray as the man staggered backwards, mouth unhinged, gurgling, and before Rogers could catch him, Ensign Randy Corbin toppled over the rail into the churning sea below.

Ten minutes later the Commander, via marine radio, informed Wilmington of the accident, and relieved himself of duties. His last official act as commanding officer was ordering a search and recovery operation from one of the helicopter crews stationed in Wilmington to assist with recovering the body of the man he'd shot and killed. Per regulation, Brooks assumed command and after ordering the search for the body to continue, he and a shaken Thompson retrieved command logs and made their way inside to the galley's broad table. There they began documenting their own accounts of the incident for the investigation. Quiet minutes passed, both writing feverishly, when suddenly, a loud volley of voices came from the roof. Pens hit the table, and both ran down the hall onto the catwalk and up on the platform. Rogers met them halfway across, babbling hysterically. Tears rolled down the ensign's face as he finally stuttered something about the water and what they'd found.

Brooks grabbed the man by the shoulders and gave him a good shake. "Slow down and talk so I can understand you. Did you find the body?"

Rogers unconsciously rubbed the back of his hand across the heavy splatter of Corbin's blood staining his shirt, "Not the body, sir. We've got *him*. He's alive."

"What?" Thompson and Brooks said in unison.

"We found him floating in the water," Rogers said, then pointed at the two men operating the hoist on the edge of the platform. "They're bringing him up in the cargo net now."

They stood at the I-beam where the hoist cable met a single large pulley then turned downward towards the water. Thompson stood silently, his face was pasty white watching the last twenty feet of cable come in. Brooks was still talking to Rogers—trying to make sense of it.

"If you saw what you said you saw, there's no way that Corbin's alive. You said he had a hole in his throat big enough to stick your fist in."

Rogers stammered back, "I know what I said and I know what I saw, sir, but I swear to you, he is."

When the cargo net swung over the side, Brooks and Thompson pulled two men away who had ridden up with Corbin. What met their boggling eyes was nothing short of miraculous. Brooks stuttered something incomprehensible, and Thompson went down to both knees, drew a shallow breath, and fainted. Ensign Corbin stared up at the junior officer—quivering hands partly covering a bloodless, gaping hole in the center of his neck.

Brooks crossed himself and said, "Holy God!"

April 8th 2017

The fishing reel screamed. Off the back of the boat, the heavy line straightened, then relaxed, then straightened again, forming a translucent laser beam between the rod tip and the large fish hooked on the other end. Frank Russo, who was affectionately called Frankie by his friends and fatso behind his back by everyone else, reeled down two, three, four cranks, then set his heavy bulk against the staunchness of what was likely a decent tuna. Forcing the rod upward, he gained on the fish, then slowly lowered the rod tip again, cranking the line onto the quarter-filled spool. The fat man continued to work the rod and reel, but knew that something was wrong. The foam on the chop beside them wasn't moving. The captain was holding the boat steady rather than backing towards the fish. Either the guy didn't know what he was doing, or perhaps it was a test to see just how experienced they were before things really started cooking.

More line sizzled from the reel, and Frankie glanced back to the boat's center console. The captain's concerned look said it all, and the fisherman easily read his thoughts. *Why in God's name did I let these Yankees talk me into going fishing without my first mate? They said they'd been deep sea fishing more times than they could count, and the big guy knew how to tie a Bimini twist . . . but what if they can't handle it, or fall off the boat, or hook themselves in the hand or throat or something? Dammit, this is the last time that sorry, boozing first mate of mine misses a charter.*

Frankie hadn't lied to the captain. Even though he was a hundred and fifty pounds heavier than anyone who ought to be seen on a sleek fishing boat, he and his two friends Pauley and Sal had cut their teeth on the water in the early days when the organization was operated solely out of New Jersey. They'd fished together for more than a decade, and knew quite a bit about saltwater fishing. Frankie was a quick learner, and after winning a slightly used twenty-four-foot fiberglass beauty in a poker game and taking subscriptions to *Sport Fish, Marlin Quarterly,* and *Gulf Stream Fishing,* in no time he ascended to what most would call an accomplished fisherman. The big bosses didn't seem to mind either. To them, having a guy like him in the ranks was, if nothing else, convenient. Frankie's ability to captain a discreet vessel large enough to go offshore made him the go-to man for making things disappear. It was true that hits weren't ordered as often as they had been in the past, but there was still the occasional body to dispose of. The sea rarely gave up her dead, and Frankie somehow had a knack for knowing exactly how far out he needed to be before donating another soul to the Atlantic.

Frankie knew almost everything there was to know about saltwater fishing, but the unrefined business of people handling was where he really shined. No one else in the Wilmington fishing fleet would have agreed to take three landlubbers out on a fishing charter without the help of a first mate, yet Frankie had found a way. When they arrived at the marina that morning, the captain tried to cancel, but Frankie's cool conversation and the offer of adding an extra grand to the charter fee was all it took. Money has a funny way of speaking to people, and those additional ten crisp one-hundred-dollar bills practically sang a love song to the captain who was only fifteen payments in on his boat loan. Frankie knew that an extra grand would get them on the boat, and he also knew (feeling the soreness in his knuckles each time he turned the crank on that Penn reel) exactly why the captain's first mate hadn't shown up, or even bothered to call that morning before they left the marina.

The stout offshore fishing rod flexing heavily excited the big fisherman, but it only seemed to make the captain more nervous. The line pulsed a few times, and Frankie braced, perfectly still and calm, as the fish began another run. More line stripped from the reel, and behind him he could hear the captain suck in a deep breath.

"Okay, big guy. Hold her steady and be gentle. Let him have a little fun, but don't try to gain back line while he's acting foolish."

Not saying a word, Frankie held his ground. After a solid minute the fish tired, and before the captain could tell him what to do, he started applying pressure and reeling again. Quickly and calmly, he recovered the lost line like a true veteran sport fisherman.

Pauley, the skinny man with crazy eyes, leaned and said with a low voice, "I think you've won him over. He still looks like he could bite a nail in half, but I can tell he's more relaxed. He knows this isn't your first boat ride."

"He should. That hook-up was as smooth as butter and if he's paying any attention to the reel, he knows that I've had him on for less than twenty minutes, and he's halfway in already."

Frankie cranked the reel and watched the line quickly come in. "He's getting tired. Probably not as big as I first thought." He looked at Pauley with cold, steely eyes. Eyes that said that pleasure had just taken a backseat to business. "Get ready. It won't be long now."

Five minutes later, the fat man leaned over the transom and caught a glimpse of a silvery-blue streak twenty feet beneath the surface. The rod tip immediately bent again, as the tired fish tried one last time to escape the hook. Pauley's crazy eyes scanned across the ocean. They seemed to look every direction at once. There were a few boats on the horizon, but none were close enough to see them without an exceptional set of binoculars. "All clear," he said softly, so that only Frankie could hear him.

The fat man winked and nodded, then turned to his other friend, Sal, and did the same. At the sign, crazy eyes turned to the captain sitting in the cockpit and yelled that the fish was close to the boat. The Captain smiled a nervous smile and hollered back, "Easy now guys, let's do it just like I told you. I've got a reputation back at the marina to keep."

On cue, Sal took a deliberate step towards the rear corner of the boat and clumsily bumped into the two rods resting in their holders. Making it look like an accident, he tripped the release lever on one of the big reels, and the line began to free-spool as the weighted lure splashed in the water and dove beneath the boat. In a matter of seconds, and with a bit of disguised help, the lines were hopelessly tangled. The captain cut the engines and cursed. Instantly he was at the back of the boat, yelling for everyone who wasn't fighting a fish to get out of the way. The tangle was a colossal mess, and in one quick motion a blade appeared and the slack line was cut; the expensive lure disappeared into the depths.

The captain cleared the remaining tangle, slid his knife back into the sheath on his belt, then turned to Frankie. Angry blue veins exploded across his forehead. "That idiot just lost me a fifty-dollar lure, and nearly cost you your fish."

"Yeah, sorry about that. Maybe he hasn't been out quite as many times as Pauley and me." He cranked the reel a couple of times, looked at Sal, winked, and said, "Thanks for nearly costing my fish, newbie."

The captain looked surprised. "Newbie! I thought you said y'all had fishing experience."

The rod dipped hard again, and Frankie held it steady as he chinned towards the man on his left and said, "Me and slim over here have tons of trips under our belts." He turned back towards Sal, "Don't worry. I'll make sure he knows what to do from now on."

The captain was a volcano poised to erupt. "Just back away from the transom, *newbie,* and don't touch anything until we get this fish in." He turned to walk back to the console, muttering something about his missing first mate when the butt of a large pistol suddenly hit him in the back of the head. The stunned captain's eyes rolled white before he landed face first in the bottom of the boat. All three men glared for a moment, admiring the sprawled captain. A trickle of blood emerged from the hairline at the base of his neck. There was no movement, only a drawn out, sickening moan.

Nodding, Frankie cut the line, releasing the fish, and stepped over the captain to the controls. "Damn fishing tournaments. There wasn't a boat to rent within a hundred miles of Wilmington, and we get stuck with Captain Ahab's apprentice here, and this little puddle-jumper. We'll probably be beat to death before we get there." He took a handheld GPS unit from his pocket, punched a few buttons, then turned the wheel and rammed the throttle forward.

Fans of salt water sprayed from either side of the bow as Sal made his way to a forward compartment near the bow and located a large duffel bag. Pauley knelt beside him as Sal took a short piece of PVC pipe from within. 'Van Dorn Water Sampler' was written in small block letters on the side of the tube. Those crazy eyes seemed to momentarily focus, and using his best joke college professor voice, he said over the wind and noise, "Tell me, Rochester . . . how does this sampling doohickey work again?"

Sal shook his head laughing and pulled another water sampler out of the duffle bag. "Still don't get it, huh?"

Pauley shook his head.

Sal pulled on the trapdoors of the sampler, opening both ends of the tube. Using two small attached wires, he connected the spring-loaded doors to the trigger mechanism in the raised handle portion at the center of the tube. "You see, after setting the ends open like this, you just lower it down in the water with this long cord to whatever depth you want to sample."

He pointed at the small doughnut shaped weight that was at the tag end of the attached coiled cord. "When it gets to the depth you want, all you do is just drop this weight down the line, and when it hits the unit down under the water right here," he nearly touched his finger to the flat trigger mechanism that was built into where the cord tied onto the tube, "the doors shut, sealing the ends of the tube. And just like that, we have a water sample."

Sal tapped the trigger. The small wires released, and the trapdoors slammed shut.

Amused, Pauley's crazy eyes almost crossed, "Then you just pull up it up?"

Sal nodded and said, "That's all there is to it. It doesn't leak or anything." Nimble fingers reopened the trap doors. "You see that rubber grommet along the edges? They keep the water you want in, and the water you don't want out." He checked and double-checked the connections on the water samplers, then focused on the captain lying on the floor. "You cracked him pretty good. You think he's going to buy the 'line breaking and the rod hitting him in the back of the head' story?"

Pauley reached into his jacket pocket and held up a small medical vial. The clear fluid inside shimmered in the sunlight like quicksilver. "After a dose or two of this, he'll believe anything we tell him."

Frankie double-checked the GPS, made a slight course adjustment, then hollered, "Quit fooling around up there Pauley and make damn sure our captain's asleep. I don't want him coming out of it while we're working. GPS says twelve miles, so hurry up and get everything ready. If we don't come back with a good water sample from the light station, Geno will cut all our throats."

Chapter 2

The calendar said it was the middle of June, but Jackie LaRue didn't believe it. Chilled and damp, she rode out wave after wave in the back of the twenty-eight-foot Grady White as it cut a white line across the Atlantic. The boat pitched and yawed and tumbled over the waves like a runaway rollercoaster, making her seat on the large burlap sack filled with supplies for the light station even more uncomfortable. The cold sliced right through the layers she was wearing, forcing her teeth to chatter. She sank deeper and deeper into the stern, knees pressing against her chest, trying to dodge the relentless wind.

While she shivered, a waxing half-moon blinked through the broken high clouds above. Even though the dawn was fast approaching, the intermittent moonlight produced enough light to see. The cold front had come through hours earlier leaving a vicious six-foot chop on the water, but her grandfather, Hoyt Bennett, a thirty-year veteran sport fisherman, stood tall at the controls. The ordinarily rock steady Grady White he named 'Show Time' was plugging along through the rough seas. A few of the waves were so large that when the boat surged across the crest and fell into the deep troughs behind them, Jackie could only see walls of water rising above the gunnels. The twin 225 outboards behind her whined loudly, and the wind hissed constantly in her ears. The sea seemed to be a living, breathing thing, and in the spooky dimness cast by the moon it was more than just alive . . . it was angry. Jackie tried to hide her fear, but each minute that passed brought her closer and closer to full panic.

It was a terrible, jarring cycle, making the boat's fiberglass pop under her, and every muscle in her body tense. She hadn't noticed before, but her jaw was sore from forcefully clinching her teeth together, an involuntary response to the impacts. She massaged both sides of her mouth and looked at her grandfather. The old man had both hands on the wheel and rode out each wave, as if he was perched on the back of the most dangerous bull of the rodeo. With slightly bent knees, his lanky frame expertly absorbed the repeated shocks. Jackie noticed him smiling, and once, when the boat had fallen into one of the deeper troughs, and the wind suddenly died, she thought she heard him humming a tune. He seemed to be enjoying it.

Visiting the Atlantic with her grandfather was nothing new to Jackie. She'd been fishing with him at least once every summer since she was eight years old. That first time had been unplanned and very memorable. Jackie's mother was getting ready to show a middle-aged couple a four bedroom, two and a half bath Victorian on the north side of town, when the babysitter called in sick. Most of the commission she would make on that sale had already been spent, so begrudgingly, Caroline Bennett picked up the phone and called her father. Hoyt was about to leave the marina with an inshore charter, and after explaining the situation to the fishing party, they all decided that Jackie could ride along. After she realized that they weren't going to sink, Jackie spent a surprisingly pleasant day watching the waves break against the boat, helping bait the hooks, and admiring the pretty Spanish and king mackerel that were caught. She was in the way more than anything else that day—she saw it in her grandfather's eyes—but after enough fish were caught to call it a successful trip (and with a little encouragement from the group) she finally got over her shyness long enough to reel in the two smallest fish of the day. She had come a long way since that first trip, but the Atlantic was forcing her to hate it again.

From her burlap nest, Jackie felt the boat cross a big wave, and instantly Hoyt yelled for her to hold on. She grabbed a cleat on the gunnel, and waited for the drop that never came. He expertly fought the wheel and feathered the throttle, making the boat crab down the backside of the wave, managing to miss the jarring landing at the bottom. The big engines bellowed, making their way up the next crest into an unprecedented stretch of flat water. Jackie had never once felt a single ounce of seasickness, but this trip was making her stomach do jumping jacks.

The frightened teen gazed across the bow, staring intently at the white boils of water around them. Even growing up on the east side of Wilmington, a beach town where the ocean was a way of life for most, she had always been leery of the water. She thought of that first fishing trip. Then, it had been as smooth as a sheet of glass, but in her mind, the sea was nothing more than an endless pit covered with a pretty blue sheet that could, in an instant, be jerked away revealing the trap. Sure, it was pretty to watch from a distance, and the sound of the waves crashing on the beach while she played safely in the sand as a toddler was music to her ears, but deep down, she'd never quite gotten over the 'what-ifs' that accompanied it. She learned from her fourth-grade history book that this watery nightmare living just a few miles away from her own bedroom was affectionately known as the Graveyard of the Atlantic, and was responsible for countless shipwrecks ever since Columbus had convinced Queen Isabella that the world was indeed round. Even more terrifying, it had claimed the lives of at least two swimmers each summer since she was old enough to pay attention to the news. At the tender age of ten, she declared that Jacqueline Anne LaRue's obituary would not be appearing in the newspapers anytime soon. She was fourteen now, wiser, stronger, and blossoming into a young lady poised to enter high school in a couple of months, but she'd never forgotten the day she took that oath.

The boat rocked and quivered, and looking over her shoulder, those big green eyes stared blankly across the open sea. There was a certain hopelessness that accompanied the view that was undeniable, and all at once nothing about being on a boat in the

Atlantic seemed right. She didn't like the sea. She didn't like the cold damp that made her shiver. She didn't like the sour smell of wet burlap. She didn't like staring directly into a wall of water off the front of the bow when the waves were big. She didn't like wondering if they were going to float or sink. And despite agreeing to help her grandfather for three more days on the light station, she didn't like being that far out.

How much farther? How much farther? How much farther?

She tried to remember the distance. Straight southeast from Wilmington towards the Gulf Stream . . . what was it? Twenty-one and a half miles? Yes, that was the number. Twenty-one and a half hard-earned, rear-end smashing, sea-sickening miles would have them at the leading edge of the Frying Pan shoals where the light station stood sentinel, like it had done for the last fifty years. As spooky as the sea was, her mind nearly rejected the notion that relief could come once aboard it. They had floated past it a few times fishing when she was younger, and each time, the eerie structure seemed to call to her. It was fascinating in a haunted house kind of way. Looking at it from a distance, it reminded her of the pictures of the oil rigs in the Gulf of Mexico she'd seen in books and on television, but up close, the large platform living area was very obvious under the raised tower that housed the search light. Perched so precariously seventy feet above the ocean, it was hard to believe that servicemen used to work and live there.

Who in their right mind would willingly come out here in the middle of the ocean for a few days? Nobody, that's who. And he expects people to pay to do it?

A light tap on her shoulder gave her a start. Hoyt was smiling, and motioned for her to get closer. She waited for a moment, and after they crested the next wave, she stood and scrambled across the boat's wet deck.

Almost in her ear, he said, "How are you doing so far, beach girl? You hungry yet?"

"I'm fine, and I think I can wait to eat until we get there. My stomach's not quite right, and the way this boat's shaking, I'm not sure I could hit my mouth with anything anyway."

"Yeah, the forecast said that it was going to be choppy, but I think it's a little rougher than they predicted. It'll jar your teeth, but I've been in worse. The front is past us, so it's supposed to be easing off by mid-morning."

The boat charged up another tall wave and popped into the depression behind it. Jackie held tight to the console's cold chrome frame. "I don't like it."

"It'll test your mettle, but don't worry, you come from good seaworthy genes. You'll pull through."

They stared across the bow together, and off to their left, ghostly clouds began to part, revealing a familiar orange glow spreading across the sky. Hoyt said, "Looks like we've got another front-row seat for the show."

Five waves later, the top of the sun peeked over the horizon, intensifying the cheerful hues of oranges, pinks, and reds that accented the entire eastern sky. It was mesmerizing watching the beginning of a new day in such a way, and both of them seemed to get caught in the moment. It only took those few seconds of lost focus before the boat began to yaw. Hoyt bent his knees and yelled, as the boat rode a strange angle up a bigger than average wave. He spun the wheel quickly, making the correction, and they both braced as the twenty-eight-foot slab of fiberglass shifted back into position at the crest, and coasted into the following trough. Wide-eyed, Jackie stared across the bow at an approaching wall of water. She started to scream, but felt the bow rise quickly, meeting the leading edge of the wave. A cold spray bathed them, but what had looked like certain death pushed harmlessly under the boat.

Jackie, not realizing she was holding her breath, finally exhaled. "Even when you're a little off, they still aren't as bad as they look, are they?"

"Nope. A little bit off here and there is expected and manageable, and sometimes fun, but hitting them sideways is a no-no—a sure way to wind up swimming. And just so you know, it's worse sitting down low like that. The lower you are, the bigger and nastier they seem." Hoyt tapped the wheel, "Up here, you can see better, and you're up above most of it. Even the big ones can be tamed as long as you keep the bow facing them. Why don't you take over for a little bit? You've done well in the bay and flat water, might as well get some training in stuff like this. I'll be right beside you."

Jackie hesitated. She didn't want to do it, but when her grandfather released the wheel and stepped to the right, she felt herself quickly step behind the controls, putting her left hand firmly on the wheel, and her right hand on the throttles.

"That's my beach girl," Hoyt said. "I'm going to make a sea captain out of you yet."

He stepped back close to her, dodging the sea spray, and pointed towards the GPS unit on the console. The display showed two dots. One was stationary and the other was moving slowly, a small digital representation of their boat's position. He tapped the upper right portion of the screen where the digital data was displayed. The bearing read 137 degrees, and the distance was a little over eleven miles.

He leaned closer and said into her ear, "Now hold her steady on bearing, one-three-seven. And always remember this: when this fancy doodad craps out, you can always get home the old-fashioned way."

Jackie looked further down on the console and saw her grandfather tapping the black fluid-filled compass. It was far from steady, rolling around in its housing. One eye on the sea, and the other on the compass, Jackie realized that it was steadily bouncing between 134 and 140 degrees. Before she could ask he said, "When it's rough like this, you have to average it out."

She checked the GPS again, and squeezed the controls. The cool chrome felt good in her hands, and it was almost no trouble at all to keep the boat facing the incoming waves, yet remain almost perfectly on bearing one-three-seven. She was doing it. She was piloting a twenty-eight-foot boat offshore in the Atlantic Ocean, and from the relaxed look on her grandfather's face, she must have been doing it well. She glanced again to the left and saw that the sun had broken almost completely free from the horizon. Its warm rays felt good on her face.

It was the third day in a row Jackie LaRue had seen the sun rise.

Chapter 3

Jackie piloted the fishing boat for twenty minutes before giving the controls back to her grandfather. Standing behind the wheel in those conditions for even that short time had been the most exhausting thing she'd ever done. Her muscles were pulsing steel cords holding her, the boat, and the rest of the world together. When she was sitting on the burlap again, catching her breath and nerve, Hoyt leaned and playfully ran his fingers through her damp hair. The air was changing, and what was forecasted by both Hoyt and the weatherman was beginning to happen. The Atlantic was well on its way to becoming friendly again.

The boat was riding smoother, and Jackie dozed in her burlap nest. She was on the verge of dreaming when Hoyt bumped her on the leg. Yawning, she rubbed the sleep from her eyes, and then she stood and saw it. On the horizon, maybe four miles ahead, stood the stilted metallic oasis. The movement of the boat, the thousands of rhythmic waves between her and it, and the fact that she was still partly asleep, instantly produced an optical illusion, making it look like the Frying Pan Shoals Light Station had fallen off its supports and was floating on the water like some ill-designed ship. The light tower lurched skyward off the flat roof, and even though the light had been out for years, she easily imagined what relief sailors in a pre-GPS world might have thought seeing it for the first time. Going from hundreds, and sometimes thousands of feet of water almost instantly to a mere twenty to thirty feet over the shallowest part of the shoals would definitely make for some interesting sailing. Falling into a deeper than average trough at full steam during low tide would certainly spell disaster for a vessel's hull . . . the boulders, coral, and sand that comprised the hidden shoals didn't give like seawater did.

Hoyt bumped her arm, then patted the wheel and moved to the right. Without hesitation, she slid behind the console again, taking dead aim at the structure. He leaned and said, "It's going on nine o'clock. After we moor the boat, we'll eat breakfast, then we'll get her unloaded, and we can take a quick walk-through, just to make sure we don't have any damage from the storm. If all's clear, we can get back to work."

She nodded and glanced across the bow at the light station, then down at the old black compass. It was welded tight on bearing one-three-seven.

"Hey, you were right," she said, pointing at the bezel. "That old compass is still reading the same bearing."

Hoyt smiled. "It's the mark of a good sailor. Being able to maneuver through seas like that and still hold a tight bearing is almost a lost art these days. And remember, you helped me do it."

The compliment made her tingle all over.

Hoyt face suddenly changed. He turned to Jackie and asked, "Please tell me we put the snorkel masks and flippers in with the rest of the stuff."

Jackie nodded.

"Good. If the weatherman is right, after a few good hours of work, we'll stop for a late lunch, get in a quick swim, and with any luck, we'll catch our supper."

Jackie made a face. They had caught fish off the platform before with rod and reels (she had thrown hers back), but what he was talking about wasn't conventional fishing. He was talking about a much more sinister way to catch fish, where releasing them afterwards wasn't an option.

Hoyt saw the look. "I think it's about time for me to introduce you to the sport of spearfishing."

She tried to sound confused. "What?"

"Spearfishing. You mean to tell me that you've lived in Wilmington all your life, and never even heard of spearfishing?"

A brightness came to her emerald eyes. It was as if sheer defiance was taking the form of a teenage girl. "I've heard of it, but I'm not doing it. Can't release a fish with a hole in it and expect it to live. And once blood is in the water, sharks show up fast. I let you teach me how to swim, and I might swim a little around the tower, but you're crazy if you think I'm going to get in the water way out here with fresh blood in it."

He laughed. "I don't think we'll have to worry about that. I've only seen two sharks, and they were all small ones looking for scraps of fish, not arms and legs."

"Just the same, I'd rather not."

He looked back toward the tower and pointed. "Hey, we are close enough to see the words now."

Across the waves, the illusion of the platform sitting on the water was gone. There was a hearty amount of sky now visible between the sea and the rig, and in big white letters just under the mail level of the platform, she easily read FRYING PAN.

While they were staring at what was to be their home for the next two days, he leaned down and said, "I know this isn't your favorite place, but there's just something about it I like. My old bones don't ache as bad when I'm out here. The water even feels warmer than it's supposed to be, like a big hot tub. It's almost therapeutic."

Jackie just stared at the big white letters.

"Even if you don't try to shoot anything, I'd like for you to watch. Should get a pompano or maybe a sea bass in no time. That'll make for some good eating this evening. It's a challenge to hit a fish, unless you are really close. I bet if you give it a try, you'll like it."

Jackie still said nothing.

Hoyt shook his head. "There ain't a thing wrong with catching your own supper, you know—to make your own way. A good fisherman, whether you hook them or spear them, at the very least, is self-sufficient. And you'll find out soon enough that independence will carry you a long way in this world, beach girl."

Jackie shrugged her shoulders.

Hoyt licked the salt spray from his lips. "Remember, the water's not deep out here, and the bigger fish from off the shoals come close chasing the smaller ones that try to hide along the pilings. All you do is float on the water, and when you see one checking out the baitfish, you take a deep breath and go down to meet him. Sometimes eight or ten feet is all you have to go, and the flippers will get you down and back up in a hurry. The spear gun is simple to use. I'll show you."

Her green eyes gleamed. "You aren't talking me into it."

Sharply, Hoyt said, "Just like you didn't let me talk you into learning how to swim?"

The comment stung and Jackie looked at her feet as she twisted a toe into white fiberglass. She hoped that her grandfather didn't see her blushed face, but she knew he did.

She piloted the boat to within a hundred yards of the light station before yielding the controls back to her grandfather. He expertly guided it to the lee girder where one of the stout mooring ropes dangled freely. At almost an idle, Hoyt passed the bow within two feet of the girder, and Jackie easily reached the rope and quickly tied it to a forward cleat. With the bow secured, he turned the wheel, and feathered the engines. In the roll of the waves, the boat slid sideways under a support beam, completely under the platform. At the stern, Jackie reached for another mooring rope attached to a secondary steel crossbeam. She quickly made figure-eights around one of the stern cleats, and neatly looped the last one tight. Her grandfather killed the tired engines, and the Grady White rocked harmlessly along with the waves fully secured to the support structure.

Hoyt stood on the gunnel and grabbed a jumbled portion of rope ladder that was looped on a piece of rebar welded to a crossbeam. A flick of the wrist unfurled it; the last two rungs splashed in the water beside the boat. They both donned their backpacks and slowly climbed the ladder twenty feet before gaining the bottom of the welded steel staircase that ascended to the steel piling forty more feet to the catwalk circling just under the outer edge of the main platform. Jackie had made that climb four times in the last month, and each time, she thought it was the tallest sixty feet on earth. They caught their breath on the steel walkway, then made their way up the short staircase to the main door of the platform.

When Jackie first set foot inside that dark corridor some four weeks ago, it was like stepping into the past. What greeted her then was an eye-watering olfactory overload of mold, rust, and the sea. Yet, intermingled within those smells was something else . . . something that jumped out at her, nearly grabbing each side of her face and drawing it into its very walls. It was more of a feeling, or perhaps an apparitional presence than something that was real. And even now, after several trips out there, she wasn't sure exactly how to describe it. Somehow, someway, it was the feeling of being surrounded by sweaty, military men. The strange smells conjured strange memories—memories that weren't her own. Walking down the stuffy hallway, she could actually see them. Uniformed men with unshaven faces and sweat-stained shirts came and went down the long, empty hallway headed to their work stations. Men seemed to muster from every room while the phantom bells and whistles sounded, signaling the approach of a supply ship, and near the galley, she found herself standing among them in chow line waiting for the Thanksgiving and Christmas meals. Jackie heard the voices, she smelled the musk, she saw the salutes made when a new commanding officer was welcomed aboard. She somehow saw all those things as clearly as if she had lived there her entire life.

Now, standing beside her grandfather on the catwalk, Jackie watched the door open again, exposing the dark, musky hallway and all at once those strange sensations flooded her senses. She seemed to feel the wind change as memories of men quickly walked past her, headed for some assigned task. It was a little different this time, though. Those sensations were not nearly as strong as they had been the first time. They walked down the dank hallway towards the galley, and instead of choking on stale, musky air, the aroma of new paint and air fresheners filled their nostrils. The phantom memories she had once strongly felt were now fading. It was as if their work was erasing history.

The galley door creaked open, and they sat their bags on the table. Hoyt asked, "Remember how to open the windows?"

She nodded.

"I'm going back after the food. Open all the ones you can, and I'll get the tough ones later. This place will look and feel a lot better with a little unfiltered sun and the sea breeze coming in."

Hoyt disappeared back down the hallway headed for the stairs, and Jackie went from room to room, carefully examining each exterior wall for leaks and damage, and easily opened all but one window that a new coating of rust had afflicted. She was sitting at the galley table when her grandfather walked back in, two soft-sided coolers hanging off his shoulders.

"Let's hurry up and get these ham biscuits down and get to work. A big school of fish was already around the boat. Let's have a look at how much rust is in those two rooms we prepped last weekend. If it's bad, I'll have to work them over with the wire brush and re-treat them. If not, you can just start painting. I'll get busy in the other rooms, and when you catch up to me, we'll take a break for lunch. After that, we'll spear us some supper."

They busied themselves with their late breakfast, and Jackie, after polishing off half of her biscuit, noticed her grandfather thoughtfully staring out of the open window. Her stare followed his, and through the portal, the rolling swells were slowly making their way towards the coast.

She almost didn't ask, but finally did. "Whatcha thinking about?"

The question broke his stare. He took a sip of orange juice, and propped his chin on his hands. "Oh, nothing much." After a big sigh, he looked again through the window. "I can't help but wonder if we're doing the right thing here."

Jackie was surprised to hear a hint of reluctance in her grandfather's voice. "The right thing about what?"

"I don't think I told you, but I used to bring supplies out here for the Coast Guard. They had their own supply ships, but they also contracted with civilians. They guaranteed one trip a month, but it was usually more than that. It was good money, and it helped fill in the gaps between charters.

"At first it was just supplying a light station—a job. But after a few trips, there was something about this place that just felt right. There were a few times I came aboard to take care of some personal business while the men unloaded the boat," he patted his belly and smiled. "I even gave a fishing lesson or two to some of the guys out here. Then one day I had some engine trouble. I thought I was going to have to paddle the last mile, but made it. I wound up staying overnight. I used their radio and called a captain friend of mine that was planning to fish out here the next day. I got him to bring the part I needed the next morning. The food was terrible, but when it got dark, I swear to you, I've never seen the sky look like that. No smog, no lights, no noise . . . there were millions of stars in places you've never seen stars before. The Milky Way was a giant smear in the sky. You could just about reach out and touch it. I remember thinking then that if there were good food and soft beds, it would be a heckuva place to spend a quiet evening."

Hoyt shook his head and ran his finger around the rim of his glass. "No doubt, it's a gamble, and it's been a lot of work, with more to come before we can start selling weekends. There is one thing that makes me feel good about it, though. I heard after the auction that a bigwig out of Morehead City sent a guy down here to bid on it. He didn't show in time . . . car trouble or something. Word is he would have tripled our bid. It makes me feel better that there was a bigger outfit willing to spend that kind of money on this place. But I guess it's still a little scary.

"Your mom didn't want anything to do with it at first. I had to do quite a bit of fancy talking to get her on board. We didn't run ourselves completely dry, but the down payment sapped us pretty good." He suddenly slapped his hand down on the table. The *pop* echoed loudly through the bare room. "I just have to believe that there are a ton of people out there that would jump at the chance to experience this place. It's just too pretty out here. There are folks who pay way more than what we are going to charge to fly to a tropical island and sip Mai Tais while choking on car exhaust from busy streets. Not to mention fighting their way through the tourist crowds for a mediocre supper somewhere."

He cleared his throat and started with what sounded like a paid advertisement infomercial. "Come on out to the Frying Pan Tower. See the stars and the Milky Way like you've never seen them before. Bring your fishing rod and catch your own supper. Bring your scuba gear and spend the evening exploring the shoals. Or just bring a good book, a couple bottles of wine, get away from it all, and enjoy quiet solitude at your new home away from home."

Jackie giggled.

Hoyt smiled and said, "Hey! That was pretty good!" Then he picked up his glass and held it up as if giving a toast. "And here's to all the fools who went through years of college to get a job in advertising. Eat your heart out, suckers."

She giggled again and took a bite of her biscuit.

"Well, I guess we'll find out if I know what I'm talking about soon enough. You know, this refurbishing really hasn't been all that bad. After thirty minutes on this thing, I knew that it wasn't on the brink of becoming an artificial reef anytime soon, so it was just a matter of turning an old work station light house into something decent. A place like this doesn't have to be a four-star attraction, but it needs to have working toilets, a couple of reliable generators, clean water holding tanks, and a galley that works. The essentials are, well, essential, but paying customers aren't going to be happy with rusty holes in the wall. They'd want nice, fresh coats of paint on everything, drapes and blinds on the windows, doors that lock, heck, even a few nice pictures on the walls . . . you know, things that make a house a home."

Hoyt's eyes narrowed, and with a fingernail, he touched the wall in front of him, pulling off an ancient paint chip, "I figured giving this place a face-lift was going to be a headache, but a little nip and tuck here and there, a little TLC—it really hasn't been that bad. We've only been working on the interior for a few weekends, and we've got a third of it done. And I've got two more rooms nearly ready for you to paint."

Jackie swallowed the rest of her biscuit. "Who was the guy in Morehead City?"

"His name is Geno Mancini. I've read about him in the papers some—a transplant from New York, or New Jersey, or somewhere up there. He's supposed to be a real estate developer, but it's rumored that he still has ties to the mob or what was left over of the crime bosses from the old days. He's still in cahoots with the guys who used to dump bodies in New York harbor."

"Wonder why he wanted it?"

Hoyt shook his head. "Beats me. Maybe he likes stargazing?"

Chapter 4

Jackie and her grandfather finished breakfast, and after tinkering with the generator for a few minutes it finally started. The supplies were hauled up from the boat with the help of a cargo net and the same antiquated electric hoist used to extract Ensign Corbin from the sea. Gallons of paint, paint brushes and rollers, electrical wiring, welding rods, new light fixtures, the big burlap sack of curtains, and several small pieces of furniture ascended to the platform a little at a time. Jackie moved the things she could carry up the stairs and into the hallway. The heavier things came up last, and together, they hefted them inside. With all the heavy lifting done, Jackie popped the top off a new gallon of paint and spent the rest of the morning turning the brown walls of a bedroom a cheerful aquamarine.

It was almost one o'clock when Hoyt, covered in a rusty dust, walked into the bedroom. "Take a load off for a few minutes, and let an old man show you how to sling paint," he said with a big grin on his face. Jackie sat cross-legged on the floor, and watched him dip the roller in the tray and put a long stripe of fresh paint from floor to ceiling. He said, "You know, I don't think I've ever asked you what you think about this place. I know you don't like that it's so far away from everything, but you gotta admit it's kind of neat."

Jackie shrugged her shoulders. "I guess it's okay. Feels a little rickety when the waves are up, and sometimes the creaks sound creepy, especially at night. I just don't—" She shook her head and looked down and picked at a piece of rust stuck to her kneecap. "I just don't like being this far out—out here by ourselves, east of nowhere. What if we get sick or hurt and need help?

Hoyt shook his head and rolled another stripe of paint on the wall. "You and your mama. Y'all worry about stuff they haven't even invented to worry about yet."

It was as if Jackie had spoken it into being, and at that moment, the light station creaked loudly and shifted—the product of a big wave pushing its way across the shoals. Jackie's eyes widened, and she put both palms on the floor beside her trying to stabilize the tons of steel.

Hoyt laughed, "I can rest your fears about the swaying and creaking. This place was inspected by a structural engineer. His report was in the bid packet, and it said that the Frying Pan Shoals Light Station is sound as the Brooklyn Bridge. The government allowed us the opportunity to hire someone to back their claims, but your mom and me didn't have a lot of extra money laying around for that. We decided to rely on the G-man's report. Some of the others did have that kind of money, though, and they still bid on it."

The roller was running out of paint, and Hoyt peeked out the small window. "Hey," he said turning back to Jackie, who'd given up on keeping the structure from swaying, "the water's getting nice again, just like the forecast said. Why don't you go get into your bathing suit and we'll see if there are any fish hanging around the pilings."

Despite Jackie's apprehension about spearfishing, after several hours of mindlessly watching paint transfer from roller to wall, a nice swim was a welcome suggestion. She quickly changed and beat her grandfather out to the catwalk. While making her way down the metal stairs, she could see what looked like massive underwater rain clouds moving with mesmerizing precision around the boat and the pilings. It took a moment, but she finally saw what was driving the movement. Each time the mass changed directions, there was a flash of silver in the water. Once in the boat, she could see the small individual fish that made up the swarming schools. In large masses of thousands or perhaps tens of thousands of individuals moving as one, they darted back and forth from under the boat, out to the piling, and back. Jackie was still unsure what the silver streaks were, until one swam close by the boat. They were medium sized barracuda, and they were moving so fast it was hard to count them. They darted around in and out of sight so often it could have been as few as three, or as many as ten. Regardless of how many there were, they all were taking turns snatching and devouring the unfortunate smaller fish along the periphery.

"Hey. Get out of here," she said loudly, waving her hands over the edge of the boat.

The feeding frenzy ignored her pleas, then something even larger came from the depths and plowed through the mass. Whatever it was quickly disappeared, and the hole it had created in the middle of the school closed, and the thousands of small fish retreated back to the security of the piling. It was like the school of fish had sutured up a wound in the middle of its collective belly, and went on merrily with the business of living . . . like nothing had happened. The barracuda also fled, leaving no trace of their voracious appetite.

Jackie's mouth hung open. How could something move that quickly and strike that fast? The ones the larger fish got couldn't have known what hit them, and a gnawing anger began to build. The feeling passed quickly though, as her mind gave birth to a second thought.

At least the big one scared off the barracudas. It stopped the feeding frenzy.

She was still watching the cloud of fish huddled against the piling near the boat, when she heard the rope squeak, and something flop into the boat behind her. Jackie turned and saw a pair of flippers lying on the fiberglass deck, and her grandfather descending the last few feet of the ladder. He was carrying the speargun in his left hand.

"Did you see that big barracuda hit the school?"

Jackie looked surprised. "The big one was a barracuda too?"

"A five-footer. The fighter jets of the ocean . . . at least that's what I've heard them called."

Jackie peered blankly at the water. She could feel a tingle in her belly were the anger had been. Emotions rose, but she stopped it before tears formed. Life for small fish in the ocean was cruel. One minute, you are having fun swimming around with your friends, and then wham-o! The next thing you know, you're being ripped to shreds by some bully that comes out of nowhere. Death lived in the water she could touch with her fingertips.

Jackie whispered, "Barracudas are mean."

Hoyt put his flippers on, and laid a spear on the rail of the gun. "Well, they get hungry too, you know."

Her eyes widened, considering the thought. "It still doesn't seem fair. Why can't they eat something else?"

"What else are they going to eat? There are a lot of things I don't know, but I am fairly certain about one thing. Nothing about life in the ocean is fair when you're an eight-inch fish."

Hoyt double checked everything, and then showed Jackie how to load the speargun, and explained the triggering mechanism that made it work. He pointed to the small hand-turned reel and said, "You have to be careful with this. The line has to pan off smoothly with no tangles or the spear might come back at you. It sits on this small rail, and after the bands are locked into place back here," he pointed at the catch at the back of the gun that held the stout elastic bands in the locked position, "all you do is aim down the shank of the spear and pull the trigger."

She nodded, feigning interest, and Hoyt positioned his mask, sat on the gunnel, and flipped over the side. She slid her own mask in place, adjusted it a little, clearing her hair from the sides, and stepped over the transom onto the boat's small ladder. The water was warm and it made the hair on her neck and arms tingle in their follicles. The gently rocking waves and the light current wanted to push her away from the boat, but she easily corrected that by holding on to the last rung of the ladder. Small fish darted around her, traveling from underneath the boat to the support piling. It was a brilliant flash of orange and yellow against a hazy blue canvas. Jackie smiled and probed deeper with her eyes, scanning for something else pretty to look at.

Floating on the surface, the visibility was excellent, but down below things rapidly changed. There were perhaps only ten feet of clear water before things started getting blurry. Ten feet past that point, the water quickly blurred into obscurity. A smile pressed against her snorkel, letting a couple of jets of water in, as she watched more small fish dart back and forth between the piling and the boat. Then a large mass swam just below her. Moving as one, they seemed to surround the piling, nibbling on the barnacles growing on the metal. Several lingered off the edge of the school and swam by her, revealing more brilliant colors that, up close, seemed to reflect from every scale. From a distance they were simply a mass of fish, but at arm's length, each individual's beauty was strikingly obvious.

One curious little fish swam by her mask. Jackie froze in the water, enjoying the close encounter. Its working pectoral fins appeared to be waving at her, as it held steady in the current. She was about to extend her hand to see how close she could get when it darted away. To her right, her grandfather splashed on the surface, and after a couple of kicks, he turned downward just beyond the piling. Down he went, five, ten, fifteen feet—at some point she lost the estimate when he turned in the water, almost in a standing position. He pointed at something, and through the murk, at the outer edge of her vision, she saw it. An African pompano made tighter and tighter circles around him, apparently still keeping an eye on the small fish it was hunting. The big fish turned again, feeling out this new living addition to the rig, and in one decisive movement the gun came up and the spear blurred forward. Jackie blinked, missing the impact, but when her eyes opened, there was a quivering slab of silver with a thin, sharp spear sticking all the way through its body. Her grandfather cranked the reel a few times, then secured the line and angled upward and kicked. He and the fish slowly ascended, leaving a greenish trail of blood in the water. He broke the surface next to Jackie, and while holding onto the boat's ladder, he reeled in more line, eventually grabbing the end of the spear. The fish still quivered, but now at the surface, the blood pouring from the wound was a deep crimson. Hoyt raised the spear, hooked a foot onto the ladder, and heaved the prize over the transom into the belly of the boat. Jackie followed, and watched in amazement as her grandfather removed the spear, opened the fish box made into the side of the boat, and dropped in the pompano.

"Looks like we are eating good tonight, beach girl," he said rewinding the loose line back onto the reel. "You want to give it a try?"

Jackie shook her head. "There's a lot of blood. I'm not even sure I'm going back in."

"Would you quit worrying? The conditions are really good down to about twenty feet. Below that, it's iffy. The storm must have stirred up the sediment from the bottom. Still, it's good enough to get a kill. I bet you'd have another in five minutes."

"Nope."

"Well, if you aren't going to catch your own supper, the least you can do is get back into the water and keep watch for me, just in case Jaws decides to show."

Not even looking back to see if she was coming, her grandfather turned, pulled his mask down over his face, and flipped back into the water.

Chapter 5

While Jackie was watching her grandfather trying to spear their supper twenty-one miles off shore, Mason LaRue paid his bill and walked out of the Wagon Wheel Café, onto Emerald Shore Avenue. The glaring sun shut his eyes and beads of sweat immediately formed on his forehead. Mornings had been cool for the last few days, but something told him the relentless summer heat had come to Morehead City to stay. Raising a dirty hand to shade his eyes, he turned east and walked down the sidewalk, looking for loose change or, if he was lucky, a cigarette or something else to smoke that had been prematurely tossed.

The job site was six blocks away, and he casually strode along, not really caring whether or not he was going to keep his roofing job for the small construction company that had picked him up as day labor a few weeks prior. The town houses they were working on were no more than two miles from the beach, but strangely, he hadn't felt a bit of sea breeze that typically started mid-morning and lasted through early evening that close to the water. It was a hot job, even for late spring, and he hated every miserable second of it.

Mason LaRue couldn't catch a break . . . not even with the weather.

Despite the heat and the growing dread of climbing back on that roof, a decent lunch and a few beers put a spring in his step. He'd made it three of the six blocks in a better than average mood when a shiny black Chevy Tahoe pulled up beside him. The engine revved a couple of times before the passenger window lowered and the dark figure inside mumbled something to him.

Mason cupped a hand to his ear, "What'd you say? I can't hear you over that damn engine."

The voice came back, this time loud enough to hear. "Sir, can you help me with this map? I'm trying to find Dolphin Street."

Taking a step towards the SUV, he gave the stranger a sour look. "You're way off bub. Dolphin Street is on the other side—"

Mason froze. Just above the lowered window there was movement, and he quickly recognized a dark, metallic eye—the business end of a large pistol. The hole in the end of the barrel looked large enough to pass a roll of dimes. The back door of the Tahoe opened, and the man in the passenger seat coldly said, "Get in."

A drop of sweat trickled down the bridge of Mason's nose. Behind him, a car went down the street that needed a new muffler. He almost bolted after it, but thought better. Trying not to move his head, he swept his eyes to the left and right, surveying the street and considering the options. There were alleys on either side of the bakery he was in front of, but he'd have to run at least fifteen yards in the open before making either corner. And even if he could do that before catching a bullet, he wasn't intimately familiar with this part of town. The alleys could have just as easily been dead ends as providing clear access to the next street over. Being cornered by an angry man holding a gun wasn't what he considered a good way to start the afternoon. Mason's eyes settled again on the pistol, now wagging towards the open door. The voice said, "I don't think you want to do that, Mister. Get in."

With nowhere to run or hide, Mason felt the lunch in his belly quiver as he reached for the door.

The stranger wasn't kidding. He was indeed looking for Dolphin Street, and after a silent twenty-minute ride the Tahoe stopped in front of a small Italian restaurant named 'Mr. G's.' The guy in the passenger seat turned and pointed the gun at Mason's belly and told him to get out. Mason thought about bolting when his feet hit the pavement, but just then, two goons stepped out of the restaurant in cheesy pinstriped suits. One was north of three hundred pounds and sweating, the other had a slim frame, but something was off about him. It took a second look to notice that the guy's eyes were too close together. And to top it off, they seemed to operate independently of each other. He could have been a freak show circus act—the human chameleon.

The fat guy snapped his sausage sized fingers a couple of times and said, "Hey, greaser, the boss wants to talk to you. He's very busy today, so let's not keep him waiting."

Mason didn't move. "What if I don't want to talk to him? You guys haven't been too friendly, sticking guns in my face and making demands. Who's in there, anyway? Who's your boss?"

It wasn't the first lie he'd told that day. It had been a long time, but the man who owned the restaurant was Geno Mancini—a man who he'd done business with in the past—a man who, apparently, he was still in business with.

The big guy patted his jacket pocket, a likely place to hide a gun. "You really need to get out of this heat, greaser. It's affecting your memory."

Mr. G's might have looked like a hole-in-the-wall eatery from the outside, but once through the door, and around the small baffle where the hostess greeted the patrons, there was a cozy line of booths along either wall, and three rows of tables, six-deep, occupying the middle of the open floor area. Each table was donned with a brilliantly white linen tablecloth, a small lit candle, and a fresh rose. Even though it smelled of stale marinara and beer, the place didn't look half bad. Geno was a hardliner, carrying all the Yankee swagger he could muster from his days in Jersey. He'd broken more fingers and wrists and arms and legs than anyone could count (and had ruined an occasional smile with a well-placed swing of a beer bottle), but even on his worst day, Geno Mancini had class.

The big guy walked behind Mason, punching him in the sides, guiding him towards the back of the room. Behind the big suit walked the guy with the freakish eyes, and behind him was the gun-carrying bully from the Tahoe. Mason didn't believe he was in danger just yet; after all, he was in a public restaurant in the middle of the day. But the uneasy feeling that came when he first saw the pistol had not completely gone away, and he began to scan the interior looking for two things: witnesses and exits. There were only two occupied tables on the far-left wall, both were aging couples that seemed to be minding their own business. At the bar, a guy in a suit sipped at a beer. He looked like an extra from one of the Godfather movies—clearly one of Geno's men. Mason swallowed hard, and even in the air conditioned building, another drop of sweat trickled down his forehead.

They walked along the right corridor next to the booths, past a few secluded rear tables, past the restrooms, towards the rear of the restaurant. The kitchen entrance was just ahead, when a big fist smashed the right side of his ribs. Mason doubled over, choking, and the fat man grabbed him by the arm and slung him through double swinging doors that opened into a small private room. Mason tried to straighten, still wheezing, and when his vision cleared, in front of him was a small table covered with a red and white checkered cloth. The table was tastefully decorated like the ones in the main dining area, harboring a narrow vase holding a single long-stemmed rose, and beside it, a tall candle flickered. To the right of the candle, there was a small chess board, its pieces situated in a half-finished game. On the other side of the flower and candle, facing them, sat Geno Mancini.

Geno looked up from a newspaper, raised a hand and said as if he were talking to a child, "Is that any way to treat our guest, Frankie?" He turned his eyes to Mason and shook his head apologetically. "I'm sorry for my man's crudeness, but I'm afraid he still remembers the sharp kick to the groin you gave him back when we were wrapping up our dealings with that—" he paused and rubbed his forehead, thinking, "that delicate matter with our friends down at city hall. You do remember that, don't you Mister LaRue?"

With most of his breath back, Mason's eyes focused across the table. Geno had changed very little since that first job. He was still a compact man, but even mostly hidden behind an immaculate custom suit, Mason could tell he hadn't succumbed to fat-cat living that plagued most aging business men. The only thing that had changed was that his once dark crop of Mediterranean hair now took on a salt and pepper look.

Being delivered to a meeting in such a manner was emasculating, and Mason scrambled, trying to gain back some of his composure. He hooked a thumb over his shoulder and said, "That's Frank Russo?" He turned and ran his eyes up and down the mountain of flesh standing behind him, then looked back at Geno and shook his head. "You've really got to lay off the buffet policy here. He was big then, but damn!"

Geno laughed out loud. "You see, Frankie, this is why I like this guy. He makes me laugh."

Frankie emitted a low growl and cracked his fat knuckles.

"Not now, Frankie," Geno said, then looked again at Mason. "I'm afraid we still have a little business left to conduct, Mister LaRue." He motioned to the chair across from him. "Please, sit down. I'll have my people bring you something to eat. Would you like a beer?"

Mason shook his head, and after running a careful eye over the room and the chair, he reluctantly sat down.

Geno's face hardened as he glanced at his men, still standing at the door of the little room. A sweep of the hand was the signal, and all three slowly retreated—the two men in suits manned their post on either side of the double doors in the hallway. They had no sooner vacated the room when an attractive waitress in a short skirt came through the door carrying a plate of pasta and a glass of wine. She sat them down on the table, smiled at Mason, and backed out of the room.

Geno stared at the glass a moment, then picked it up, swirled it, and took a sip. A satisfied look followed. "Are you sure I can't offer you anything? I don't remember you being a connoisseur of fine wine, but we do have an excellent selection of draft, and the meatballs are exceptional today."

"Sorry, I just had lunch. And if it's all the same to you, I'd rather just get this over with—whatever *this* is." Mason pressed a hand against his ribcage and winced, "I thought we were finished after our last deal, Geno. If I remember right, you got what you wanted, and I got paid. Wasn't a seat on the city council good enough? Jesus man, I gave you the whole north shore of Beaufort on a platter. I see your name everywhere up there: Mancini Towers, Mancini Breeze, Mancini Dunes—"

Geno looked pleased. "It has a nice ring to it, doesn't it?"

Mason continued, "You wanted Tankersly gone. I made it happen. You paid me. It was a good deal, and more importantly, a *closed* deal."

Geno picked up a fork, and surveyed the plate of spaghetti on the table. "And if the word on the street is worth the water this pasta was cooked in, you got a little something unexpected out of the job as well."

Mason was silent for a moment, then said, "I didn't know she hated her husband. When she walked in on me wrapping him up in that blanket, I thought I was going to have to kill her too."

Geno twirled the fork in the spaghetti. "I scarcely think killing her is what it's called, Mister LaRue. Tell me, did you two really ... oh, how shall I put this . . . *celebrate* Mister Tankersly's untimely demise in their bed, while he was still cooling off on the floor?"

Before Mason could answer, Geno abandoned the subject, "I suppose it doesn't matter. It all seemed to work out in the end, and you are right, *that* matter is closed. There's a new item of business that has come to my attention. Something that I believe you can help me with. I received a phone call from New York earlier this week about it. My investors seemed highly motivated for me, or us, rather, to revisit something that, regrettably, slipped away from us a couple of months ago." Geno took the bite off his fork, and chewed thoroughly. It and a big gulp of wine went down. "Have you heard about the old Coast Guard light stations offshore?"

"Diamond, and Frying Pan? Yeah, I've read about them in the papers."

"Well then, you're probably also aware that the US Government sold both of them. They were suffering from neglect, and I suppose some committee in Washington finally decided to cut their losses. Pretty interesting history stuck way out there in the Atlantic, though. Sometimes the charter guys target them. They seem to attract a wide variety of fish. Have you ever seen them in person?"

Mason shook his head.

"Frankie carried a few of us out to have a look. They really are something. The one off Hatteras is in bad shape, and I'm afraid the poor guy who bought it is going to die out there when it finally collapses. However, the Frying Pan is still operable. Headquarters was, and still is interested in it."

"Why are you telling me this? If it was for sale, why didn't you and headquarters buy it? You got deep pockets."

Mason thought he saw a flash of hatred in Geno's eyes. "Well, Mister LaRue, we were poised to do just that, but the US Government would not accept anything but a hand-delivered sealed bid at the time of the sale. No call-ins, faxes, or email transmissions. I was planning to go myself, but something popped up at the last minute, so I sent one of my men. The incompetent boob was twenty minutes from Wilmington when one of his tires blew. Apparently, he couldn't operate a jack."

Mason smiled. "I guess he got a raise then?"

"I'm afraid not. We had a stern discussion about accountability, and a few weeks later he and a couple of the boys chartered a boat for a fishing trip. It was his birthday, I believe. Somewhere on the edge of the Gulf Stream, he got tangled in the line, and was snatched clear. I hear the marlin he was fighting at the time was a potential world record. It's a shame he didn't get him in." Geno sat back in his chair, and touched a linen napkin to the corners of his mouth, "The Coast Guard called off the search for his body two days later. It was a terrible tragedy. Frankie took it especially hard."

Mason cut an eye over his shoulder at the smiling fat man peeking over the door and wondered what it would be like dying attached to nearly a ton of blue marlin dragging you down into the deep. He shivered, then came back to himself, looked at his watch and said, "Come on Geno, let's get to the point. What does all this have to do with me?"

"A couple of locals from Wilmington bought the Frying Pan rig. Got it at a very good price, actually. I think you might know them."

Mason looked dumbfounded. "How would I know—"

"Hoyt Bennett. He and his daughter Caroline bought it together. I believe you know her especially well—formerly Miss Caroline LaRue? I understand she goes by Bennett now. Tell me, just how soon after the separation did she revert to her maiden name?"

Mason stood up, his eyes widened, and the center of his brain began to throb. Geno had always been very thorough, but how could he have known about him and Caroline? It's not like they had been the center of the well-to-do cliques around Wilmington. At best, they had been only one step above common trailer trash.

Before he could say anything, Geno continued, "Our sources in Wilmington say they've been working on it extensively, trying to get it set up for some kind of overnight fishing bed and breakfast destination. A kind of offshore adventure hotel."

Still in shock, Mason gulped down a mouthful of stale air as his mind began to tackle the other impossibility. *How could they afford it? How could they secure a loan from anyone who worked at a reputable bank?*

He stood there completely flummoxed. Geno sipped loudly from his glass, and Mason blinked his eyes a couple of times. "Are your sources smoking what you used to sell out of the trunk of your Cadillac? When I split, Caroline was all but washed up trying to get her real estate license, and Hoyt was the worst fisherman in the charter fleet, captaining a sinking ship. We were all living from minute to minute off what I could hustle every night from bums on the street. We barely could keep Jacqueline fed."

Geno leaned and raised a magazine from the chair next to him. He glanced at the front page and tossed it across the table. The candle flickered as it went by. "I take it that you've not kept up with them since you . . . how'd you put it? Split?"

Mason shook his head, and reached for the magazine. It was the latest issue of *Cape Fear Living,* and right there on the front page was Caroline Bennett standing next to a big red and white realty sign on a brilliantly green lawn. She was applying a large 'SOLD' sticker diagonally cross the company's name; behind her was nothing short of a small mansion.

Geno waited, letting it sink in. "As you can see from the cover, Caroline did finish getting her license, and has become quite the hustling agent. Also, Hoyt bought himself a better boat, and with a bit of luck I hear, has built a decent reputation and clientele running inshore and offshore fishing trips."

"But still," Mason said looking up from the magazine, "Uncle Sam just didn't give that thing away, and it's only been, what, three or four years? How could they have come up with a down payment for something like that?"

"I'm afraid you're missing a good bit of time in all this. It's been nine years since you left your family and Wilmington. Caroline got her license a year after you left, and she's been immersed in the real estate market down there ever since. I believe she paid off all her debt, including the lawyer's fees from the divorce within two years of selling her first house. She's been in the top ten in sales everywhere she's worked." Geno pointed at the magazine in Mason's hand and said, "Looks like the all-American girl. Smart and successful, and if I might say so, quite attractive. Wasn't she a cheerleader at East Carolina, too? Tell me, what caused you to file for divorce?"

The throbbing in Mason's head intensified. "Long story. Tell *me* something, Geno. You still haven't told me what I probably just got fired over. What do you want from me?"

"It's a unique situation, really. If it had been any other family, I'd seen to this myself. However, it just so happens to be your family. I'm fully aware that you're probably not on the best of terms with them, but when it comes to business, especially real estate transactions, oddly enough it's been my experience that family, even ex-family, can get things done quicker than strangers can, no matter how much money is waved in front of them. Since you have nothing better to do," Geno smiled across the table at Mason, "I want you to take a trip to Wilmington and see if you can convince them to sell me that light station. We were prepared to offer two hundred thousand dollars for it at the sale. Public records tell us that they bought it for sixty thousand. I have been authorized to offer up to a hundred, twenty-five thousand, plus whatever costs they've accrued via repairs, sight unseen, just like it sits. You are guaranteed five thousand if you swing the deal, plus ten percent of whatever you can get it for under our maximum set price. But, Mister LaRue, we need you on this now. Not tomorrow, not next week, not in a couple of months. *Now.*

"I understand that Mister Bennett and your daughter have been working on it on the weekends, going out Friday evenings and staying overnight, and coming back in either late Saturday or Sunday mornings. They've ramped up their efforts, now that school's out, trying to get a lot of the work done before the meat of the charter season hits. Your daughter has been accompanying him quite a bit. In fact, they went out this morning before light with a loaded boat.

With them out of the way, I think this evening will probably be a good time to bump into Miss Bennett in Wilmington, don't you agree? One-on-one—greasing the wheels a little?"

Mason LaRue sat back down in the chair. He couldn't believe it had been that long. Nine years had gone by in a blink, and now Caroline was a real estate mogul in Wilmington? He envisioned her closing deals and cashing big checks, and then a big check floated by in front of his eyes. This one had his name on it. Geno's offer was pretty good . . . unbelievable, actually. Mason didn't believe that an ex-husband had any advantage swinging deals with former family, but then again, he did have a way with Caroline—Hoyt, not so much. Maybe they could meet somewhere alone, have a few stiff drinks, and see what happened? If nothing else, she wasn't wearing a ring on the magazine cover, maybe there was a chance to do more than have a few drinks. At one time, she was voted the best-looking legs at East Carolina, and if the photograph hadn't been photoshopped, that hadn't changed. Maybe this was it? For the first time in a long time, maybe Mason LaRue was about to catch a break.

Mason scanned over the magazine one last time, then laid it on the table. "Make it ten thousand, plus the difference, and you've got a deal."

The response came without hesitation. "Let's split it and say seventy-five hundred." Geno seemed to emphasize it as a statement, rather than a question.

Mason smiled and stood up, offering his hand to his host. "It's good to be back in business with you, Geno." And while they were shaking hands, Mason asked, "Now just for shits and giggles, what in the hell are you and a bunch of washed up fat-cats from Yankeeville gonna do with a run down, rusty old light station twenty miles off the beach?"

Geno released Mason's hand and sat back down. He swirled the last bit of wine around in the glass thoughtfully. "I'm afraid that's privileged information, Mister LaRue, and something you needn't worry yourself with. Right now, you need to be focusing all your energy and creativity into determining how you're going to approach your former family about this. And from the look of things, upgrading your wardrobe might be the best place to start. Looks aren't everything, but in situations such as these, it does seem to help. What does your bank account look like?"

"Not as good as yours."

"I see." Geno took his wallet out of his jacket's interior pocket. Five one-hundred-dollar bills landed on the table. "Consider it an advance. You can pay me back, with a little interest of course, when you swing the deal. Now, do you have any wheels that can get you to Wilmington, or are you going to need a ride too?"

Chapter 6

Mason LaRue had never had a good and wholesome idea in his life. The possibility of doing something simply for the greater good of mankind had never once entered his devious mind. Everything he'd ever done—decent, bad, or indifferent—was ultimately for himself and himself only. As Hoyt testified at the divorce hearing, if Mason LaRue had spent half the time devising ways to be a decent human being as he spent trying to con people, the Rockefeller Center in New York would have been petitioned for a name change.

Mason's twisted gift was the ability to manipulate people. Even as a young kid, he'd learned that he was able to get most things he wanted by simply acting a certain way, or crying at just the right time. He began to hone the talent early on, and from the third through the eighth grade, he seldom completed an entire week at school. His best amateur performance came the day after he found out that a mushy, chewed mixture of saltine crackers and milk looked fantastically similar to vomit. His mother happily obliged when he asked for that combination to carry with him to school for breakfast, and while the other kids were enjoying stale jelly on dry toast, a young Mason LaRue opened pack after pack of the dry crackers, placed them in his mouth, cracked them up with a couple of chews, then filled the rest of the void with milk. No one thought twice about his slightly bulging cheeks, or about how unusually quiet he was walking back to class. A few minutes into the math lesson, the teacher called on Mason to answer a problem on the board, and instantly he made a face, grabbed his belly and began to blubber. The mixture began dribbling down his chin, and with a little encouragement, it quickly turned into a forceful spew. In seconds, his desk and the pretty little blonde girl that sat in front of him were blanketed with a warm, white chunky soup. Smiling, he was whisked away to the nurse's station . . . his school day quickly over before it had even started.

The complexity of his abilities grew throughout his teen and young adult years, and by the time he was thirty, Mason prided himself on his ability to talk himself into and out of any situation. The con he bragged about the most came quite easily to him one night in a twist of fate so bizarre he could barely believe it himself. After spending a mediocre hour with a less than enthusiastic hooker, Mason LaRue actually got *her* to pay *him* by convincing her that he'd found a lump on her left breast. He assumed correctly that she'd not been the class valedictorian, and without even a trace of cocaine or heroin in her system, the ditsy, but unbelievably stacked blonde savagely groped herself in a type of crude breast exam. Once her fingers located the phantom lump she sprang from the bed, and after an uncharacteristically thoughtful pause, began to wail uncontrollably. Mason somehow held back laughter as he feigned consolation, then on a whim, he decided to see just how far he could take it. Without hesitation, he reached for his wallet and handed her a business card of what he called the most prestigious front-end specialist in Norfolk. She snatched the card from his hand as she shimmied up her panties. Snuffing back tears, she read the large print 'Best Balance, Alignment, and Rotation in the Tidewater.' She stared helplessly, trying to make sense of it, and Mason, hardly believing the words coming out of his own mouth, told her it was simply a buzz phrase that floated around every breast oncology and reconstructive surgery conference. He popped the top on another beer, and with an air of confidence that would have turned every politician in DC green with envy, he coolly told her that he usually collected a twenty-dollar referral fee, since he, too, was a doctor. As close to stunned as he'd ever been, Mason watched the poor girl fish through her purse and then slap a crumpled twenty-dollar bill in his hand. He was still staring at it when she flew out the door, harboring a bogus case of breast cancer and a business card that would get her in touch with a master mechanic. He brayed laughter, envisioning what the guys at the shop would think when that call came in.

Mason had a gift, all right. And that, along with a few other crude attributes he possessed (necessary in the raw and unforgiving circles of high stakes, organized crime) was why Geno Mancini had called on him. Brute force and scare tactics could go a long way, but there was something about the subtle way Mason LaRue could get things done that seemed to fascinate Geno Mancini.

Two hours after Mason and Geno shook on their deal, Pauley Bertanelli, Geno's man with the strange eyes, met Mason outside a department store in town. Mason jumped into the passenger seat, with a fresh haircut, and wearing a very nice selection that hinted at professionalism, but was also casual enough to be worn at a Hawaiian luau. The two men seldom spoke, and in the miles between Morehead City and Wilmington, Mason had plenty of time to think. Not about how good it would be to see Caroline again or the possibility of seeing an up-to-date picture of his only legitimate daughter—no, he was racking his brain, running through potential conversations he and his ex-wife would likely have about the light station. They sped past a New Hanover county line sign, stating that they'd reached the *Gateway to Wilmington,* and Mason sat a little taller in the seat, almost in a panic. Two hours they'd been on the road, and nothing worth a second thought had come. His devious mind kicked into overdrive, hashing and re-hashing idea after rotten idea. There *had* to be something that would work, something that would convince Caroline that he had changed and was now one of the good and honest people in the world.

Looking out the window at the countryside, he realized that the petty little schemes that he'd managed to hatch probably wouldn't fool a first grader. Mason shook his head and frowned. It would take more than schoolboy lies and excuses to fool Caroline. She'd put up with some of his best work before, and likely would be on guard from the first moment she laid eyes on him. The divorce had been messy, and there towards the end, he and his sleaze-hole of a lawyer were lobbying hard for full custody. But Mason's desire to have Jackie wasn't for the ordinary reasons a father might want his daughter. He didn't want her because he loved her, or because he wanted to watch her grow up and be a part of her life. No, Mason wanted his daughter for the most important reason he could think of—financial gain. He looked at her as a prospective investor might consider a certain stock while the price was low, expecting it to soar later on. The entire family was living on crumbs at the time of the divorce, but Mason knew that if Caroline ever passed the realtor's exam and began to sell houses, there would be the potential for monthly alimony checks. He wasn't convinced that she'd ever do it, but at least he'd have Jackie and some guaranteed money every month if she did. Unfortunately for him, the court didn't see it his way, and he completely washed his hands of the entire situation.

As the 'Welcome to Wilmington' sign flew past his window, his wonderfully wicked brain finally sparked. Mason was sure that just coming right out and asking Caroline to meet with him for any reason was never going to happen, so there was nothing left to do except trick her. And since she was on the real estate hot-seat in Wilmington, what better way to accomplish a rendezvous than pretending to be a potential buyer of one of her listings? The idea was so simple, he found himself second-guessing it, but the more and more it rolled around in his head, the more and more he realized that it had a better than average chance of working. It wasn't going to be easy, but if the ruse could get his foot in the door, and if he could catch her at just the right time, and pitch something juicy to her in just the right way, Caroline might be swayed. That left Hoyt. Mason's crooked smile almost fell off his face, fighting back a sudden attack of depression.

Hoyt, Hoyt, Hoyt.

The old man was going to be a tough nut to crack. Mason had never been able to get him to see things his way, not even early on in his marriage to Caroline when they pretended to like each other. There was one thing that would work for him if things fell into place. If he could just get Caroline on his side, maybe she could help soften the old man. Hoyt had always been a sucker for anything she wanted. Daddy's little girl. If he could get her to start tasting money, she might be a valuable ally. Money always seemed to change things. The thoughts kept sparking in his mind, and the blueprints of his plan slowly started to come together. First, he had to get Caroline to meet him. If he could talk with her, there was a chance to lure her in with the money. Then came the really hard part. He'd have to make contact with Hoyt before Caroline did. If he pulled that off, then it would be the classic 'both ends working against the middle' scenario, where he could try to lead them both through the gauntlet, one right behind the other. There was always a chance for a slow developing plan to blow up, but Mason knew that none of it was going to have a chance to work unless he could speak to each of them separately before the other knew about it.

One step at a time, Mason. One step at a time.

He pointed at a used car lot up ahead and told Pauley to pull over. While the Tahoe idled, he stared straight ahead through the window at a late model midnight blue convertible. Mason wasn't seeing the car though, his mind's eye was staring at a great moving flowchart of possible inputs and outcomes. Consideration was given, retracted, then regiven, and as a sign of final decision, he turned to his chauffer and said, "I think I've got it. Gimme your phone."

Chapter 7

The conversation with Geno went better than expected, and as soon as the call ended, Mason opened Google on the smartphone and searched for Caroline's office webpage. He glanced at the listings and found a nice little bayside cottage at the end of a cul-de-sac that needed new shutters and a paint job. Caroline's name and number were there on the webpage, and he quickly reached for a pen and jotted the cottage's address and the office number down on his hand.

Mason turned to Pauley and said, "I'm going to get Caroline on speaker phone and then you are going to talk to her. It's been a while, and I'm not sure she'll recognize my voice, but there's no need to risk it before I can get in the same room with her."

He and crazy-eyes rehearsed it a couple of times, then Mason punched in the numbers.

The speaker buzzed once, then twice, before a perky voice answered. "Pickett and Bennett Properties. Jeanine speaking, can I help you?"

Pauley's voice cracked faking the southern accent, "Um, yes ma'am. My name's Thomas Martin. I'm interested in a listing of yours." He squinted at the ink scribbled on Mason's palm. "It's on Quarter Main Loop, 485 Quarter Main."

The secretary seemed to flip through some papers on her desk, then said, "I believe that's Miss Bennett's listing. Let me see." A flurry of keystrokes flooded the line, then the voice was back. "Oh yes, here it is. The three-bed, two-bath cottage. Yes, that's Caroline's. Can you hold for a moment?"

Less than a minute later, the worst elevator music he'd ever heard faded away, and then a familiar voice came on the line. "Mister

Martin, I'm so glad you called. My name is Caroline Bennett. What would you like to know about our listing at 485 Quarter Main Loop? Besides the fact that it's a very nice home that boasts a fantastic view of the bay."

Mason nearly spoke, but caught himself and punched Pauley on the arm. "Oh yeah, well, I've looked at all the pictures on the website and would like to see more, but I've got business in Miami and will be leaving in the morning. I do happen to have a couple of hours this evening to look at it in person, but I'm not sure if you'd be willing to meet me on short notice like this. If I don't look at it today, I'm afraid it'll be a couple of weeks before my schedule opens up again."

Mason could hear Caroline sweating on the other end of the line.

"I was trying to finish up some paperwork here in the office—been a busy week. What time is it now? Ten after four, hmmm. Well, I usually don't like to work late on Friday nights, but my usual Friday night obligation is busy helping her grandfather. Let's try to squeeze you in. When can you be there?"

Mason smiled and held up his hand and flashed five fingers, then four, then five again.

Pauley said, "Five-forty-five work for you?"

There was a brief pause, "An hour and a half. I think it will—that might even be enough time for me to finish up here. See you there, Mister Martin. Be sure to bring your checkbook, because you are going to love this cozy bay-view home."

* * *

The black Tahoe parked on the side of the street four houses from 485 Quarter Main. The quaint neighborhood was all neat, cottage-style homes with freshly mowed lawns and immaculately trimmed hedges. Mason briefly daydreamed about all the scams he could pull on the brainless suburbanites who lived there. Starting at quarter after five, the two men watched car after car roll past them, pull in to their respective homes, then leave twenty-minutes later.

61

Mason coldly said, "Looks like all the leg on this street have forgotten how to cook." More cars passed them and rolled back by a short time later. "Jesus! Is everyone here propping up the local restaurant economy or what?" Mason hadn't had anything as extravagant as a five-dollar quarter pound burger in a long time, but the Friday night ritual of the well-to-do on Quarter Main Loop was working to his advantage. The houses on either side of 485 looked dark and empty. He looked at Pauley and said, "Let 'em all go get a damn steak. If nobody's around, then they can't call the cops if this goes bad."

At five-thirty, a white Subaru SUV drove by with a Pickett and Bennett Properties sticker on the side. Mason watched in awe as the door opened and two long legs dropped to the street. His ex-wife emerged from behind the door wearing a lacy cream-colored top with a casual business length crimson red skirt. Her long wavy blonde hair unfurled to her shoulders and, holding a large leather satchel, she stepped down the walk and keyed open the front door. For a moment, all Mason LaRue could see was a shaft of divine light descending on her from above.

Pauley stuttered, "You . . . you were married to *her?*"

"Shut up you cross-eyed punk."

The minutes crawled by. Mason impatiently checked his watch. There was no need to startle her doing whatever last second preparations real estate agents do before showing homes . . . he wanted to walk in that door to a totally relaxed ex-wife. It was the only way he saw it working.

Five more minutes passed, then he stepped out of the Tahoe and made his way down road. At the door, he dumbly stared at the big numbers 485, as a shaking finger found the doorbell. Inside, chimes rang and footsteps sounded. Mason took a deep breath, trying to calm the butterflies.

Chapter 8

When the door to 485 Quarter Main Loop opened, Mason LaRue was nearly overcome with what he saw. Caroline hadn't changed a bit. There standing in the small foyer was the twenty-year-old cheerleader that he'd met for the first time singing karaoke on stage at the Pirate's Cove in Greenville. Like a highlight reel stuck in fast-forward, the time they'd lived, loved, and finally hated zipped by.

Mason snapped out of it when Caroline's shrill voice pierced the silence.

"What the hell are *you* doing here?" Her voice echoed down the vacant hallway, then he saw her face change from a look of surprise, to complete exasperation. "Oh—I get it now. Thomas Martin, huh? You made that crap up just to get me out here by myself."

She turned and ran back into the kitchenette. Her hand disappeared into the satchel, and emerged again holding a snub-nose revolver.

Mason's mind finally caught up with that was happening. "No, no, Caroline. It's not like that!"

He took a step into the foyer, waving his hand from side to side. He began to take another step, but stopped cold in his tracks. For the second time that day, Mason LaRue was staring down the barrel of a gun.

Caroline's voice was determined, and surprisingly calm. "Turn around and take your lying, conniving, worthless ass right out that door, and I'll think about not calling the law. And if you don't move in the next three seconds," she waggled the revolver in front of her, finger on the trigger, "I'll kill you right where you stand."

Shocked and impressed, it took everything he had not to smile. Caroline Bennett had only flashed bits and pieces of this kind of attitude, sass, gumption, or whatever you wanted to call it in the last few weeks before their divorce was final. When she was mad, she was beautiful, but standing there in the lacy-cream top and crimson skirt with those long legs pouring out of it, holding a gun and cursing, she was more than beautiful . . . she was bombshell sexy. He felt the front of his pants tighten as the highlight reel kicked again, this time replaying scenes from the bedroom, laundry room, kitchen, and every other place in the house they had maddening, wild sex. Just for a moment, he actually believed that what was hiding behind that skirt was worth getting shot over. He came back to himself—remembering the plan—and instantly worked the percentages. What were the odds of covering the eight steps before she convinced herself to shoot? Disarming her would be easy, if he could just get there.

Mason shifted his weight ever-so-slightly, planning a running start, and almost as quickly Caroline responded by thumbing back the hammer on her revolver. The dull gray hollow-pointed bullets peeked from the front of the cylinder's chambers as it rotated into position.

"No, Caroline. I promise you, it's not like that!" Mason said it louder this time, and with a more concerned voice. "I'm here on business, that and, well—I did want to see you again. My God, you are just as beautiful as you were back at East Carolina."

Caroline's eyes seemed to burn holes through him. "Cut the crap, Mason."

"It's not crap. It's the truth."

"You think I'm going to believe anything you say after what you did to me. To *us?*" The revolver was still aimed at the center of his chest.

All at once, Mason's scheming mind began to produce. He turned his wrist slightly and glanced where a watch would've been had he owned one. "Well, frankly, I don't have time to care if you believe me or not, but if you don't, you're about to miss out on the biggest deal of your life."

Caroline just stood there looking at him.

He cleared his voice and continued. "I'm here about the light station. On behalf of a business partner."

Caroline erupted. "Shut up, turn around, and get out!"

"Hold on a minute." Mason gambled and took a step towards her, getting fully inside the door. "You've gotten good at this real estate game. I see your signs all over town and I hear you're doing pretty good for yourself, but I know this light station deal is going to be a drain."

Caroline shook her head. "Somebody's been feeding you bad information."

"I don't think so. I've been working as a silent partner up the coast for a big outfit out of Jersey. Mainly Virginia Beach to Hatteras. You know how those Yankees love the Outer Banks." He stopped for a moment, giving this newly minted information a chance to sink in. "We have ears up and down the coast, all the way to Savannah, and they don't miss a trick. To be honest, I don't know how they pull it off. The things they hear." Mason's voice was now smooth as butter. He actually smiled at her. "You've hit their radar screen, Caroline. They're tracking you and your business partner. You're impressing them."

It was so subtle, he didn't know if it was real or not. A slight softening of the eyes, or perhaps it was a longer than average exhale, but Mason thought he sensed his ex-wife relax. She turned her head to the side in a thinking posture, and the revolver lowered slightly. Maybe it was working. Maybe he'd finally found a chink in her armor. The glimpse of whatever it was didn't last long. Caroline blinked twice, and the revolver was back up again, trained on his chest. Mason could still feel it, but the hardness that came back to her eyes didn't seem so harsh.

That's what I was looking for. That's a good girl. Now let's see what kind of damage I managed to do.

Mason took in a deep breath and released it as a long, smooth sigh. "Look, my people want that thing. They didn't tell me why, and I didn't ask. I also told them that sending me down here wasn't going to work." Mason shook his head and mumbled, almost talking to himself. "Send me down here to talk with you, as much as you hate—" He laughed a little and said, "If I told them once, I told them a hundred times. But I gave my word to give it a try, and here I am. You see, I've grown some too in the last, what's it been, nine, ten years? I learned the hard way what happens when you disappoint your partner."

Mason looked into her eyes, eyes where he'd seen the fires of passion and also the cold sting of hate. "So here I am, Caroline. Standing here staring down the barrel of a gun, hoping to get something from you to take back."

There was no answer.

Mason's evil mind sparked again. "Let me say my piece, and then I can at least go back and tell her that I tried."

Caroline's mouth unhinged. "*Her?* Your partner is a *woman?*"

Mason tried his best to look modest, but on the inside, he was smiling the biggest smile he'd ever smiled. That was it. He knew he had her now.

"Yep. A crackerjack too. But she don't hold a candle to you."

Caroline's eyes dropped to his left hand. "No ring?"

He shook his head. "Nope, business only. I told you I've grown since I made both of our lives miserable."

Mason nearly screamed out loud. He hadn't planned on bringing up their painful past, but he'd said it before he could stop himself. He quickly changed gears. "I talked with Hoyt a few days ago about it."

"You . . . you talked to dad about this?"

"Only for a few minutes over the phone. Our people did make one mistake. We were told that he'd bought it by himself. I did a little digging and found out about you. I figured you were a silent partner being so busy with all this, so naturally, I was thinking he was the one to talk to first." Mason chuckled. "Man, oh man, am I glad that conversation didn't happen in person. He cussed me for the first three minutes straight. But he finally ran out of steam, and I got him to listen to me for just a minute."

Caroline shook her head. "I don't believe it."

"Believe it. And I'll tell you something, ole Hoyt hasn't changed a bit, but when I told him that he could very well double his money . . . well, let's just say that he was way more accommodating."

Stunned, Caroline's arm dropped to her side, pointing the gun harmlessly at the floor. "*Double* the money?"

"Sure. Our offer is twice what you paid for it, but as the old saying goes, all good things must come to an end. There's a shelf life . . . or there was a shelf life. Hoyt said that he wasn't going to do anything without consulting you first."

Caroline blankly stared past him. "How long ago was this?"

"Three days. We didn't hear back from him, so we figured that either y'all decided not to sell, or that maybe for some reason he didn't want to tell you about it." Mason looked to either side of him at the walls of the foyer and waved his hands again, "And that's why I took my partner's advice to come see you like this. I knew you'd never meet me any other way, but what I had to say, I thought, was important enough to risk you calling the cops, or," Mason's eyes went to the gun in her hand, "getting shot."

When he first knocked on the door of 485 Quarter Main Loop, Mason was sure it was going to take a miracle to make something happen. And when the door opened and Caroline began screaming, he actually could feel his heart beating in his neck, but those smooth lies that he'd somehow always been able to conjure at just the right moment had slowly taken their toll. Now, he was relaxed and loose and well aware that the last two minutes had been some of his best work. Just like old times, in the clutch, Mason LaRue had found yet another way to manipulate the situation. In a matter of minutes, he had reduced his once irate ex-wife to putty, and the only thing left to do was to make her do what he wanted her to do. Applying just a touch of pressure in the right spot would likely do it. Not enough to make her bolt—no—too much would ruin what he'd been able to accomplish. She only needed to feel a small pinch here and there to know that a decision needed to be made. Sooner, rather than later.

Mason stuck his hands in his pockets and stared at the tops of his shoes. "The offer will expire, Caroline. In fact, the delay with Hoyt may have already have done it. But even if it has, I can still help you. If I tell them you're interested, I believe they'd make it good. If not, I know the second offer will be very handsome."

Caroline shook her head again, speaking more to herself than to Mason. "Somebody actually wants it worse than we do?" She mumbled a few other things that Mason couldn't understand, then said, "I wonder why dad didn't say anything?"

Mason's brain, which had been following the loose outline he devised before walking through the door, went absolutely rouge. He stifled a laugh, impressed at his own insane brilliance. He'd been tiptoeing all around her feelings the entire conversation, but the idea that had just manifested itself in the most devious part of his brain would bring her to her knees—it would be the final nail in Caroline Bennett's coffin.

He straightened and said with as much fake dignity as he could muster, "Can't say why he kept it to himself, but I'm definitely glad I came out here to see you. I still have a little interest in all this too."

Immediately, he sensed her entire aura change back into business mode.

"Oh yeah? Whatcha going to make off this deal?"

Mason followed his instincts, pursing his lips and staring at the tops of his shoes. "Initially, seven percent. But I just couldn't do it. I asked her for just enough to cover my gas and time getting down here, but she insisted on two."

Caroline covered her mouth with her free hand for a moment. "I don't believe you. Why would you cut your own throat like that?"

"Like I said, for my other interest in this deal."

"What other interest?"

"Jacqueline."

* * *

Mason LaRue appeared at the door to 485 Quarter Main Loop, closed it behind him, and confidently strode down the street. He quickly covered the distance and climbed into the black Tahoe.

Pauley looked at his watch and said, "All that in just twenty minutes? I didn't think she was going to let you in the door. Didn't I see a gun?"

Mason LaRue smiled a smile that would have turned fresh milk sour. He reached for Pauley's cell phone and said, "Get me to the airport, freak-show. I've got a helicopter to catch."

Chapter 9

Playtime was officially over on the Frying Pan Shoals Light Station. Jackie continued to roll fresh paint on the walls, but her mind was totally consumed by the pompano her grandfather had speared. She hated to see such majestic fish die, and she almost cried watching it being cut up, but the thought of those fillets sizzling on the grill doused in a bath of garlic butter made her mouth water. At the expense of a couple of innocent pompanos, they were going to eat well that evening. But what really astonished her were the smaller fish. Those hundreds of greedy little mouths seemed to appear out of thin water when Hoyt tossed the carcasses overboard. It was like watching a small pack of piranha feed. Humans were wasteful, she knew that, but small ocean fish didn't spare a single ounce of anything edible. The clever slogan she'd heard on TV 'waste not want not' had taken on new meaning.

Jackie dipped the roller in the pan and laid the final column of paint to finish the first coat on the new wall she was working on. While she waited for it to dry, she put together new bed frames in the two finished bedrooms, and one by one, she placed the mattresses that they'd brought on a prior trip in place. When she was finished, she opened the new linens from their shrink-wrapped packages, and began making the beds. It was boring work, but it made for plenty of time to think. The biology lessons the sea taught weren't as neat and tidy as her teachers and textbooks made them out to be. The frantic way the small fish fought over the carcasses was startling. And thinking like a scientist, an interesting question settled in her mind. Were they just fighting over the free meal, each trying to out-eat its neighbor, or were they trying to minimize their time out in the open to keep from becoming a meal themselves?

Pondering that, another thought manifested itself. Her grandfather said that life in the ocean wasn't fair, and after watching it all happen, she had no other choice but to agree. The ocean was strictly an 'eat or be eaten' world, and sometimes both happened within seconds of each other.

Jackie was making the last bed when the cooling breeze wafted an overwhelming aroma of grilled fish into the room. A hunger pang rippled deep inside her, working its way all the way up into her throat. Saliva glands were triggered, and swallowing a big gulp, Jackie quickly spread the light blanket over the freshly made bed and pulled a new case over the last pillow. Out the window, white wisps of smoke blew over the edge of the platform, and the sun dipped low on the horizon. Jackie's stomach growled again, and she was out the door and down the hallway, headed for the roof.

Hoyt stood at the grill, flipping fish fillets in a pair of Bermuda shorts, and a red Hawaiian shirt. Beside him was a cooler filled with drinks, and a few steps away sat a small wooden table centered between two lawn chairs. The table and chairs were weighed down by small, discreet sandbags.

"Ah, there you are beach girl. I was just about to call for you. Supper's almost ready."

Jackie smiled then looked to the west. The sinking sun was a bloated red disk suspended over the sea—the refraction from the atmosphere easily made it appear three times its normal size. As far as sunsets go, Jackie knew that it couldn't get any better. She remembered thinking that morning while being beat to death on the boat how nobody would want to put up with the trouble of getting out here just to spend the night in the middle of the ocean. The freakishly large sun saying its farewells to the day made her realize that perhaps she was wrong. Maybe the old light station did have a few endearing qualities after all. She collapsed into one of the chairs, released a big sigh, and watched a handful of terns hover in the sky above a handrail along the edge of the platform. One by one, they descended and found the rail. Each ruffled their feathers, then seemed to sigh themselves.

Jackie pulled a lock of hair behind her ear and said, "The sunsets are the best thing about this place."

Hoyt casually gazed at the horizon over his shoulder. "Sure is pretty. Not much better than grilled pompano and a sunset out here on the edge of the Frying Pan."

After a long day of work, it felt good just to sit still. And after a couple of long blinks, she felt her chin touch her chest. Forcing her eyes open, Jackie noticed that the sun was just touching the sea. She'd never forgotten what her grandfather said about it when she was a kid. On his knee at the controls, coming back in from a few of the evening trips that went long, he'd leaned close and told her that the sun put itself out every night when it slid into the ocean. She'd naively believed that was true until a science teacher had taught her otherwise. The wind wafted the sweet smoke in her direction and a new flush of saliva coated the inside of her mouth. She gazed at the big red disk again. Back on land or out here on the shoals, the sun meant everything to everything. Warmth, food, light to see . . . it was life itself in its simplest form. The pompano had been delivered to the grill because of it too. Sunlight shining through the water grew seaweed and plankton. Small fish ate that, and then some of them were eaten by bigger fish like the pompano. Then along comes Hoyt Bennett with a speargun on a sunny day, and suddenly she's feasting on a fantastic supper.

If only life was as simple as believing that the sun put itself out every night when it dipped into the sea.

She snickered at the red disk, now beginning to disappear, taking its cool dip in the water.

Hoyt asked, "What's so funny beach girl?"

"Oh nothing, just watching the sun get wet."

Hoyt smiled and lightly pressed a fillet with the spatula. The extruded juices sizzled loudly on the charcoal. "You hear that, dontcha? You didn't believe me, but you *can* hear it sizzle going under."

They both shared a laugh, and she watched him, in quiet admiration, while he flipped the fillets one last time and reached for the platter. There was no doubt she loved her grandfather. He had been there every time Caroline needed him while finishing her realtor license. Jackie and he had spent many hours on the water together, fishing, talking, and living. Hoyt had totally taken the place of her father, who, according to her mother, had abandoned them both when she was just a toddler. She asked about him often when she was younger, but Caroline always managed to change the subject. The notion of her father completely faded away over the years, while her grandfather filled the void in their lives. While other charter captains were out squeezing every last cent out of lengthy fishing trips and enjoying a few libations at the local watering hole after a long day at sea, Hoyt had managed to grow his fishing business, and at the same time help raise Jackie. He was there almost every day in the evenings, helping her with homework, cooking supper, showing her how to swing a softball bat and shoot a basketball. He had become the relief valve they so desperately needed.

A tern landed on platform a few yards away, and begged for handouts as the two dined. The grilled fish was tender and delicious—some of the best she'd ever had. Hoyt mopped his plate with a piece of bread and said, "Did you feel anything while you were in the water?"

Jackie thought for a moment. "Not really. I kinda felt bad for the fish you shot."

"Not that. Remember earlier when I told you I felt better after a swim here? My joints didn't ache, and whatever soreness in my muscles, well, sort of went away?"

She nodded.

"It happened again. I was fighting a sore wrist while I was treating the walls, and after that swim it was good as new." He squeezed his right wrist with his left hand, and flexed his fingers several times, working them in all directions. "I couldn't do this at lunch. Must've slept on it wrong or something. Feels right as rain now though."

Jackie said, "Maybe it was all that movement and flexing you did while you were working. That could've loosened it up."

She yawned and stood up, intending to deposit the paper plate in the trash bag tied to the cooler's handle. Between her chair and the cooler, her right foot awkwardly found one of the tie-down loops welded to the metal sheet roofing. Jackie's ankle buckled, and reflexively she dipped her right side, trying to stay upright. Her arm straightened, searching for anything to steady herself with, and the only thing there was the grill. Jackie screamed as she pressed her forearm down on the hot lid. Instinctively, she rolled hard to the left, off the grill, leaving pieces of her sizzling skin on the hot metal. In just seconds, the emergency that Jackie had worried about before they swam that afternoon had happened.

"Jackie!" Hoyt screamed, bolting out of his chair and grabbing her arm. The burn was savage. Already a nasty, five-inch long white blister had formed underneath the shredded layer of epidermis between her elbow and wrist.

Jackie was still wailing as they hurried down the stairs, into the hallway, headed to the galley. There, Hoyt found some medicinal aloe in the supplies, and he carefully smeared it on, then wrapped it with clean gauze. Then he poured a small glass of milk and gave her two Tylenol.

"It's not too bad," he finally said.

Jackie, snubbing tears, noticed the inflection. She'd been able to tell when he was keeping something from her and her mother for a couple of years.

Hoyt pasted on the best smile he could muster. "Probably going to be sore for a few days. We've had a busy day, and I saw you dozing some up there while I was finishing up the fish fillets. Let's give those pills a few minutes to start working and get you to bed. I bet you'll start to feel better in just a bit. Try to get some sleep, and we'll see what it looks like in the morning. I can handle the clean-up."

He hurried down the hallway, and came back holding a small prescription bottle. He shook a single small pill out in his hand, placed it on the counter, and cut it in half with his pocket knife. "Here, give one of these a try. Low dose sleeping pills. The doctor gave them to me when I started coming out here. Sometimes I get too sore to sleep after a full day's work. They'll help."

Jackie washed it down with a splash of milk, and walked beside her grandfather to her room. He kissed her on the forehead, and told her he'd come by and check on her when he was done tidying up. Lying in the dark, her arm pulsed like a siren, but strangely, it didn't hurt enough to make her cry. She'd learned about burns in school, and she knew that what she had was likely a second degree version of one. The window was open, letting the cool breeze blow through the room, and off in the distance she heard a strange sound. It started out as a light hum, and with every passing second it became more of a constant buzz. She blinked heavy eyelids, and listened closely. It sounded like a lonely cicada on a warm summer's night, but she'd never seen any bugs this far out. It had to be an engine . . probably a yacht coming north from wherever yachts come from. The sleeping pill was working, as the steady engine buzz, the occasional metallic creak, and the light waves rhythmically slapping the Grady White's fiberglass below her all harmonized at the right moment. It was an irresistible lullaby that seized her mind with the force of a steel grapple.

Jackie forcibly opened her eyes. The pills were softening the pain, but she still felt horrible about the accident. Tripping over a tie-down loop on the flat roof and turning her ankle was embarrassing and juvenile, bordering on sheer stupidity. Her grandfather had allowed her to come out with him to work on the tower, he'd tried to teach her how to spearfish, he'd even let her pilot the boat in less than perfect conditions—and she proved after all that, she was nothing more than an uncoordinated child.

Jackie tried to be disgusted with herself, but found that she no longer cared. She drifted, letting the new, soft mattress soothe her body and mind. Off in the distance, the yacht was still there, but the low roar of the engines now seemed to be fading into the distance.

Chapter 10

The engine on the small Robinson R-44 helicopter was louder than Mason LaRue expected. Even with the headset over his ears, the constant roar leaking through the thin fuselage and the pilot's constant babbling about flying Blackhawks in the first Gulf War was the perfect cranial storm. Mason's head was beginning to throb.

The fact that the small cockpit was cramped with two grown men didn't help. He had never felt the slightest inkling of claustrophobia before, but crammed in that little glass globe watching the instruments spin and twirl while rubbing elbows and thighs with this blowhard who must have single-handedly airlifted every wounded soldier out of Baghdad made him feel like he was slowly being chewed to pieces inside a blender. Mason slipped off the headphones, and looked over his shoulder and saw two charter boats on the horizon heading in for the day. Past them in the sky, the sun was already beginning to set. The engine was loud, the conversation was septic, but at least the view was nice.

Mason watched the boats blink out of sight, wishing he was on one, when he felt the pilot's knee bump his. He snapped back, facing forward, and slid the headphones back into place.

"You see it out there? The blinking light?"

Mason strained his eyes and nodded, even though he saw nothing but water.

"That's the navigational light on the top of the tower. We're fifteen minutes out. Should be there with some daylight to spare."

Mason refocused his eyes and finally saw it. There was an uneasy feeling in the pit of his stomach.

Hopefully the old man won't greet us with a load of buckshot.

* * *

The helicopter hovered thirty feet over the platform. There was enough light to see, but the pilot flipped a switch on the instrument panel, and a sharp beam of light hit the center of the flat roof below. A cooking grill and a few chairs and table were over by the rail, but the landing area was clear. There was a dark silhouette making its way up the stairs with a flashlight, and after blinking it back at the helicopter several times, the pilot began slowly descending. Permission to land, at least for now, had been granted.

Just before the skids contacted the roof, Mason turned and saw his crouched ex-father-in-law staring a hole through him. He quickly turned back to the pilot and said, "Keep this bird running, just in case things go south."

Mason stepped clear of the cockpit, but before he could stretch all the kinks loose, Hoyt advanced.

"What the hell are you doing here?" What was left of the old man's hair whipped almost comically in the rotor-wash. "There's no need to get comfortable. Quit stretching, get back on board, and tell the pilot to get that thing off my platform."

Mason ignored the banter and glanced at Hoyt's empty hands. Satisfied he wasn't in danger, he said, "I've got some information for you, Hoyt. Something that I think you'll want to hear."

"You flew all the way out here just to tell me something?" Hoyt's face flushed. "What in hell's name could you possibly have to tell me?"

The engine whined relentlessly. Mason motioned for Hoyt to follow as he backed away from the helicopter, towards the edge of the platform. "I was hoping that we could at least be civil," he said, watching Hoyt's face turn a deeper shade of red.

"Civil? We burned that bridge a long time ago, sonny."

Mason arched his back, stretching the final kinks loose. "I have a message for you from some friends of mine up in Morehead City. They are interested in this," he looked down and tapped his toe a couple of times on the roof, "piece of rusty steel."

"Rusty steel!"

"Yes sir. I know a few people who would like to take this thing off your hands. I've put them off, and put them off—been trying to tell them for weeks now that you probably wouldn't be interested. I talked with Caroline about it recently and—"

"You did *what?* What are you doing talking to Caroline about anything? After what you did to her and Jackie, you don't have a right to be seen in the same time zone with them. Don't you remember what the Judge told you?"

The hatred was still there. Even over the whirring helicopter rotors, he could hear the old man breathing hard. His blood pressure had to be spiking. For a split-second of sheer fantasy, Mason LaRue saw his ex-father-in-law suddenly clutch his chest, turn pasty white, and fall over dead. Massive coronary. He'd dreamed of this exact scenario hundreds of times when he and Caroline were married, but had never attempted to carry him that far. Maybe it was time to do just that.

Mason came back to himself. "No, Hoyt. This is strictly business. I spoke to her briefly about it. Now, she didn't come right out and say it, but the impression I got is that she thought it was interesting. She didn't seem to mind talking about it when I told her that she might double her money on this thing. I figured that if Caroline was interested enough to hear me out, then you might be too. I wanted to break the ice and see where you stood, and when I didn't find you in the normal spots around town, somebody down at the marina told me you'd come out to work on it this weekend. I thought about chartering a boat, but the boss let me borrow his whirly-bird. Time is money you know."

"You . . . you . . . you came out here to . . . to tell me that? That you want to broker a deal for this tower?"

Mason tried to look innocent. "You mean Caroline didn't say anything to you about it?"

Hoyt started to answer, but Mason cut him off. "Well, I guess she didn't think the time was right yet. She said that this was your baby, and that she was merely a silent partner on it."

Hoyt seemed to mentally crack. "You know what I think, you sorry piece of shit? I think you are playing games. And that's something we don't need 'round here."

The old man took a couple of steps towards Mason, fists clinched.

"Now wait a minute, Hoyt, I'm telling the truth. I know some folks who want to buy this tower and are prepared to pay you handsomely for it. I think they are trying to work some kind of deal with several oceanographic departments. You've seen Shark Week on the Discovery Channel? Well, scientific research in that type of thing is big right now. If you know the right people and have the right connections, certain parts of the government, universities, and maybe some marine institutes are going to be interested in something like this. That's not even counting the global warming wackos. I hear that's going to be big research in the upcoming years, and I think there's a chance that they'll want to use this thing for a home base of operations studying all sorts of stuff. My friends have the inside track with people in Washington that award research grants for stuff like that."

Hoyt ground his teeth. "Why can't we line up the researchers? We can certainly advertise this to those big shot scientists. Your folks aren't the only ones who can make phone calls to Washington."

For a moment, Mason didn't have an answer. He stuck his hands in his pockets, and tried to look in control. Then, right on cue, it came.

"It's a matter of funding on your end. These people need more than just the basic amenities to do their work. They are going to need power and communication upgrades, cold storage, and a few other things that, I'm sure, you and Caroline aren't going to be able to financially provide here. My people have more capital to invest."

The old man suddenly sprang forward. His right arm cocked, then released, landing a deceptively powerful punch in the corner of Mason's mouth. Bells rang and fireworks exploded inside his head. For a moment everything blurred, and the coppery taste of blood flooded Mason's tongue. Dazed, he staggered backwards and went to a knee. He was shaking his head, trying to clear the cobwebs, when instinct told him to move. Hoyt was closing in for another volley, and quickly, Mason was on his feet and ducked just in time to miss a haymaker. The old man's momentum almost spun him completely around, but he regained his balance and closed in again. This time, Mason was ready. Instead of ducking, a big hand opened and caught the old man's fist.

"Stop it, Hoyt," he said feeling a trickle of blood running across his swelling lips. "I'm not looking for trouble, but if you try to hit me again, I'm going to fold you up like a cheap road map and toss you over the rail."

The warning worked . . . at least temporarily. Mason felt Hoyt's hand relax. He released the fist, and both men took a step away from the other.

Mason ran a knuckle under his busted lip, and surveyed the red stain smeared across his hand. A vein materialized on his forehead, and heat began to rise in his neck. "Why you old bast—"

Okay, okay. Calm down. Killing him right now is not going to solve my problems.

Mason shook his head, gaining back his faculties. "Okay, okay. I deserved that one, I'll give you that. And now that you've got it out of your system, I need you to calm down and listen to me. I know you still hate me, and quite frankly, I don't give a damn. But you are about to let your emotions screw up a pretty good deal here. These guys are based in Jersey, but have satellite offices up and down the coast—they're big time."

Mason could see something change in Hoyt's face. The old man blinked twice and said, "Mancini?"

"You know him?"

"He's the one who wanted to buy the light station at the auction, but his man didn't make it in time."

Mason nodded. "Then you've heard of Mancini Towers, Dunes, and all that up in Beaufort right? He practically owns all the beach up there. How much do you know about him?"

Hoyt sneered. "I've heard stories."

"Then you know what this guy and his backers are capable of. He might not lower himself to personally break legs and arms anymore, but you better believe he hires it done."

The old man squinted, peering at his ex-son-in-law. "If you are trying to scare me, you better try a little harder."

Mason shook his head. "I'm not trying to scare you, and I'm not trying to hurt you. If anything, I'm trying to keep legs and arms *from* being broken."

"Quit wasting my time, and hop back on that helicopter and go tell him that we aren't interested. He missed his chance, and if he wants to send more muscle out here to try to convince me, he'd better send more than just you."

"But Hoyt—"

The old man's face changed. At first it looked like a smile, but on second glance, it was the look people get when they get a call from the IRS. "You're done here, sonny. Now shut up and get off my platform."

Mason was nearly in shock, processing just how terribly the last few minutes had progressed. Things had gone so well with Caroline earlier, he'd foolishly convinced himself that Hoyt would probably be a hard sell, but not impossible. And the old man had proved him absolutely wrong; cussing him, threatening him, and actually punching him in the mouth. It probably could have been worse, but what had just happened didn't miss worse by far.

Mason stood there for a moment trying to devise the next lie. His manipulations were gold most of the time, but this time nothing seemed to be working. He'd only really had his back against the wall a few times in his life, and it was during those select times he'd resorted to stooping to the absolute lowest of the lows. In those dark moments the absolute last resort was simply the truth. Mancini hadn't said it explicitly during their chat back in Morehead City, but the old man said he had heard some stories. He'd have to know that at some point threats would be made, and more muscle would be deployed.

Mason casually shrugged his shoulders and started to turn back to the helicopter, but stopped. "Okay, Hoyt. I'll tell him. But you need to understand something. Mancini and his business partners—they're used to getting what they want."

"A man in hell wants a glass of ice water, but guess what."

Mason shook his finger at Hoyt, then pointed down at the platform. "Jacqueline is down there somewhere, right?"

Hoyt's eyes widened.

"I'll take that as a yes. You need to start caring, old man. I haven't been much of a daddy to her, but I never put her life in danger. I relay this back to Mancini, and that's exactly what you're doing. You, Caroline, and Jacqueline—all of you will be in terrible danger."

Hoyt didn't blink.

Mason was on the verge of conceding, but he quickly remembered that Hoyt didn't flinch when he mentioned doubling the money earlier. Maybe he hadn't heard him? Making money was always worth bringing up again. "I thought I was doing you a favor coming out here like this. Let me remind you that you stand to double your money on this piece of crap, you stubborn son of a—" Mason forced himself to stop. He felt certain nothing was going to happen today, but after reminding the old man of that juicy little morsel, something might happen in the future. Caroline liked the money. Even if Hoyt wasn't interested now, she might be able to sway him. Double the money. That's all the old buzzard needed to hear. He could assume the rest.

"Have it your way old man. But when bad things start happening, make sure to tell Caroline I tried to warn you."

Mason turned back towards the helicopter rubbing his swollen lip. Other than Frankie tickling his ribs at the restaurant, it had been a long time since someone had laid a finger on him, and not had to spend a few days in the hospital as a consolation prize. As bad as it hurt, it was necessary. The pieces of his plan were set now. And keeping cool after that sucker punch might just put a wad of cash in his pocket—just a little collateral damage to plant the seed. It might take a day or two, but Hoyt and Caroline would talk, then he'd cave. He always did.

Chapter 11

Jackie woke abruptly to a dark room. Through half-open eyes, the glowing display on her watch said it was ten minutes until two—way too early to wake for no reason. The wet, salty breeze blew in the open window, and in her ever-increasing state of awareness, Jackie quickly understood why she was awake. Her arm hurt. The Tylenol and sleeping pill were long gone, and her pain receptors seemed to be making up for lost time. As a big tear rolled down her cheek, she remembered something that perhaps could help. Jackie scrambled for her flashlight.

Down the hallway, Hoyt's snoring sounded like a blaring car horn, but Jackie could barely hear it over her own mind crying out. Her backpack was lying in the corner and she frantically unzipped it and searched through the compartments. Her hand brushed against a plastic baggie at the bottom of a small interior pocket, and reluctantly, she grabbed it. A raucous, jerky snore erupted from down the hall, and she froze, listening. Regular snores soon followed, and she directed the light down in the bag and three small, roughly hand-rolled marijuana cigarettes came into view.

The painful clawing gave way to what felt like an out-of-control conflagration. She laid one of the joints on the lamp desk next to her bed, then closed the bag and stuffed it and the remaining two in her pajama pants pocket. She ran her hand back through the backpack's main compartment, and found a lighter. Cradling both in her left hand, whimpering in pain, Jackie hurried down the hallway towards the catwalk.

She sat, legs crossed on the leeward side of the platform, considering what she was about to do. It was irony in its grandest sense. The first time she'd ever seen a joint was in December—

halftime of the last boys' basketball game before Christmas break. She and two of her friends had wandered outside to get a lungful of air that wasn't stale and sweaty. They walked along the sidewalk, chatting, when suddenly a strong and strange smell stopped them in their tracks. For a moment, Jackie thought that the gym might be on fire, but then someone hiding behind the row of hedges giggled. Twin boys in her class, Reggie and Ronnie Davis, were hunkered down behind the wall of vegetation, smoking a joint they had lifted from their older brother's stash. They were giggling, coughing, and choking, but they were getting enough of the smoke into their lungs to do the job.

Reggie and Ronnie motioned them behind the shrubs and dared the girls to take a puff. When all three of them shook their heads, Reggie, the class smart aleck, said something about the girls being chicken. He handed Ronnie the smoking joint and pulled his hand to his armpits, flapped chicken wings, and clucked a few times. "See, Ronnie," he said laughing, "I told you they all had yellow feathers stuffed in their training bras and panties."

Her two friends looked scared and still shook their heads no, but Jackie stiffened. Nobody called her chicken, especially the likes of the Davis twerps. Her reaction was instant. Jackie felt herself snatch the joint out of Ronnie's hand, and after three big puffs and a massive cough, she threw what was left of the joint back at them and said something that unhinged everyone's mouths. "I ain't chicken, and if you say it again, Reggie Davis, so help me, I'm going to kick you right in the balls . . . like this." Jackie turned and in a blur, pumped her size eight sneaker right into Ronnie's crotch. She parted the shrubs and stormed off, leaving them all stuttering and slobbering, watching Ronnie rolling on the ground, red-eyed and gasping for air.

She had only smoked it one other time, and that was because Reggie (apparently impressed that night behind the gym hedge) had made it a point to introduce her to his older brother. She'd done it then mostly out of defiance too, but what had found its way into her school bag and onto the light station was not of her choosing. During the last week of school while changing classes, Reggie pulled Jackie into the boy's bathroom. After blankly staring a moment at the two bulges pressing against the front of her shirt, he told her that his mom had almost caught him with 'the goods' as he called it the night before. He pulled a plastic bag out of his pocket, and Jackie's eyes widened, looking at three hand-rolled marijuana cigarettes. "Mom's on the warpath, and I don't have anywhere to hide it that she won't find it," he said almost in a panic. "We're going to camp Saturday morning. I'll get them from you Friday after school. I can keep them in my underwear for one night."

She wanted to protest, but didn't get a chance. Reggie smiled as he stuffed the bag in her hand and pushed her out into the hallway. The last thing he said through the door was, "And just don't throw it away, it has your fingerprints on it now. They'll find it and come after you."

Jackie kept it buried deep in that small interior pocket for the rest of the week, and Friday afternoon, Reggie never showed. So much for trusting the Davis twins.

Now, with her arm feeling like it was stuffed in a kettle of boiling water, she sat in the dark, back to the wind, slowly rolling the joint between her index finger and thumb. She liked the 'I don't give a shit' feeling it gave her, but what she so desperately needed was relief from the pain. A flame quickly flared from the hand-cupped lighter, and smoke began to flutter. Feeling like she'd somehow let the entire planet down, she gently squeezed her burned forearm, closed her eyes, and inhaled deeply. Two inches past her nose, the end of the joint glowed bright orange, as the dried leaves popped and hissed. A few deep breaths and stifled coughs later, the pain in her arm began to wane. She drew twice more on the joint, then strangely, her sense of hearing began to change . . . enhance. Under her, the steel structure squeaked like a mouse and at the same time purred like a stroked kitten. The wind seemed to whisper her name and the gentle waves below, lapping against the steel pilings and her grandfather's moored boat, tapped out a strange drumbeat that sounded too musical to be mere coincidence. She hated herself, and at the same time, she was thankful.

The sensory effects were one thing, but the drug was working its primary purpose. Impaired synapses registered less and less pain, and forgetting about her arm, Jackie's mind began to wander. She thought of all the mean kids at school that all seemed to magically turn into barracudas. They made their living devouring the weak or the strange, or pretty much anyone who was different than them. Oh, how she wanted to line them all up and give them the Ronnie Davis treatment, but much like their fish counterparts, they were masters at swimming up and down the school hallways snatching the weak ones from the edges. They never stayed in one place long enough to get caught.

It was the thought of her science teacher that kept her from crying. Miss Rollins was the only teacher that had ever given her a reasonable answer to how she felt about her friends, school, and life. All of the rest of her teachers had told her that as long as she kept a good attitude and behaved, everything would be all right—but not her. No, Miss Rollins, young, energetic, charismatic lover of the environment, had been the first to tell her that things in the world, at times, were not going to be fair. And she blew Jackie's and the rest of her student's minds when she told them that was perfectly normal. She told them that it was easy to get down on humanity, with all its blatant social injustices where only the rich and powerful were guaranteed to win.

Just like the barracudas.

To make matters worse, the battle between good and bad didn't just stop in school. There were barracudas all over the world . . . people who mined coal, jewels, petroleum, and other materials, upsetting the balance of the planet and making the ecosystem angry.

Miss Rollins had shocked them even further when she said that there were even barracudas who lived right there in New Hanover County. They tilled the earth, growing things using inorganic fertilizer and harmful pesticides, poisoning the environment. And there were barracudas that grew cattle, pigs, and chickens in cramped, deplorable conditions, only to have them hauled off and slaughtered in even more cramped and deplorable conditions. And worse still, the most hated barracudas of all were the ones who served in political office that allowed and actually applauded these horrible things. They even had the audacity to promote such savagery, claiming that it was good for growth and prosperity.

The drug was flooding her system, and Jackie's confused mind settled again on Miss Rollins. Jackie wanted to believe her, because after all, she was a grown-up, a college graduate, and a teacher. Teachers weren't hired because they were stupid . . . she had to be right about the barracudas. But Jackie also remembered things that her grandfather had told her about: piloting a boat in the sea, how to make a living fishing, being independent. And then there were the intense and larger than life biology lessons she'd seen earlier that day that he'd summed up so perfectly. Deep down in the folds of chemically-inspired logic, she knew that he was right too.

Granddad and Miss Rollins are so different. How could they both be right?

None of it was easy to understand, but the only thing she knew for sure was that the pain in her arm was completely gone. Jackie took a last puff, felt a jolt of heat on her fingertips, and looked down at the stub of a joint that remained. She flipped what was left over the rail, then fished the plastic baggie from her pocket, considered it, then balled it up and tossed it to the wind. Above, the stars danced and swirled around what she assumed was the North Star, a time lapsed picture of celestial movement every amateur astronomical photographer attempted. The longer she watched the more the round rings pulsed in circular motion until the image above formed itself into a three-dimensional cone-shaped vortex. But it wasn't just mesmerizing to the eyes. Somehow the vortex produced a kind of attraction that Jackie could clearly feel pulling her upwards—trying to lift her from the light station. She kneeled and held onto the chained railing, and almost laughed out loud.

It's trying to suck me back into science class.

Jackie held the chain and mechanically walked towards the stairs, applying as much downward pressure with her feet as possible. She giggled, imagining what it would be like flying into the sky, through the coned vortex, landing right in her old seat in science class, or perhaps somewhere in Oz itself. The scene played out over and over, and each time a new set of giggles and laughter almost crippled her. It was a grand feeling, but her impaired senses and hallucination didn't allow her to notice the dark silhouette peeking over the top of the platform from the metal staircase. The shadow was gone by the time she reached the stairs, and she descended them clumsily, swaying to and fro, giggling at everything and at the same time, nothing. When she gained the catwalk, she thought she felt something cold and wet on her hands. At first glance nothing was there, but strangely, they both smelled like seawater. Double checking what her nose told her, she ran her palm across her tongue and tasted salt. The detail was quickly forgotten, and she continued to her room, somehow making it all the way there without waking her grandfather. Before she fell asleep, on the ceiling she clearly saw the same swirling vortex that had been in the sky outside. Except now, there was nothing pulling her upward. She laughed trying to make sense of it. The ceiling wasn't able to block the view of the sky, but it had somehow managed to block the attraction she'd felt coming from the heavens.

Chapter 12

It wasn't the pulsing pain in Jackie's arm that woke her two hours later. The drug had given her a couple of hours of deep sleep, but with it came horribly vivid nightmares. The one that finally vaulted her from sleep was of her falling from the light station, landing not in the ocean, but on a flaming bed of hot coals in some massive cooking grill. The oversize briquettes were glowing orange, but when she landed in them, strangely, there was no impact or pain or heat, but only an intense sizzling sound. There was the unmistakable smell of cooking meat, and when she realized that it was her own flesh sizzling, she awoke, bolt upright in bed, sweating and gasping, just short of a scream.

Jackie regained her composure, then gingerly squeezed the bandage on her arm, feeling the blister move underneath like a compressed water balloon. Her watch said ten after five, and she laid back down trying to go back to sleep. The buzz was completely gone, and after twenty minutes of pulsing pain, she knew it was no use.

Jackie slid on a t-shirt and a pair of shorts, and walked down the hallway, passing her grandfather's room. What she heard coming from within sounded more like a revving chainsaw engine than an old man snoring. Managing a smile, she continued down the hallway, making her way up the set of stairs leading to the roof. The moon was far in the west, leaving the business of producing what little light there was to the stars. Knifing its way across the expanse was a narrow, almost filmy streak of light—the Milky Way. She had never noticed it before, and she stared at it in a kind of blissful awe. Twenty-one miles offshore, there was no light pollution. She was viewing the night sky as it had been seen originally, by early man, who had not yet hoped to dream of something as complicated as the common light bulb. She leaned her good arm on the rail, picking out constellations, and eventually, the eastern sky slowly began to lighten. She caressed the bandage again and sighed.

Looks like it's going to be four days in a row.

She was patiently waiting for the dawn when something caught her eye out in the water. She didn't know what it was at first, but a few moments later, it happened again. This time, it was closer, and she immediately recognized a splashing pod of dolphin jumping and cutting through the water. She counted five individuals, and they were coming straight to the structure.

Jackie forgot the pain and almost tripped again on a tie-down loop as she sprinted across the platform. She ran down the stairs, through the hallway, and into her room where she found and frantically changed into her bathing suit. The mask and fins weren't there though, and it took her a minute to remember they'd left them in the boat. On the way out, she stopped in the galley and stuffed three pieces of leftover buttered French bread from supper into a small plastic bag. She stopped just for a second outside her grandfather's room. She wanted to tell him her plan, but the snoring was as loud as ever. Not wanting to miss an opportunity to swim with dolphins, she flew down the hallway and out the door.

Jackie stood on the boat's gunnel watching, waiting. Minutes went by, but she saw nothing. They had simply disappeared. In every direction, there was only the gentle waves of the Atlantic. Tears welled in the corners of her eyes, when she finally heard a splash. There it was! To her right and slightly behind, another dolphin's back appeared; its flat tail slapped the water, making that familiar *pop*. As soon as that one was down, another breached, then disappeared into the waves. They had already passed the light station, and were continuing on their way. The pain in her arm seemed secondary to the hurt she felt missing the opportunity.

Jackie stamped her foot, slung her gear down, and slumped on the deck of the boat.

If I had of just grabbed the bread, instead of wasting time putting on my bathing suit.

The anger quickly subsided, and Jackie stood and scanned the water, hoping to see another dolphin breach in the distance. Hopeful minutes went by, and she finally huffed a contemptuous breath at the ocean and turned for the rope ladder when she nearly tripped over her snorkel gear lying in the floor of the boat. She kicked at it, sending the mask flying. It thumped against the fiberglass, and the sound caused a few small fish to dart from the edge of the boat. Jackie saw the flash of silver scales and another plan formed.

I bet I can get those small fish to come right up to me with the bread. Maybe the dolphins will come back.

She cocked the mask on top of her head, and stepped onto the transom ladder. The water felt unusually warm and soothing, and lowering herself to the last rung, the gentle waves sloshed well over her knees. The sun was just starting to peek over the horizon, and the direct light allowed her to clearly see a school of fish swimming around the boat's engines. The dolphins were quickly forgotten and a smile touched her lips. Pulling the mask and snorkel down over her face, Jackie slid into the water.

The ocean's new addition spooked the school, but a dozen were quick to return. Swaying with the swells on top of the water, with one hand she steadied herself against the ladder, and extended the other, offering the tasty morsel to the closest fish. It took just a moment of temptation before her new friend swam in close. Its two large eyes goggled to the left and right, up and down, staring at the bread, her fingers, her arm, and the rest of her lying on the surface. It fluttered its fins, and came within arm's reach, then quickly retreated. Seconds later, it came in for another look, but abandoned the attempt. She laughed to herself imagining thought bubbles above the fish's head. In a fishy language no human had ever translated before, the bubbles filled with dialogue.

Is this real? Whatever this is, it's offering me something that smells good, and I'm just supposed to take it? What's the catch here?

Back and forth the small fish swam. Two, three, four times. With each pass, it came closer and closer to the morsel that was now getting soggy and was starting to disintegrate. Finally, the temptation was too great. Her fishy friend lurched forward, snatched the piece of bread form her fingers, and darted back towards the engines. It was instantly mobbed by other fish, but it managed to gobble down the prize in two bites. It seemed to be trying to decide if what had just happened was a good or bad thing when Jackie slowly reached back to the transom and tore off another small piece of bread.

Charlie. Yeah, that sounds good. Charlie's a good name for a little fellow like you.

Her fishy friend boldly came back. Without any hesitation, it took the piece of bread from her fingertips.

Jackie smiled.

Charlie was nibbling at his third morsel, when something long and silver flashed in front of her. Jackie recoiled in the water, and when everything made sense again, a three-foot barracuda swam away from them, working something in its mouth. She turned back to her new friend, and there, in a light cloud of red-tinted water, gills still fluttering, was what was left of Charlie. In the blink of an eye, the barracuda had chewed the small fish in half, leaving only his head, gills, and only part of a pectoral fin.

Mortified, Jackie scrambled back into the boat. She rocked back and forth on her knees while her thoughts ran wild, hoping that what she'd just witnessed was a dream. But there was no mistaking the reality of cold death. She wiped away the tears, and her grandfather's speargun came into focus, lying on the seat towards the bow. A million thoughts ran through her head, all of them summed up in one word, revenge. She scrambled forward, loaded the spear, set the thick rubber bands just like Hoyt had shown her. Muttering an oath, she slid back into the water—speargun in one hand, a piece of bread in the other. It took only a few minutes for the rest of Charlie's gang to show up, and as another bold fish nibbled at her fingertips, she stalked with her eyes the heartless barracuda circling the rear of the boat. It was hard to see him at first, but with each circle, he closed in on the oblivious feeding fish. There was no doubt, it was calculating its next move . . . its next kill.

Another small fish finally took a morsel from her hand, but Jackie barely saw it. She was completely focused on the barracuda, now only fifteen feet from the back of the boat. The predator turned towards her, and paused.

This is it. He's coming for another one.

It was as if the thought itself commanded the fish. Jackie's blood chilled as it darted toward them, and a new part of her—a part she never knew existed—took over. She aimed the speargun, and the sudden movement spooked the barracuda, and it veered sharply away from its intended victim, giving Jackie a perfect broadside shot. Tracking the fish, she kept the points of the trident aimed at its hateful eye. Logically, what she was doing went against her very soul, but the weapon felt good in her hand, and the aim seemed so natural there was only one thing left to do. The mental signal blinked green, and in a moment of what she hoped would be a slow death of painful justice, her finger squeezed the trigger. A large red cloud erupted in the water, and from it swam the speared barracuda. It plunged deeper, trying to escape, and the line began panning freely from the reel. As more water separated the fish from the surface, the leaking red cloud slowly faded to green. She grabbed the line with her hand and pulled.

You aren't getting away that easy.

Chapter 13

The barracuda lay bleeding in the bottom of the boat. Its gills worked, trying to breathe, and its slender body twitched, still trying to swim. Jackie stood over it, the sea's salt water dripping from her chin, fingertips, and hair, while her own salt water coursed from her two green eyes. She hated the sleek predator for killing Charlie, but the longer she stared at him, strangely, the hatred that was once firmly focused on the killer, slowly began to transfer to her own heart. How could it happen? How could she have killed an animal like that? A shy, fourteen-year-old girl whose worst offense was smoking three joints and kicking Ronnie Davis in the balls?

Those horrible feelings had suddenly erupted from a strange and dark place, and it scared her. One moment, she was in the water screaming at pieces of Charlie, and then, in some weird twist of distorted time, there was a barracuda in front of her trying to swim away from a bloody cloud with a spear shish-kabobbed through it. Then everything fuzzed out again, and there it was lying in the bottom of the boat at her feet. She couldn't remember actually shooting the fish nor getting it into the boat, but it apparently happened. Even scarier, no matter how it happened, a big part of her relished the murderous act. It was like she was a human tuning fork tapped against the cold steel of the fish spear—every molecule of her being vibrating together in the harmonizing, natural frequency of revenge. It was the sweet feeling of swift justice.

She was still standing there staring into that killer's big hateful black eye when she heard a voice behind her.

"Whatcha got there, beach girl?" Hoyt stepped off the rope ladder into the boat, and then saw the speargun still in her hand, the spear lying on the boat's white fiberglass, and finally, the dead fish lying in its own blood.

"What the—" he said, utterly surprised. "I didn't think you wanted . . . or could. How did you? A barracuda? That's one of the fastest fish around. How did you manage to—"

Jackie screamed, "He ate my . . . my . . ." she wanted to say friend, but stopped herself after realizing how silly it would sound. "He ate a little fish I was feeding, right in front of me."

Hoyt rubbed the stubble on his chin, unable to say anything for a moment. He nudged the fish with his foot a couple of times. "Well, looks like Mister Cuda got to enjoy one last meal before it all came to an end." He glanced at her hand, tightly grasping the speargun, "I was beginning to think you didn't have it in you."

"Have what in me?"

Hoyt went to his knee and pulled the spear out of the fish. "The ability to kill."

"Why do you keep pushing this on me?"

Hoyt sighed, "Killing is a fact of life. Every animal in the wild kills, and that includes us in the not-so-wild. Male, female, big, small—it doesn't matter." He opened his mouth, and touched the tip of his right canine tooth with his index finger. "You see this? A lot of folks will tell you otherwise, but these beauties were put here for a reason. The Man Upstairs knew what he was doing when he designed pointed teeth—he made them specifically to rip meat. Ask any biology teacher. Animals that eat plants don't have them. They have flat and wide pearlies that do a bang-up job of grinding vegetation, but the tiger, the lion, the bear, the jaguar, heck, even the T-rex skull at the museum all have pointed teeth. And guess what they all eat, or ate?" He stood and wiped the blood from the spear, "Meat. And don't listen to those wacky vegetarians about animals and feelings, and that all killing is bad. They still kill—it's just plants instead of animals. And I'd bet my boat that they kill poisonous snakes in their yards, and cockroaches, and mosquitos, and other vermin in their houses." He raised a bony finger in defiance to all who may disagree, "And beach girl, no matter the reason, no matter the cause, killing is killing."

He stepped to the console and laid the spear and the gun on the seat. "And before you get on your high horse, I'll be glad to remind you about all the hamburgers, roasts, fried chicken, grilled fish, and on and on and on you've eaten over the years. Folks have moved so far away from the farms, they've forgotten that hams, chops, and chicken wings once were parts of living animals. A butcher doesn't wave a magic wand and *poof*, neat cuts of cellophane-wrapped meat just magically appear in the grocery store." He shook his head, "Folks just can't go around letting others kill for them, then spit at them for doing it. No ma'am. At some point, folks have to do their own killing. Remember our talk yesterday about being self-sufficient?"

Jackie stared at her grandfather as he positioned the dead barracuda on top of the fish box and pulled his knife from the sheath on his belt. He lightly touched the edge of the blade with his thumb, checking the edge. "Pay attention, because you are going to fillet the other side."

He pressed the blade, cutting the meat behind the gill, all the way down to the fish's spine. Hoyt tactfully rotated the blade towards its tail, and slowly and deliberately sawed the knife down the fish's body cleaving the solid slab of meat away from its spine. He stopped the blade just before it came through the skin at the base of the tail, and he flipped the slab of meat over, skin down on the fiberglass. With the blade pressed lightly against the skin, he quickly and effortlessly freed the entire meaty fillet. He raised the long slab of meat and inspected both sides, deemed it acceptable, and leaned and rinsed it in the water beside the boat.

"There aren't many who eat these, but I know a few folks that can make a respectable meal from it. Luckily, they've let me in on the secret. And since you killed it, we are going to eat it. That's one thing I won't compromise."

He flipped the barracuda over and handed Jackie the knife. "Now let's see what you've learned."

While Jackie slowly worked the blade, she told him how it all happened. When the story was finished, he paused thoughtfully before telling her that feeding the small fish likely had baited the larger predator in close, expecting an easy meal, and her reaction to Charlie's unfortunate circumstance had ironically given them both a chance at a meal. Jackie almost started crying again. Charlie's death was on her hands, but she managed to keep her composure by concentrating on working the fillet. The blade sliced between the meat and the skin beautifully, and she handed her grandfather a very large and very eatable slab of fish.

"Not bad," he said proudly. "Not bad at all."

She watched as Hoyt leaned and rinsed her fillet off in the sea water. It was as if someone had rung the underwater dinner bell. A school of small fish appeared next to the boat, nibbling at the small droplets of blood and giblets of meat that were washed off. In a matter of seconds, the leftovers had been consumed and the school retreated back to cover.

Hoyt pointed at the skeletal remains lying on the gunnel. "You wanted revenge on this one for eating the small fish you were feeding?"

Jackie nodded. "I suppose."

Hoyt stuck the tip of his knife into the gills of what was left of the barracuda, and flipped it into the water. "Revenge you'll get then."

She watched in amazement as hordes of small fish again materialized. The cloud of scales and fins swarmed the carcass as it slowly sank in the water, meticulously excising bits of meat from every crevice. Before sinking completely out of sight, the hateful murderer had been reduced to bone. Bone, and that big empty black eye, that Jackie now thought didn't look so hateful.

* * *

Jackie and Hoyt made it back up the ladder and Hoyt disappeared into the galley with the barracuda fillets while Jackie wandered into her room. A few minutes later, she heard the familiar hiss of bacon in a hot pan, and her stomach began to growl. She toweled off, dried her hair, and dressed. Her arm didn't hurt as bad as it had when she woke that morning, but it still hurt. The wet gauze was still tightly covering the burn, but it looked soggy and swollen from the sea water. Jackie was brushing her hair when the smell of bacon finally reached her nose. She couldn't help thinking about pens of friendly pigs destined for the slaughterhouse, as the sweet smell of frying pork oozed into every corner of her room. Her belly growled loudly, making her forget the mental image. The only thing she could think of was how good three pieces of crispy bacon would taste wedged into a buttered biscuit.

By the time Jackie made it to the galley, the bacon was done and the biscuits were just coming out of the oven. Hoyt, on the way out the door to kill the generator, told her to take the bandage off so he could inspect it while breakfast was cooling.

The tape easily came off, and the soggy bandage unraveled, leaving the gauze stuck to the burn. Carefully, she peeled the layers away, and stared at amazement at what was once was a second-degree burn. She was still staring at it, speechless, when Hoyt walked back into the galley.

"Let's take a look at it. I've already decided that we need to pack things up and head—" He stopped mid-sentence as he held up an almost completely healed arm. The blister was gone, and in its place was something that appeared to be just a mild case of sunburn. Hoyt looked at it from every angle, and she winced only once when he lightly ran his finger down the middle of the newly formed, tender, pink skin.

Hoyt said, "This beats all I've ever seen. Did you do anything else to it last night?"

Jackie could still taste the marijuana smoke on her tongue, but just shrugged. "No. I was tired. That pill you gave me must've worked. I think I went right to sleep."

"You didn't mess with it?"

She shook her head.

"How'd the blister heal so quickly? Does it hurt?"

"A little."

Hoyt poured two glasses of orange juice, and while Jackie was eating, he retrieved the tube of burn ointment from the medicine cabinet. Looking at the label he said, "We might have gotten the best run of this stuff that has ever been produced, beach girl. That was a nasty burn. I've never seen anything work that fast."

After breakfast, more from habit than need, Hoyt applied more medicine and rebandaged her arm. They went back to work, and with every passing second, the phantom pain in her forearm grew fainter and fainter. After painting the first wall, Jackie had forgotten that she'd even been burned.

Chapter 14

The sun was peeking through the ragged shades of the motel window when Mason LaRue was awakened by a sharp knock on the door. His head buzzed, his breath stank, his tongue felt like it was wearing a fur coat two sizes too big. He groaned and groped for the phone, knocking an empty liquor bottle off the table by the bed. The receiver only blared a blank dial tone. Stupidly, he stared at the wall, wondering through a heavy mental fog who had tried to call him there when the knocks came again. It sounded like somebody was pounding a steel fist directly on his brain. He stood beside the bed on wobbly legs for just a moment before a key entered the lock from the outside. A faint sound came from the tumblers, and with a hard push, the door flew open, letting a shaft of blinding light into the small room. Mason shaded his eyes, but the pain accompanying the brightness felt like a wedge slowly splitting his head open. Frankie was the first man through the door, still dressed in that ridiculous pinstriped suit. The fat man lumbered across the threshold, a mad bull roaming the streets of Pamplona. Following close behind was the human chameleon.

Mason felt his nakedness and scrambled for the bed sheet. He looked up in time to see Geno outside the door, speaking with a well-dressed, olive skinned man holding a big ring of keys, presumably, the motel manager. They shook hands, and the manager withdrew, folding several green bills that seemed to have magically appeared. Frankie and Pauley assumed their sentinel positions, while Geno almost tiptoed through the door, stepping over a torn bra and a handful of beer bottle caps that laid strewn across the dirty linoleum.

"Good morning Mister LaRue. I trust you had a good night's sleep?"

Mason tried to clear his head, but everything was still garbled.

"Pauley, stand by the door. Our new friend is going to be back in a few minutes with a pot of coffee. When he knocks, please receive it, and by all means tip him well."

Mason tried to say something, but wasn't able to get everything out in the right order. Geno paced around in a small open spot on the floor listening to the gibberish, and when Mason ran out of words, he said, "I've had some time to think about our phone conversation last night, and judging by the state of affairs this morning, I can only assume that we've come to an impasse. If Mister Bennett is adamant, then we must up the ante. No doubt you're familiar with the old saying when at first you don't succeed, try, try again?" Geno looked around the room, then flashed a disgusted look back at Mason. "I'm afraid this doesn't qualify as trying."

Geno nodded at Frankie. Immediately Mason's breath left him as the fat man's right fist smashed into his ribcage. It could have been the fist that sobered him, or perhaps it was the sudden rush of adrenaline, but when he regained his wind, Mason clearly said, "If fatty hits me again, I'm going to saw his head off with a piece of used dental floss and mail it to Jersey, COD."

"I don't believe you'll have the time to do that, Mister LaRue, because you are about to engage the second part of your plan in this matter of the Frying Pan Shoals Light Station."

"What?" Mason shook his head, and quickly regretted doing so. "There wasn't a second part to it. Listen to me, Geno, I knew Hoyt wasn't going to go for it. At least not right away. Isn't that why we went to Caroline first? She's interested, and even back when we were married, Hoyt always caved when it came to his little girl. Open your eyes, man. This is a touchy matter that's gonna take some time. I set everything in motion, and now all we have to do is to let the pot simmer. They'll talk, probably today, and Hoyt will put up a good front, but in the end, he's going to do what his little girl wants. It might take a few days, but he'll come around."

Geno took an immaculately folded, unnaturally white handkerchief from his lapel pocket and brushed off his jacket sleeve. "I figured that was what you were thinking. But time is of the essence, so I've taken the liberty to develop a plan B for you. I have payment for the light station in a briefcase in the car. I'm going to visit your ex-wife around noon today and invite her to take a little helicopter ride with us out to the rig. Once we have them all together, we'll sit down on whatever they've got to sit down on out there and hammer out a little deal."

Mason saw his broker fee growing a set of wings and flying out the window. "He'll never agree to it. It's too quick. Too forceful. You've got to give Caroline some time to work her magic. I saw it in her eyes. She doesn't like that thing, and what woman doesn't like money? She'll do the dirty work for us, we've just got to give her a chance. You run in there making demands and waving guns, and you're just going to piss him off."

Geno slowly put the handkerchief back in his pocket, making sure it looked just right, then nodded again at Frankie. Before Mason could react, the big body guard had him immobilized in a sideways bear hug. He struggled against the man's giant bulk, but couldn't move. Geno stepped forward and forced his palm under Mason's chin, and mashed his cheeks between his thumb and fingers, exposing the busted lip. The pressure forced the split back open, and Mason's eyes widened then went into a hard squint.

The deceptively powerful Italian said, "Looks like you've already pissed him off. How old is he, sixty-five, seventy? Pity that a middle-aged man in relatively good health gets bested by a senior citizen."

Geno released him, and Frankie's sharp elbow caught Mason on the other side of his mouth. The blow almost knocked him to the floor.

"Mister LaRue, what you don't understand is the time frame I, and therefore you, are dealing with here. I need that light house signed over to me *today*, and we are going to make sure that happens. And somehow, I've got a really good feeling about it. I believe that Mister Bennett and your ex-wife will be more than willing to comply once we get there and explain everything. Especially since they'll have young Jackie's condition to consider."

"Condition?"

Geno smiled, "Oh come now, Mister LaRue. A light station out in the middle of the ocean. Sharp metal edges everywhere, and a clumsy teenage girl? Unfortunate things happen in environments like that all the time. Injuries are common, even for seasoned oil rig workers. A silly young girl surely will be subject to more peril than usual. I suspect she's going to have one of these little accidents while we're there, and you know how much of a philanthropist I am. I'll be more than happy to offer them a ride back to the mainland for whatever treatment is needed, but an emergency helicopter ride, even operated by rescue personnel, costs something. And since I don't take any medical insurance plans," Geno straightened, and looked pleased with himself, "well, I'm sure you see where this is going."

Mason's voice quivered. "What are you going to do to her?"

Geno shrugged his shoulders. "I don't know. But Frankie's ability to predict stuff like this is absolutely uncanny." He turned to the big bodyguard. "Frankie, what untimely calamity do you think will befall the young lady this afternoon?"

Frankie chuckled. The fat hanging off his cheeks and under his chin shook in unison with his distended belly. "I'm still working on that, boss."

Geno turned back to Mason. "I'm sure he'll have something in mind by the time we arrive."

"You son of a bitch."

Geno shook his head and walked to the door, stepping back over the bra and beer bottle tops. "Really, Mister LaRue. You haven't seen you daughter in nearly a decade. There's no sense in pretending you care now. What you should be caring about is that my time here is just about up. What I need from you now is a simple answer. Are you still on board, or are you jumping ship? I don't believe that I need you any longer to make all this happen, but we have a fairly good history together, and I'd hate to throw that all away. I've rolled the dice and come up snake-eyes before, but that doesn't mean that our partnership is completely dissolved. I'm quite certain that I'll have some work for you in the near future. So, I'm giving you a chance to see this through." Geno paused, thinking. "Although we might have to renegotiate your settlement in this matter."

Mason was dumbfounded. Oh sure, earlier in his career Geno would have forced his hand and abducted Caroline, gotten everyone out on the tower and started shooting until both of them signed. But Geno Mancini had mellowed. Taking things by an act of brute force just wasn't his style now. Geno had become a thinking man, and with money and power backing him, he usually got what he wanted by being bigger and smarter than his opponent. Everyone knew that the only thing Geno liked better than a good red wine was chess. The game suited his personality perfectly. Over the last decade, business had become nothing more than elaborate chess matches, where he thrived at meticulously dismantling the opponent with smart and concise moves. The Tankersly job was a prime example. Geno had destroyed the poor guy long before Mason executed the hit. He'd been hounding business deals and stealing clients for the better part of three years. Tankersly went from having lunch at the Emerald Coast Club five days a week and owning the largest construction company in eastern North Carolina, to eating sardines on crackers at home, while supervising a two-wrecker, fly-by-night vehicle repo business. The hit, Mason had thought, was really just an act of mercy. He probably could have just walked in, handed the guy a gun with a single bullet, and told him that it was a present from Geno—a gentlemanly gesture—and the guy would have happily obliged. But what Geno just suggested was no chess match. His plans for Hoyt, Caroline, and Jackie out on the light station was borderline barbaric.

The bigwigs up in Jersey must want that thing really bad.

It was a hard pill to swallow, but Mason knew he was now just a pawn on Geno's chess board, and he was about to be tucked in the corner, never to be touched again. There wasn't much he could do about it either. None of it sounded good, especially since the commission for the deal was currently growing wings. He liked the idea of Hoyt being pushed around or worse, and Caroline could use fifty dollars' worth of rough treatment, but the queen left on the board wasn't Caroline, it was Jackie. She was to be leverage, plain and simple, and if he could get to her first, then he might just be a larger player in all this than Geno realized. He had to be on the light station to have any chance at all at what he wanted most . . . what was sitting in Geno's briefcase out in the car.

Mason weaved together a conceding smile. "I'm still in. What do you have in mind?"

Geno cleared the door, took a deep breath of fresh air and turned back around. "Good decision, Mister LaRue. You've, no doubt, heard of the good cop bad cop routines? I think we shall give that a try. When I start making brash demands and begin to educate them on what skill sets Frankie has, you can step in and act as a moderator. They'll think you're on their side, especially if you look concerned and perhaps shed a tear at the appropriate time, but we know that won't be the case." Geno pointed a finger at Mason. "You are going to play the role of double agent for me this afternoon. And with all double agents, you'll be granted a certain amount of leniency in your actions. But please don't get any wild ideas. You're still working for me, and if you want to live to see the sun set, you'd better be convincing."

Geno took a step towards the Tahoe, and before anything else was said, the motel manager appeared beside him, holding a dingy wooden serving tray supporting a decanter of black coffee and several Styrofoam cups turned mouth-side down.

Geno hooked a thumb over his shoulder. "The patient is in there." He turned back to Frankie. "Sober him up and for God's sake make sure he showers. It smells like he's sweating straight liquor. I'm leaving you the other car. Be at the marina at one-thirty, Sal will have the boat fueled and waiting. If I'm delayed, I'll contact you with instructions on the radio." He opened the door to the Tahoe, and said with his back turned to them, "Mister LaRue looks like hell already, but it'll probably be best if he has a few more bumps and bruises—you know, to really sell the performance. Take care of that for me, would you Frankie."

The big bodyguard smiled, grinding a balled fist into his palm.

Chapter 15

Jackie painted for the next hour without a break. By nine o'clock, she'd worked up a good sweat. Her arm wasn't hurting, but it tingled and itched the way cuts do while they are healing. She stopped and sighed, looking down at the new package of narrow sponge brushes. Of all the work she'd done, there was nothing worse than painting the corners. All of it had to be done from an either frequently moved ladder, or from the knees. She shook her head thinking that this was likely the only reason why her granddad brought her. Stooping, squatting, leaning, and constantly moving a ladder around the room chasing the unpainted spots was all difficult work that made even the youngest backs hurt.

She moved the ladder to the corner, considering how many more Tylenol she'd likely need again tonight. Through the window, she spotted a boat out on the water. It was close, and two forms stood at the transom. One was holding a bent, quivering rod, and the other was standing beside him with a big landing net.

These guys must be rookies. A landing net, instead of a gaff? Even I know better than that. How did those two goobers manage to get a boat way out here?

Whatever it was on the end of the line must have been big— snapper, or perhaps an amberjack—and she found herself a little jealous despite their apparent stupidity. They were having fun, and she was painting a stuffy room.

The fish splashed behind the boat, and on the second swipe, the guy with the net lost his balance and almost fell into the water. Jackie laughed out loud and shook her head. At least she was being entertained. She brushed more paint, but her smile soon went away, thinking about the splashing dolphin pod. Missing them hurt, but it didn't hurt as badly as what happened to her little friend. She still hated the fish for killing Charlie, and herself for the killing the barracuda, but maybe it somehow was all meant to be. She had entered a new world, and almost instantly had found a new friend. And even though he'd been snatched from her, there were lots of others down there. After it happened, she wasn't sure that she needed to get into the water anymore, but now, she found that all she wanted to do was to feed the fish. The thought was so opulent, she barely could concentrate on the mundane act of painting. She stared at the sponge brush, at the wall, then out the window again. The sky was blue, the water was bluer, and the guys on the boat were still trying to fish. It was time for a break.

She found Hoyt in the head, lying on the floor next to the toilet. Everything above his waist was buried in a small square hole, and from inside the wall came tinking sounds—the sounds pipe wrenches make when working on water lines.

"Hey, granddad. You mind if I take a break and go for another swim? Maybe feed a few more little fish?"

"Did you finish the room?"

"All but the high corners. There's a boat out there, looks like they are catching a few fish. Can we try to catch some this evening? We don't have to take the boat out, we can just fish from the catwalk."

His voice lightened from behind the wall. "You're reading my mind. I've been wanting to wet a line all morning. If your arm is feeling up to it, go ahead. I don't know how long it's going to take me here, but I promise I'll be down there in less than an hour, whether I get this stuff fixed or not."

Jackie smiled and ran back down the hallway to her room, and quickly put on her bathing suit. She stopped by the galley to get another piece of bread, and jogging down the hallway, she heard Hoyt say, "Keep an eye out for anything big. We haven't seen a shark yet, but that doesn't mean they're not out there. And don't try to bait in any more barracuda. I don't think they'd take a swipe at you, but you never can tell."

Chapter 16

Jackie slid into the warm water. The fish were still there and it only took them a few minutes to finish off the bread. The water was unusually calm, and she swam around under the platform admiring all the sea life. Gaining confidence, she made it to the opposite side of the structure and touched the steel piling. Peering into the water through the mask she saw another small barracuda snatching another quick meal from the hundreds of living snacks swimming below. She felt bad for the little fish, but after the talk with her granddad, she realized that the barracuda didn't have a grocery store to buy pretty, pre-packaged meals. The area under the platform *was* the grocery store, and the barracuda, a more primitive being than herself, had processed the small fish in its own way. There were no knives, no clean cuts—the fish processed its meal strictly by grabbing and snatching, swallowing chunks of meat whole.

The barracuda turned to make another pass through the cloud of fish. It darted through, and it emerged on the other side without a prize. The mass of countless small fish scattered, disappearing into thin water. Oblivious, the barracuda swam away from the structure, then quickly turned again, preparing for another pass. It approached the deserted piling and stopped. Jackie could see its large eyes moving in their sockets. Nothing else was there to eat, so it simply swam away into the vast blue expanse.

Her grandfather was right. The ocean was an eat or be eaten world. The barracuda was a large fish, doubtless it would take several Charlies to fill its stomach. She almost felt sorry for it. It would have been like Jackie eating a single French fry for lunch, before someone snatched the rest of the meal away. The fish went away hungry, and Jackie wondered how far would it have to swim before it would eat again . . . or be eaten?

It didn't take long before it finally occurred to her that perhaps she'd been too quick to judge the predator. After all, the smaller fish had to live when she wasn't there to feed them. Charlie and his friends just moved up and down the steel, pecking at the barnacles and harassing the smaller fish that lived there. They were killing, same as the barracuda, it just wasn't as flashy and as visible and to the scale of what she'd witnessed. Why hadn't she felt bad for the barnacles and other small things Charlie and his friends were eating? Why hadn't she hated Charlie for killing them?

Jackie was still floating on the surface thinking about life and death, when she felt a warmness surround her. The burn on her arm, or where it once was, felt hot and she looked down to rub it when she noticed a stream of small bubbles clinging close to the piling rising towards the surface. The bottom was well out of view, and she couldn't pinpoint what caused the release. She took a deep breath and went down. Jackie followed the piling eight, maybe ten feet, and the bubbles kept coming. The deeper she went, the warmer and more satisfying the water felt, and the more sensitive the burn on her arm became. She stopped at what she judged to be twenty feet below the surface, and although her ears and head were popping from the pressure, her lungs had not yet started burning for air. She had been underwater for nearly a minute, and it was as if she had just taken a normal breath at the surface. Jackie kicked downward again. She'd never seen the bottom under the structure, but now, it seemed like a very obtainable goal. One, she felt, needed to be accomplished.

She continued to dive. Her chest was just starting to feel funny when she noticed the water changing. Near the surface, it was blue and clear, and now it was more of a turbid greenish color. She lost the feel for distance, but at some point, Jackie noticed the bubbles appeared from a single point next to where the piling disappeared from sight. It took her only a second to realize that she was staring at the sea floor. Amazed, she ran her fingers through the sandy bottom. The water wasn't hot, but it was warmer than what she felt on the surface, and the bandaged burn on her arm was stinging as if she'd brushed up against a jellyfish. Jackie's finger found the small crack in the sea floor, temporarily arresting the bubbles, and that's when she felt the corrugated surface of a partially buried sea shell. She fanned the sand away with the other hand, and more of the shell appeared. It was perfect, and larger than her hand.

I've got to get this. Granddad will never believe I got down here unless I bring this back up with me.

Something made her look up, and even through the green turbid water, she saw the surface of the sea. It looked miles above her. Instantly, her lungs began to burn, but she managed to grasp the shell, and in one great motion, turned upwards and kicked off the bottom. The light station, distorted grotesquely through the rocking surface of the sea, looked massive above her as she ascended. But what seemed like only seconds going down felt like hours coming up. The more she kicked with her flippers, the slower she seemed to rise. Her lips, toes, and fingers were tingling, and a black doughnut began to grow around the periphery of her vision. When she finally broke the surface, it was like she was looking at the world through a small pipe.

Coughing and spitting water, Jackie crawled into the boat, and collapsed on the cool fiberglass. She rolled onto her back, and stared momentarily at a wavy, distorted image of the structure's underbelly. The dark doughnut restricting her vision vanished and a gasp, a cough, and a wheeze all simultaneously attacked her chest. After a few big breaths, the blurry image contorted, attempting to smooth itself out. She closed her eyes, hoping that when she opened them again, the light station would still be there.

Chapter 17

From the moment Geno disappeared into the Tahoe, Mason LaRue could not escape Frankie's watchful eye. The large man was quick and intuitive, and every subtle, testing move Mason tried was instantly countered. Frankie was following Geno's directions to the letter, but that didn't stop Mason's devious brain from working. The cheap coffee was bad going down, but the caffeine was slowly bringing order back. Only a couple of big cups in, the fog had lifted enough for him to start planning his next move.

The plan was actually quite simple: get sober, and try not to get killed before getting on the light station. And all that hinged on something that Mason only had a faint recollection of. Sometime during the night, he seemed to remember lifting a small pistol and an extra clip out of somebody's car at a gas station. His bourbon-soaked brain wouldn't allow total recall, and he wasn't even totally sure he'd stolen it, but he clearly remembered kicking that stingy whore out of the room at gunpoint when she refused to go the extra mile after the money had run out.

If he did have a gun hidden somewhere, Mason had a good idea of where it was. Long before he met Caroline, he learned the trick of hiding small guns under toilet tank lids from a drug dealer in Greenville. Duct tape was a wonderful thing, even in high moisture environments, and it was never a bad idea to have a little bit of insurance tucked away in a safe place, just in case trouble came looking for you. Out of sight, out of mind, and out of any normal search zones—who looks under a toilet lid for anything? All of it was just hopeful thoughts, but one thing was a certainty, if he'd stowed a pistol, Frankie and the gang hadn't let on that they'd found it. That was a good sign, and it gave him hope. Getting on the boat seemed like a guarantee, but he needed that little bundle of joy to help even up the odds.

How do I get into the bathroom alone long enough to check for it? If I can, and if it's there, I'm going to make Frankie fatso Russo sorry he'd ever been born.

The fat bodyguard wasn't cutting him any slack. Frankie kept a gun on him as he paced nervously back and forth across the room, downing cup after cup of bad coffee. After Mason's piss no longer smelled like bourbon and his head no longer swam, Frankie unknowingly granted his prisoner the gift of hope. Double and triple checking the bathroom for potential weapons or anything out of the ordinary, and making sure there were no windows for potential escape, he foolishly allowed Mason a little privacy to pass what had built in his bowels, and pursuant to Geno's wishes, a chance to shower.

The steaming shower was therapeutic, and although Mason felt like he could have stayed in there all morning, with Frankie safely behind the closed door, there wasn't a moment to waste. He quickly bathed and turned the water to cold and drank heavily from the flowing shower head. The flush of clean water mixing with the bad coffee in his belly made him feel better, but it was the coldness sluicing down his hungover body that finally snapped him completely out of the fog. Leaving the shower running, he toweled off, then pressed an ear to the door. Satisfied Frankie wasn't about to walk in, he straddled the toilet and carefully removed the tank's porcelain lid. He flipped it over and sat it on the seat. And there, held in place by a spider web of duct tape, was a snub-nose Ruger .380.

Attaboy Mason! The boy scouts would be proud.

A few quick tugs, and the small pistol and an extra clip fell into his hands. Mason checked the clips, six rounds each. He fed one clip in the handle of the gun and turned and whispered to the bathroom door, "You may be big my friend, but this little equalizer will still split that fat little heart of yours wide open."

Mason replaced the toilet lid, then quickly straightened out the used tape. Carefully, he pressed and wrapped the Ruger and clip to his inner thigh. On went his briefs, and in front of the mirror, he sized himself up. The tape pulled at his pubes, and there was a little pinching discomfort at certain angles, but just the briefs did a fair job of concealing the Ruger. He slid his pants on, and it completely vanished under the loose denim. A long hike would probably kill him, but a few hours tucked neatly near his crotch like that would be very doable.

Mason pulled a t-shirt on and let the shower run for another minute. After turning the water off, he made sounds like he was getting dressed. He'd just finished brushing the fuzz off his teeth, when he heard the door opening behind him. He turned just in time to see a fist flying at his face. Then it all went black.

Chapter 18

Jackie came to, still lying in the boat. Cold hands lightly slapped each side of her face. Her fierce green eyes cleared and focused first on the iron pipes that crisscrossed the underside of the light station, but after a few blinks, the blurry blob standing over her slowly transformed into her grandfather.

"What happened, beach girl? I could hear you coughing from way up there." The concern in his voice was unmistakable.

She took a ragged breath and sat up, propping herself on her elbows. Her head was still swimming. "Yeah, I sorta got choked up there for a minute. Guess I got a mouthful of water."

Hoyt helped her up and sat her on the cushioned captain's seat. He told her to take a few deep breaths, then something caught his eye near the transom. He leaned and picked up the large sea shell. "Where'd this come from?"

Jackie's eyes widened. The shell was real. All the jumbled thoughts neatly aligned themselves and everything became clear. The stream of bubbles, the strange feeling she'd experienced as she got closer to the bottom, her arm burning . . . they all came together into a seamless memory. She'd actually touched the ocean floor under them. A few more coughs came, and then she said, "I got it from the bottom. Right where the metal goes into the sand."

"You must have hit your head on the bottom of the boat or something, beach girl. It's fifty feet deep here. I can't even make it to the bottom on one breath, and you don't even like swimming."

Jackie retold the story, and when she was finished, the color seemed to drain from his face. The look of concern he once had, she noticed, had transformed into a look of disbelief.

He said, "Let me see your arm."

Hoyt carefully unwrapped the soaked gauze and stood there, shocked, looking at a full covering of new skin, complete with arm hair. It was as if the burn had never happened. Both were stunned for a moment, then Hoyt took her by the hand. "Come on. I want to show you something."

They made their way to the galley. Hoyt poured her a glass of milk and pulled a small box from a drawer under the counter. He carefully opened it, and inside rested an old manila folder, tightly wrapped in a plastic baggie. Folded neatly inside was a bunch of archaic looking papers. One was a newspaper and under it were other official looking documents that looked to be from the same era. Hoyt laid the newspaper on the counter in front of them, and Jackie read the front page. It was the *Wilmington Star,* dated Sunday June 18, 1982. The big bold headlines read: 'Son of Sam Killer Berkowitz Sentenced to 365 Years, Vows Appeal.'

Hoyt said, "I haven't told anyone about this, because, well, there was really no need to. But when I came out here the first time, I found a few things that I assumed belonged to a Coast Guard officer that was stationed here." He reached in the box again and laid an opened pack of old Lucky Strike cigarettes, and a few Coast Guard officer's pins by the newspaper. He tapped the old newspaper lying on the counter. "Nobody saves these without a reason, so, I figured there was going to be a picture or article or something in it about this place or the guy who put it in this box."

They both stared at the artifacts for a moment before Hoyt said, "I guess the Son of Sam stuff took center stage back then, but further back, I found a small write-up about an accidental shooting that happened out here." Hoyt turned to a page and ran a finger down the small black print. "Ah. Here it is. Take a look at this."

She read the smaller bold print out loud, "Service Man Lives Following Accidental Shooting."

Jackie looked at her grandfather and said, "Somebody was shot here?"

"Looks like it."

Jackie turned back to the paper, but Hoyt interrupted. "No need to read all of it, I can sum it up for you. Years ago, they did live-fire target practice on the upper deck. Pistols mostly, and they had rigged some kind of metal fold down target holders. Well, it looks like one of the target frames jammed during practice, and an enlisted man, a young Petty Officer named Corbin tried to fix it. The guy cleared the jam, but somehow was still standing behind the target when they started shooting again. A bullet got him in the neck."

Jackie covered her mouth with both hands, and gasped loudly.

"Article said he fell off the platform, but they drug him out of the water, got a helicopter out here, and airlifted him to Wilmington. Saved his life, but the poor guy lost most of his larynx. The Commanding Officer was the one who shot him. A guy named Edwin Thompson. A junior officer relieved him of his command... a Lieutenant Brooks."

Jackie's glass stopped halfway to her mouth. "What was his name?

"Edwin Thompson and something Brooks. And look here—" Hoyt flipped through some of the other papers, but before he could find what he was looking for, Jackie jumped from the stool.

"Are you kidding me? I found something in my room with that guy's name on it. Brooks, right?" For a moment they looked at one another, reading each other's thoughts.

She disappeared down the hallway, and came back holding a small, bound leather book. "I found this behind a loose vent grate in my room last time we were here. Look inside the front cover. It's the same guy's name. I think it's his diary or something."

Hoyt opened the wrinkled leather-bound pages to the first page. There he read in faded ink: Lieutenant Jeremiah B. Brooks, Commander, Frying Pan Shoals Light Station. He flipped through a few pages, skimming the bad writing.

"Where did you find this?"

"Remember last week? You wanted me to crawl through the big air vent to see how much rust was in it? Well, it was lying in the air duct behind the vent in my room, inside an old plastic bag. I'm sorry I didn't say anything about it. I've been reading it some in my room at night. I wasn't sure if it was real or not. The stories seemed all made up."

Hoyt flipped through several more pages, mesmerized. "Air duct, huh? Your room must have been his room. I guess he didn't want anyone to find it—looks like his personal journal."

He flipped another page and read out loud, "Petty Officer J. Rogers: assigned to galley duty this morning until further notice for fighting. He punched Ensign Clausen for making him sweep the deck three times for being tardy to duty station. Rogers is an unkempt, brawling ass, and not surprisingly, Clausen isn't much better."

He looked at Jackie, with raised eyebrows, "Hey, these entries are dated too." He paused for a moment thinking, then pointed at the newspaper. "Does it have a date anywhere on that newspaper clipping?"

Jackie quickly found it.

Hoyt flipped through page after page, and was almost at the back of the book when he said, "Well, well. Would you look at this!"

He scanned through the entry while Jackie took a big gulp of milk. She wiped her lips with the back of her hand, and noticed her grandfather's eyebrows raise again. He flipped another page, reading silently, then flipped one more. His eyes went back and forth, then settled on the counter as he shut the journal.

"What'd it say?"

"The newspaper was almost two weeks behind, but it's in here all right. The Lieutenant said that two guys were working on the targets, but the bullet only hit Corbin. Said it opened up a hole in his neck the size of a large plum. The guy stumbled backwards and went over the rail. The body sank out of sight and the water turned red. They fished him out almost fifteen minutes later. Everyone knew he was a goner, but turns out the guy lived."

Jackie breathed a small scream.

"The guy was conscious and everything when they got him back up. Brooks said that the hole in his neck was still there, but it wasn't bleeding. Took forty minutes for the helicopter to get here from Wilmington, and that whole time they had him topside, the guy never bled another drop."

While Hoyt flipped back through the journal, Jackie felt like a child that had just been read a bedtime story where everyone always lived happily ever after. She took another sip of milk and rubbed sore muscles on the back of her neck. "Wow! How do you live through something like that?"

"I don't know. And look here." Hoyt shuffled through a several old papers that came from the box. "There were other reports in with the newspaper. Old medical reports that looked to be ripped out of an official notebook. Probably from the Medical Officer or medic."

Hoyt picked up the journal again, flipped back through the pages, and rattled off the highlights of four more incidents. They were all small and superficial injuries (a sprained ankle, dislocated shoulder, a busted lip and loosened tooth from a fist fight, the cook had even cut his finger badly preparing chow) but they were injuries none the less. And according to Brooks, all of them were healed miraculously with an alacrity rivaling Voodoo magic, lacking two basic things injuries need to heal properly: proper medical treatment and time.

Hoyt sat the book down and whistled through his teeth. He looked at Jackie's arm again. The skin was new, pink, and perfect; the sign of the burn completely gone. There wasn't so much as a scar there. "This can't be a coincidence, beach girl. Something's in the water out here."

122

Chapter 19

They lingered in the galley a little while longer discussing the journal and Jackie's arm. At some point, Hoyt glanced at his watch, flinched, and jokingly announced that all of this fairy-tale business was fun to talk about, but all the magic or witchcraft that existed on the rig wasn't going to finish the repairs and remodeling. Hoyt disappeared back into the head to do battle again with old rusty pipes, and Jackie walked down the hallway, where her small sponge brush waited. Work, however, was the farthest thing from her mind. What they had just discovered was important, she was sure of that, but her arm . . . there was no other explanation.

She worked in the small room for thirty minutes, and as she put the last coat of paint on the corners around the doorframe, her thoughts and curiosity finally won. The paintbrush found the lid of the paint bucket, and she propped her elbows on the window sill. It was nearly ten-thirty, and the sun was starting to climb high overhead, making the undulating sea below her shimmer a deep royal blue. The salt breeze filled her nostrils, and after a deep, cleansing breath, she noticed two fishing boats to the west. They were a subtle reminder that there was a world outside of the walls of the light station. And with that realization, she decided that just accepting the fact that strange things happen out there wasn't good enough. If the water had healed her once, it could do it again.

Unconsciously rubbing her healed burn, Jackie brainstormed about testing the water again. A broken bone or another burn was absurd—it didn't need to be that severe. She thought about the cook's cut finger and smiled. It didn't have to be big, or deep, but a simple cut in a less than critical area would do it. What was the worst thing that could happen? A small cut, even if the water didn't heal it, could easily be managed by a band aid. Jackie's eyes caught movement towards the northwest, as another white dot appeared on the horizon—another fishing boat taking their catch from the sea. It was indeed a busy day out here on the Frying Pan, but she decided that along with everything else, one more thing had to be done. She tiptoed down the hallway and stopped for just a moment to make sure her granddad was still preoccupied with the plumbing, then quietly made her way to the galley to find a knife.

Jackie descended the rope ladder into the boat with the small paring knife clinched in her teeth. She giggled, thinking she must look like a fierce teenage pirate boarding a merchant vessel. The fantasy faded, and she walked to the back of the boat testing the blade the same way Hoyt tested the filet knife. With minimal pressure, she could feel it bite into the raised ridges of her fingerprints, leaving a thin white line across her thumb. Swallowing hard, she lightly pressed the tip of the knife into the back of her hand a few times, each time feeling the sting of the point. Several fish darted from underneath the boat to the steel piling. Her eyes followed, and eventually settled on the small column of bubbles teasing the surface—the same bubbles she'd followed down to the sea floor. Her eyes went back to the knife point and the back of her hand. Intentionally cutting herself was proving to be more than bravery could overcome.

Come on Jackie. Just enough to bleed.

It was now or never. All at once, she swung her other leg over the side of the boat and stepped down to the bottom rung of the ladder. The Atlantic's warm and rhythmic sway lapped over her knee caps, and her feet and calves felt funny and tingly. Jackie relished the sensation before she gently drug the dull side of the blade across her hand. The point found the dip between her index and middle finger's knuckle, and she gingerly moved the tip down a half-inch, making sure to stay between the metacarpal bones, avoiding the big blue vein crossing the back of her hand. A quick prayer was said, then she raised the knife's handle and began to press the tip into the meaty part of her hand.

Nothing happened at first. She counted to three and applied more pressure. It still didn't cut, but after adjusting the blade angle the point finally broke the skin. It stung a little, but the pin-prick at the point of the blade didn't look big enough to her. Jackie flexed her hand around the knife's handle, and pressed down again. A drop of blood pooled around the point acting as a lubricant, and before she could stop herself, the blade buried itself deep into her hand. What was supposed to be just the slitting of the skin suddenly became much more. Withdrawing the knife, she sucked in a lungful of air and involuntarily flexed her hand a couple of times. The wound opened like the mouth of a hungry baby bird expecting a worm. A slight stinging sensation transformed into a stabbing pain as blood pooled in the void, spilled over the incision, and began running down her fingers.

There was nothing left to do. Jackie placed the knife on the transom, slid the snorkel mask into place, and stepped off the ladder.

Chapter 20

Mason LaRue opened a bloodshot eye. For a dazed moment he didn't know where he was or what was going on. He felt whatever he was laying on rising and falling, and somewhere under him was the steady hum and harsh vibrations of diesel engines . . . boat engines. The sun beat down on the side of his face, and the rest of his head felt like somebody had parked a tank on it. Nothing in his throat or mouth worked, and after several moments of intense concentration, his tongue finally moved. It probed the inside of his mouth, finding several painful splits and two loose teeth along his lower jaw. And a few minutes later, when his brain finally connected to his taste buds, there was nothing but the rancid taste of blood.

His mind began to clear, and the broken memories of what happened the night before slowly came back to him. The visit by Geno and his goons, drinking what seemed like gallons of bad coffee, and finally taking a shower before things went haywire. The awful hum of the engines compounded the pain in his head, and as he gained more and more of his senses, strangely, he felt more hungover now than he did when Frankie nearly beat the door down at the motel. There were large gaps in his memory that didn't make sense, even for a hangover. Mason wasn't even sure it was the same day. He'd never been drugged before, but he somehow knew that's exactly what had happened.

There was movement above him on the boat's flying bridge—a huge shirt covering a large belly fluttered in the breeze. A head appeared, glancing over the edge, and Mason closed his eyes, pretending to still be unconscious. Lying still wasn't a problem. Something had his hands bound behind his back, and the same thing affected his ankles. He was lying on the bow of a large boat, and like it or not, that was his only domain. The engines hummed mercilessly, but at times he could hear two distinct voices making conversation. Some of it was gibberish, and some of it made sense, but everything he heard and saw was marred by a growing annoyance between his legs. The more he thought about it the more it hurt, until at last he remembered what it was. The Ruger.

They'd missed it getting him aboard the boat, but that didn't do much for his current situation. The sun was relentless, and only an occasional passing cloud provided any kind of respite. He was on the verge of crying out, when he heard the fat man's unmistakable voice again. He was on the radio, telling somebody that he had made visual contact with the structure. Then he felt a presence close to his face and a cheerful voice said, "Time to wake up, greaser."

Something snapped under his nose, and immediately the airways leading to his lungs filled with a heavy dose of ammonia, burning the sensitive tissues along his sinus and trachea. He unconsciously took in a deep breath, eyes widened by the sudden influx of air. The form leering over him was Sal, the man who pointed the gun at him from the Tahoe at the bakery.

"I remember you," Mason said disjointedly, as the powerful Italian hoisted him from the deck. Arms twisted behind his back, Mason was pushed to the back of the boat and into the open cabin. Sal slammed him down on a chair and the pressure from the hidden pistol pinched Mason's scrotum. He swallowed a scream, turning it into a long moan, something that could be mistaken for hangover grief.

Sal said, "You don't look so good. You aren't going to puke, are you?"

Mason inhaled deeply and coughed a few times, still trying to evacuate the lingering ammonia. He hacked twice, and wad of bloody saliva hit the carpet. "Probably not," Mason said, "but you know what'd make me feel better?"

"What?"

"You, with your eyelids sliced off, tied down on the bow, admiring the pretty blue sky for a few days."

Sal laughed and yelled out the cabin's back door, "You know what Frankie? Geno was right. This is one funny dude."

Mason forced a smile, exposing blood streaked teeth. It was the same face every bar fight loser wore. Another clean, deep breath broke more cobwebs loose. "I thought it was Mister Mancini to meat heads like you."

Sal blurred a big hand across Mason's face. The sound loudly reverberated through the small cabin.

Frankie laughed from above and said, "Damn, Sal. Did you just hit him? I heard that way up here."

Sal rubbed the back of his hand and twisted a big class ring back in place, "Keep your mouth shut, greaser, and you might make the rest of the trip without being knocked back into la-la land. We talked about cutting you up into little pieces and feeding you to the sharks, but Mister Manci—Geno—wanted you alive on the light station."

Sal grabbed his face. A big thumb pressed firmly into a purple bruise that was forming on his cheekbone. He released his hold and slung a towel at Mason then pointed down the hallway. "The head— bathroom—is on the left. Last door. Clean yourself up, and when you're done with your face, clean that blood off the carpet."

Mason wiggled his arms. "How am I going to do all that with my hands tied? How about cutting me loose, unless you are planning to give me a bubble bath." Mason showed his bloody teeth again. "You look like the type that would like that."

Sal pulled a knife from an ankle sheath and tossed it back and forth between hands. The big Italian's eyes seemed to probe Mason's thoughts. The stare was cold and hateful, and after slowly running the flat part of the blade across Mason's swelling cheek, two quick swipes had his hands and feet free.

Mason rubbed the red marks on his wrist, encouraging blood flow, and watched a big .45 auto appear out of a shoulder holster. Sal thumbed back the hammer and pointed the barrel straight at the tip of Mason's nose. The hole in the barrel looked larger now than it did from the Tahoe.

"One wrong move and you'll be able to brush what's left of your teeth without opening your mouth."

"Okay, okay," Mason said, flexing his hands. He stood and shuffled down the hallway; the small pistol beginning to rub a blister on his inner thigh. "The blood hasn't made it to my fingers yet. I may need help."

Mason wasn't completely through the door when he saw the hand towel hanging next to the mirror. It was exactly what he needed. One more shuffle had him hidden behind the door frame, and he shoved his hands into his pants, ripping the small pistol free.

Chapter 21

The shot from the Ruger was nearly silent. Sal, wearing a mask of horror, stumbled backwards into the cramped hallway. His mouth worked a harsh series of guttural sounds, and he managed to raise the .45 even with Mason's feet before his whole arm trembled, then went limp. The big pistol fell harmlessly to the floor, and a stream of blood dribbled into his eye, then down his cheek from a small hole nestled in his right eyebrow.

Mason unwrapped the towel from the Ruger in his hand, and with one finger, he pushed the middle of Sal's chest. The big, stuttering Italian crumpled on the floor. Quickly, Mason balled up a corner of the white cloth and stuffed most of it in Sal's gaping mouth. He checked the Ruger's chamber and found the empty brass case. The towel had interfered with the small pistol's action, and he manually racked the slide, forcing the spent case out and a fresh round into the chamber. The pistol came up again, trained on the cabin's wide rear entrance. Mason's eyes moved back and forth, up and down, waiting for a target, but his ears only registered the muffled groans coming from the floor. It only took Sal ten seconds to die.

A muffled small caliber pistol fired in the bowels of a big boat, and fatso, topside at the controls with the wind in his ears and the engines roaring? Could the overstuffed sausage mauler even hear it?

It would only take a moment to find out.

Heart thumping and adrenaline flowing, he picked up Sal's .45 and backed into the small bathroom. There he breathed long, calming breaths . . . each filled with a healthy dose of burnt gun powder. He expected the engines to throttle back, the boat to slow, to hear yells from above. Or perhaps fatso would just abandon the controls and come barreling into the cabin, guns blazing at anything and everything just like something from the movies.

He waited.

He breathed.

Three long minutes passed, and the only thing that changed was the blood stopped bubbling in the small hole above Sal's right eye. He looked approvingly at the little black pistol. The .380 had been a perfect solution to the problem—just powerful enough to get into Sal's head and scramble his brains, yet not big enough to make a noticeable noise over everything else in the boat.

Satisfied that Frankie was still in the dark, Mason hooked the small pistol in his waistband, and holding the .45, he drug Sal to the back of the cabin. He peeked up at the flying bridge, and Frankie was there in the Captain's chair turning the dials on the radio. "Sometimes it pays to have a small pistol," Mason muttered as he hoisted the body, grabbing it under both lifeless arms. Four quick steps had Sal around the fighting chair and at the transom. With a solid heave, the body disappeared into the wake, and Mason stepped back into the cabin, pulled a beer from the small fridge, and sat down on the sofa. There was a shiny new cartridge in the chamber of the .45 and the clip looked to be full. He laid the big pistol across his lap and popped the top on the beer—for the first time since kicking the hooker out of the motel room the night before, Mason LaRue felt in control. In a strangely relaxed and satisfied voice he said, "Who's feeding the sharks now, prick?"

There can was almost empty when Mason heard the radio on the flying bridge squelch. The engines were too loud to hear everything, but someone was having a lengthy conversation with Frankie. A heavy foot stomped on the fiberglass above, and the loud thumping noise brought Mason out of complacency. The big pistol was fast in his hand, hammer cocked. Just for a moment he thought about emptying the clip through the ceiling, taking care of his last problem, then dressing in Frankie's clothes and attempting to fool Geno. It would have been a decent plan had it not been for Frankie's girth. There couldn't be enough pillows on the boat to make him look that big.

A harsh voice came from above. "Hey, Sal." That was Geno. They are a few miles off our rear port quarter. Right on time. Get that greaser ready. We're about four miles out."

A funny feeling grew in the pit of Mason's stomach. The plan he'd conceived came on the fly, and had worked well, but in his haste to toss the body Mason had completely forgotten about the helicopter. Sal could be no more than a couple of miles behind them, and the sharks probably hadn't had enough time to find him yet. A body floating in cobalt-blue water would be a flashing neon sign from the air. The element of surprise was always a good thing to have, especially when matched against someone who was physically bigger and stronger. That funny feeling nestled in his belly told Mason that he was about to experience a heavy dose of Murphy's Law. And if that happened, he was about to meet a very angry fat man, one on one, without any assistance from a thing called surprise.

With all the gumption he could muster, he pounded back on the roof of the cabin. Trying his best to sound Italian, he hollered back everything was good. Then what he feared the most happened—the radio sprang back to life. Mason stood near the cabin entrance listening, but still only was able to discern bits and pieces of the transmission. The radio went silent, and the engines died to an idle. With only a light hiss of breeze blowing, he clearly heard Frankie say, "You saw a *what?*"

The helicopter shook the boat as it flew by and heavy footsteps sounded above. Frankie was on his way. Mason turned a complete circle looking for somewhere to hide. The couch was along one wall, and the small refrigerator and a table along the other. For a split second, he thought about running down the hallway to the head. It was the only logical place to hide, but there was only one way in and one way out. Frankie wasn't a Rhodes Scholar, but if he came down and didn't see anyone, there was only one place to look. No more surprise. And if Frankie wanted to, he could easily just start sending volleys of bullets through the thin cabin walls.

Bad idea, dipshit. That's a good way to be killed without even the chance to shoot back.

Mason surveyed the open area again. The couch was jammed all the way to the door frame on the left side, but on the right, there was a small alcove between the cabin's door and the table and small refrigerator. A shift of the eyes noticed a narrow window beside the door frame facing the transom. It came down from the ceiling, but didn't extend all the way to the floor. A small area below the window was covered with wood paneling. It wasn't much, but it would have to do.

Mason jammed his back against the narrow window, and slinked to his knees. His head was barely below the window, and he sucked in everything he could, trying to stay as far away from the door as possible. Frankie's heavy steps pounded down the ladder behind him, then he was on the fiberglass deck, making his way to the cabin door. Mason held the .45 close to his chest, finger on the trigger, waiting.

One of Frankie's feet came through the opening. Nearly laughing, he blubbered out, "Hey, Sal—"

The rest of him appeared in the opening, and in one smooth motion, his massive head turned and mouth opened in surprise. Frankie's fat arm began to swing a pistol into position, and he was forming the word 'no' on his lips, but he never got to say it. Only three feet separated them, and Mason, easily estimating the aim, pivoted Sal's .45 and pulled the trigger. Instantly, Frankie's gun blew apart, and shards of metal and bullet fragments scattered into the far wall of the cabin. The fat man bellowed in pain. His thumb dangled by only a bit of bone and sinew, and he nearly tore it completely from his quivering hand as he grabbed at the wound.

Mason sneered. "I've been waiting a long time to hear you scream, you sonuvabitch."

Chapter 22

Jackie opened her eyes and right away knew that whatever that had healed her forearm was working its magic again. Her body, tight and tingly, felt energized but something just wasn't right. She had merely blinked entering the water, but when she could see again, the surface was at least twenty feet above her. Somehow, more time had passed than just what it takes to blink.

Barely aware that she was still sinking, above her, near the surface, hundreds of Charlies had gathered at the dissolving purplish cloud she had offered to the ocean. Whether they were trying to consume it or just attracted to its smell was unclear, but seeing the fish gather around the cloud of blood almost pushed her into a panic. She remembered from her science class that sharks could smell a drop of blood from a mile away. The warm tingling that was teasing her body at once turned into a suffocating feeling of dread, but before Jackie could imagine being torn to pieces by a large shark, an intense burning sensation erupted on her hand.

Twenty-five feet below the surface, the wound was still leaking a greenish cloud, but the skin around it quivered and popped, as if the flesh was trying to crawl off the bone. She waved through the water with her good hand, trying to clear the blood, and with a better view she could actually see the cut slowly mending itself from the inside out. Jackie wanted to scream, but took the pain, watching in both horror and amazement at the excruciatingly slow but steady movement of her own red, raw flesh cleaving itself together one cell, one molecule, one atom at a time.

The cut was over halfway shut and the bleeding had stopped completely when another strange thought came to her. She had been underwater for an exceptionally long time, yet she hadn't felt the need to breathe. But much like when she followed the bubbles down and found the shell, the mere understanding that a submerged human must have oxygen seemed to start an internal timer. Jackie's chest began to tighten, and her lungs pulsed. She was still contemplating what to do, when she dropped below that same inversion line where clear, blue water changed into a green murk. Just before leaving the clear water, something off in the distance caught her eye, and immediately her hand became a secondary concern. Something was there, but judging the distance was impossible. Even with the strange way billions of gallons of undulating seawater refract light, the object seemed very big and very far away, perhaps even far enough away to be out on the edge of the shoals where the depths sometimes plunged hundreds of feet straight down. She blinked and strained her eyes. It wasn't an illusion—whatever it was, was still there. It was big, and it was moving.

The frightened teen froze. She'd seen it on television—ascending and silhouetting herself against the surface would make her look like a large shark's typical prey. She had no choice, her lungs were demanding air. Jackie kicked hard, but she'd only risen ten feet in the water column when something grabbed her around the waist. She screamed, evacuating her remaining breath, and through the burst of bubbles, a hand appeared and pinched her nose shut, while another hand shoved an air regulator into her open mouth.

Chapter 23

When Jackie had convinced herself that she wasn't being consumed by a large, toothy fish, the panic eased, and she was able to take in a few breaths through the regulator. She coughed away some of the seawater that had seeped in around the mouthpiece, then, almost unbelievably, her breathing normalized. A man in a wetsuit was beside her, but she had no idea who he was, or what he was doing under the light station. Piercing blue eyes stared at her through the mask, and somehow she knew he was smiling. Taking turns breathing through the regulator, the swimmer pulled Jackie out into deeper water towards the very object that had caused her panic. The closer they came, the more it took shape—what she had seen from a distorted distance hadn't been a shark at all.

It might have been the refraction, but the submarine looked as big as a skyscraper laid on its side. The swimmer kept Jackie steady as they approached the conning tower above the main body of the vessel. Their feet touched the flat surface of the sub at the same time, and while she took another hit off the air, he opened a hatch and motioned for her to go in. He followed, and turned and closed the hatch, securing it shut. A well-muscled arm raised, pointing at a panel of buttons on the roof, then to a small grate made into the wall of the compartment. Jackie understood, and took another large breath from the regulator while the swimmer began pressing buttons. A red light blinked and the water level began to recede. Warm air whistled into the compartment, displacing the sea water, and when it was past their shoulders, they both pulled their masks off.

Jackie's mouth opened but nothing came out. There was just too much flooding her mind to organize a coherent thought. She was still gathering her wits when the man pulled back the wetsuit's hood, exposing short-cropped platinum blonde hair. He was younger than she first thought, and even though the rest of his body was covered by a plain black wetsuit, Jackie immediately deemed him attractive.

A strong baritone voice resonated in the compartment. He told her she was safe, then asked where was she hurt. Jackie still couldn't speak, barely managing to shrug her shoulders. The swimmer told her that everything was going to be okay, and he guessed that she had a thousand questions. He assured her that after her injuries were attended to, the captain wanted to meet her. Without warning, another hatched popped open on the floor. She sucked in a lungful of warm air and grabbed the young man around the waist, while the floor opened beneath them, revealing a larger compartment—the main deck of the vessel.

A man that called himself a doctor checked her head to toe, and other than a small scratch on her hand, proclaimed her physically sound. Someone handed her a towel as the swimmer lead her down the tight passageway, past sailor after sailor busy at his station with the task of operating a submarine. They stooped through several hatches and emerged into what looked to be the brain of the vessel. No less than fifteen sailors sat in small chairs along the walls staring at computer screens, each wearing a set of headphones. They all seemed to look at her at the same time, then turned back to their work, tapping out a sort of orchestral music on the keyboards. Two men sat at the far end of the room, at what could have only been the vessel's navigation controls. Behind them, sitting in a large chair watching their every move, was a man wearing an impressive naval hat. He was thin and lanky, but carried an air of importance. Jackie knew immediately that he was the captain.

The tall man motioned to them, and stood from his chair. His overbearing height occupied every last inch of vertical space, and he stepped towards them, offering Jackie his hand. "Good morning. You must be Jackie LaRue."

A big part of her was still not sure if what she was seeing was real, but from somewhere inside a small voice slipped her lips. "How … how . . . how do you know who I am?"

The man smiled. "We actually know a lot about you, Miss LaRue, but our top-secret sources insist on confidentiality." He chuckled like it was a joke and said, "Please allow me to introduce myself. My name is Robert McClendon, Captain of the USS Omaha."

At that, he swept the official-looking hat from his head, and stooped into an exaggerated ceremonial bow.

"On behalf of the seventy-five sailors on board, we bid you welcome to our little piece of sub-oceanographic paradise."

By the time he had regained his full height, two men walked through the hatch behind them. One of the men looked pleasant, but all business, while the other looked annoyed. Both were dressed semi-casually in button down white shirts, with plain khaki pants. They wore sidearms and law enforcement badges on their belts, accompanied by two sets of handcuffs in black polished holsters.

Captain McClendon said, "It seems that our top-secret sources have arrived. Please allow me introduce to you two of America's finest crime specialists from D.C., Special Agents Jason Grier, and Don Cooper. CIA and FBI, not necessarily in that order.

Both men forced a smile at Jackie, but didn't offer to shake hands.

After an awkward pause, Captain McClendon cleared his voice and looked at the swimmer. "Well done, sailor. Please rejoin your unit, but don't get lost. I suspect we'll need you again shortly." The captain turned back to Jackie, "It's fortunate that one of our men was reconning the rig when you fell into the water. But your accident, I'm afraid, has caused us to break our cover somewhat with the operation." He looked her up and down and said, "I was told there was blood in the water and you looked to be unconscious, but our doctor says there's nothing wrong with you short of a partially healed cut on your hand. Is there anything he might have missed?"

She held her hand out in front of her and noticed only a thin pink line where the gaping cut had been. She shrugged her shoulders. "No, I'm fine, and I didn't fall." Confused eyes met the captain's. "What operation?"

This time it was Don Cooper that spoke, harboring a noticeable New York accent. "We are not at liberty to discuss all the intricacies of what we're doing here, Miss LaRue. But I will tell you that we are here to apprehend a person of interest that the US Government has been monitoring for some time. We have reason to believe he will be visiting the Frying Pan today." He turned towards the other man and said, "Special Agent Grier and I have been sent here through a joint venture with our agencies and the US Navy to capture this man alive."

Before Jackie could say anything, agent Grier said, "As you can probably guess, since you are standing in a submarine, this man is not a very nice guy. In fact, we believe he's a direct link to several people in the northeast who are even bigger scum-bags than he is. But what makes this such a special case," he completed a sweeping look at the inside of the submarine, "and the reason we are crammed in this underwater sardine can, is that on top of all that, two of those men in the northeast, we believe, are closely linked with several Middle Eastern governments. Governments that do not hold the United States in high regard. We want the man who we think is coming out here today. If we get him, then we stand a very good chance of capturing the others."

Jackie thought for a moment, trying to remember the name her grandfather had mentioned—the guy that wanted to buy the light station. Finally, it came. "This guy's name is Mancini, isn't it?"

The two agents looked at each other, then back to Jackie. Grier nodded, while Cooper just stood there, eyebrows raised.

Agent Grier stuck his hands in his pockets and rocked back on his heels. "What do you know about this man, Miss LaRue?"

"Nothing much. Granddad said he wanted to buy the light station, but we got it first."

While Special Agent Grier fumbled around words trying to explain more of what was going on, somebody in a uniform stepped onto the bridge and handed the captain a piece of paper. McClendon's eyes scanned it, then he raised his hand and said, "Pardon the interruption, gentlemen. Our target and Caro—" he stopped reading mid-sentence, and cut an eye at Jackie, "Our target and his guest just arrived at the airport in Wilmington. We have approximately one hour."

Every eye on the bridge fell on the two men in plain clothes. They shared a concerned glance, then turned to the captain.

Agent Cooper said, "If there's nothing wrong with her, she needs to go back. If she is not there when Mancini arrives, Hoyt may do something foolish and make him bolt. We've all worked too hard for this to blow up in our faces now just because of her."

Jackie's voice changed. "How do you know my grandfather's name, and what do you mean because of—"

The captain raised a finger and he leaned and pressed a button on a control panel by his chair. A steady thump from a deep throated siren began blaring, and after a few seconds of regulated chaos, he reached for another button and an intercom system came to life, temporarily displacing the siren. He blew at the console, and his breath came through hidden speakers somewhere above them.

"Now hear this. All personnel: general quarters. All SEALs report to forward compartment. I repeat: all SEALs report to forward compartment." He looked at his watch and said, "The operation commences in ten minutes. That's 14:46 hours. I repeat: 14:46 hours. That is all."

McClendon turned to the two men sitting at the submarine's controls. "Have the navigational instruments settled down enough to get us closer to the station without breaching the line of visibility?"

One of the men responded. "Sir, we are still getting bogus readings, but we should be able to half the distance."

"Good. Maneuver us as close as possible so we can deploy the men, but I want us back in the soup before Geno arrives. Under no circumstances is he to see our outline."

Jackie LaRue was a statue watching the sub spring to life. The siren continued blaring in an annoying tone, and men busily shuffled through the bridge, responding to the urgency in McClendon's commands. No more than forty-five minutes ago, she'd been staring out of the window at the sea from the room she was painting in the light station, and now she was in the control room of a United States submarine preparing for some kind of covert operation. Everyone seemed to be going somewhere in a hurry except Jackie. She was still trying to process what was going on around her, when the captain took her by the arm.

"Please come with me Miss LaRue. Your head must be spinning, but I think I can explain better what's going on. The main thing you need to know right now is that you are safe, but Agent Cooper is right. We need you back on that station."

Chapter 24

They briskly wound their way back through the tight compartments. Jackie listened while McClendon talked. It was still a big blurry mess, but she was beginning to understand. When they reached the forward compartment, a dozen Navy SEALs were busy testing and retesting their air tanks and regulators. The siren, the constant keyboard clicking that seemed to permeate the entire vessel, all the movement and hustle and bustle of the SEALs and support people coming and going around the cramped space made her nauseous.

Hoping that the sound of her own voice would somehow help, she took a deep, cleansing breath and said, "So all of this is to get a guy that knows guys that have ties with some spies or terrorists from other countries?"

The captain nodded.

"And those two guys from the FBI or CIA set this whole thing up?

"More or less."

It all buzzed through her mind again, and even though she didn't know exactly why, it was apparent that she and her grandfather were somehow the bait for this Mancini guy. A flush of adrenaline emptied into her veins, and she began to feel her heart beating in her neck. The next question didn't come from the mild, unassuming Jackie LaRue. It came from the girl who had shot the barracuda for eating her friend Charlie.

"This guy has ties to terrorists, and you need us, an old man and a girl on there when he shows up? We're the bait?"

The captain's cheerful face changed. He spoke as if talking to one of his men. "He's flying in on his own bird, and we have to get him out of it and into the light station to make certain we get him without incident. He knows you and your grandfather are out here. If he sees anything out of the ordinary before he lands or before he gets too far away from the helo, he'll bolt. We've all done a good job so far keeping all this confidential, and believe me, we are very guilty of over-utilizing resources in order to complete this mission. Those extra men will be used to specifically protect you and your family. We are reasonably certain we have him cold here, but if we blow this, he'll know we're after him. If that happens, we'll never have a chance like this again."

Jackie's body began to shake. "This Mancini guy is supposed to be rich and powerful. What makes you think he's just going to rat out his friends?"

"You seem like a smart girl, Miss LaRue, so you have to realize that his business contacts aren't school yard, best-friends-forever relationships. When people like Mancini start to feel pressure, especially the type of pressure we are able to apply, they tend to spill their guts quickly. Most of the time, all they want to do is save their own bacon. Apparently, this Geno guy has done well for himself, bullying his way into a good bit of the real estate game in Morehead City and further up the coast. He's not a nice guy, and probably should already be in prison for something, but ultimately, he's just a small fish doing the will of the much larger and meaner fish up north. And those fish are connected with the biggest fish of all." The Captain looked left, then right at the metal bulkheads that held the submarine together. "An appropriate analogy, considering where we are, don't you think?"

Jackie's blood began to cool and her stomach was almost free of the knots that occupied it just moments before.

How did he know to use big and little fish as an example?

She stared blankly at the twists of pipes running along the gray painted side of the submarine. It was a lot to take in, but it was slowly coming together, piece by piece. There was one thing that still didn't make sense. She took a calming breath, and looked straight into the captain's steady eyes. "But why here—the light station? You all seem to know everything there is to know about him. Why didn't you try to get him where he lives, or at the airport at Wilmington?"

"According to our two agents," the Captain chinned towards them briefing the SEAL team, "they had a trap set for Mancini when the government first tried to sell it. Apparently, Mancini has a history of dabbling with small and unique real estate ventures, but their intel at the time said that he wasn't interested. To give him a little incentive, they cooked up this crazy story about the waters out here having some kind of special powers and spread it on the street where his men would hear it. What made it even more genius is that Grier's and Cooper's men were playing off an old urban legend about this place. Back in the seventies and eighties, it was rumored that some really weird stuff happened out here—"

Jackie's head turned quickly, "What kind of weird stuff?"

McClendon removed his hat and mopped his forehead with a handkerchief. "You ever read the Bible, Miss LaRue?"

Jackie nodded.

"Do you remember the story about Lazarus?"

Jackie nodded, absently rubbing the remnants of the knife wound on the back of her hand.

"Well, I'm not saying someone came back to life, but supposedly a guy was accidentally shot on that thing. I think it was either in the head or neck—a terrible wound—and he fell completely off the tower into the water. Yet somehow he lived. Most people claim it's an old urban legend, and that the gunshot just nicked him, but more than one eye witness reported that the guy had every right to be graveyard dead. When they fished him out of the drink, he was still alive."

Jackie covered her mouth with both hands, hiding a smile. The burn and healed cut were another couple of occurrences that could be added to the legend. She ran a finger over the scar . . . it was still there and still very real. She wanted to tell him that she had lived the legend twice and about the hidden journal. She wanted to tell him that when wounds healed, it hurt. She wanted to tell him what it felt like to watch your skin try to crawl right off your body. But now wasn't the time.

Captain McClendon continued, "So with some other tall tales thrown in for good measure, the rumors about the tower did their own impersonation of Lazarus." He nodded again in Grier and Cooper's direction, "And I'll give those guys credit for thoroughness. They did everything right. From forging and fabricating documents in the Coast Guard's public records and newspaper articles, to planting that kind of material on the light station for Mancini and the rest of them to find at the inspections. It was as good of a paper trail as you could ask for. The only problem is that it didn't work. Mancini only sent out a structural engineer to inspect it before the sale, and he was too busy looking at the supporting structure to pay any attention to the interior stuff. He didn't find the planted documents. Mancini knew about the rumors though. Cooper and Grier made certain of that.

"Mancini's ego is the size of the Bermuda Triangle, so they figured that he'd show at the bid opening to laugh off any attempts of the locals to buy it. They had everything set to take him there, but at the last minute, Mancini decided against coming, and just sent one of his men. Well, the guy never showed, and that's when your mom and grandfather stumbled onto the scene. They had the trap baited for Mancini, but your family wound up eating the cheese."

Jackie said, "So we just got in the way?"

The captain laughed. "Kinda. You see, those agents get paid to think, so they adjusted the plan on the fly and, well, I can tell by the way you are acting that Hoyt kept it quiet. They contacted him a few weeks after the sale and brought him up to speed on what was going on. Your grandfather was more than accommodating, and he didn't mind us using the light station as part of the master plan," he looked down at his watch, "that should kick off here in about three minutes."

Flabbergasted, Jackie said, "So granddad knows about this?"

"He knows we are after Mancini and that this is linked to something bigger up north, and that he was to expect some kind of communication or visit from Mancini about buying the tower, but exactly how much they told him I can't say. I do know that he would not go along with any of it without the government guaranteeing your and your mother's safety, on or off the structure."

The captain ran the handkerchief back over his forehead. "It's actually worked out quite well, given the twists and turns along the way. Out here, we are well past the threshold of US judicial protocol, operating on a top-secret, small reconnaissance submarine that only a handful of people in Washington and the US Navy even know about. We aren't handcuffed to restrictive rules pertaining to how we apprehend and treat domestic or international threats. And to be perfectly honest with you, of those few in Washington and the Navy that know we exist, only a select few of them know what we are doing at any given moment. Most just think we are testing this new little sub, that's about sixty percent of the size of a normal attack sub, mainly for research and development. When in reality, Top Secret is about three levels below us. We get orders straight from the Oval Office, and our little recon sub here can go to the bottom of the ocean and stay there for quite some time—quite literally disappearing from the face of the planet. We have clearance to operate globally, and on orders, can covertly deliver anyone to any government or entity in the world who has a sea port, helicopter, or ship. In other words, even if Mancini plays hardball with us, he's going to see the futility at some point. Then, it's only a matter of time before he tries to—"

Jackie finished his sentence, "Save his own bacon."

"Sharp girl, Miss LaRue, sharp girl." McClendon replaced his hat and said in a noticeably more serious voice. "But first thing's first. We've got to get our hands on him, and to do that, everything on the light station must be status quo. We have to get you back on it."

He snapped his fingers and a young SEAL appeared next to them. "I believe you two have already met but I doubt you've been properly introduced. Miss LaRue, this young man's name is Ethan Wade. He'll accompany you back the same way he brought you here. Please do as he says, and I promise nothing bad will happen."

* * *

When Jackie broke the surface beside her grandfather's Grady White, she took a deep breath and stuck her face back into the water and waved at Ethan Wade fifteen feet below her. He saluted, and she thought she could see smile lines around his eyes through the mask. Jackie watched as he swam back towards the submarine until his dark form became obscured by the Atlantic's refraction. A chill slipped down the curve of her spine. How could a fourteen-year-old girl get involved in a US Navy operation to apprehend a man backing terrorists? She looked as far as she could in every direction. There seemed to be nothing but water, scattered schools of small fish, and a couple of amberjacks as far as she could see. Yet, somewhere down there were eleven other SEALs with orders to take Geno Mancini by whatever means necessary.

She floated in the water tingly numb for a long moment before she heard the helicopter's whirring rotors in the distance.

Chapter 25

The sound of the helicopter signaled it was time to move, and move she did. It was as if the rope ladder wasn't even there. In what seemed like a blink of the eye, she was up the stairs, across the catwalk, down the hall, and in her room scrambling for a dry set of clothes. Out the window, the helicopter was maneuvering towards the platform and a fresh dose of adrenaline coursed. Tight muscles in her legs began to cramp, but she still managed to slide on a pair of shorts and a t-shirt with the agility of a ballet dancer. The hallway was still empty, and the room to room search turned up nothing. The galley was all that was left, and she roared through the open door, skidding to a stop, head swiveling and sucking in massive gulps of air. Leftover breakfast was still on the table, dishes from the night before still sat in the sink, and to the left, on the counter, were her grandfather's snorkel mask and speargun. But Hoyt was nowhere to be found.

Fear was slowly taking over her system and she wanted badly to just sit down on the floor and scream, but she knew that wouldn't help. Reversing direction, she quickly ran down the hallway to the outside cat walk, and up the short flight of steel stairs leading to the roof. And that's when she saw him. Hoyt was standing along the edge, holding onto the chain railings next to the marked landing area. The helicopter was slowly descending towards the platform.

This time, there was no hover and no signals were made—Geno Mancini was not asking for permission to land. Jackie and Hoyt shared a glance, and in an eerie moment that she'd never forget, she somehow felt like their minds were linked. It wasn't even her voice she heard in her own head. Hoyt's lips moved, and *his* haggard voice sounded in her mind as crisp and clear as if he was standing beside her: *Air duct. Hide in the air duct. Don't come out unless I call for you.*

Jackie nodded and reluctantly backed down the steps. Halfway down, eye-level to the roof, something made her stop. Somewhere floating around in her crazy, mixed up mind, she remembered Captain McClendon's words.

Geno Mancini and his guest? I wonder if it's one of the terrorists?

The helicopter's skids hit the landing zone perfectly, a door opened, and a lady stepped out, stumbling as if she had been pushed. The engines began to wane, and the rotor's reverberating chop that was making her chest thump began to slow. Two men stepped out, one on either side of the small cockpit. The short one was holding a briefcase, the other stooped as he came around the helicopter holding another briefcase in one hand and a gun in the other. The short one said something to the woman, and pointed at Hoyt with his free hand. They all stepped towards the rail, and the air from the rotors ruffled the lady's hair enough to see her face. Jackie gasped. Her mom, sporting a swollen cheek and fresh shiner around the eye above it, did not look happy.

For a horrible moment, Jackie's brain went blank. It was like someone had disconnected the cable plug on the television. One moment the screen was alive with a clear screen and audio, and the next it was a black and white sizzling mess. She stood there a prisoner in her own helpless body, not seeing, not hearing, and not caring. She didn't know how long the connections were severed, but it couldn't have been long. When the television finally came back on, the group was approaching her grandfather. The wind whipped again, clearly revealing Caroline's look of fear.

Terrorized by a hail of torturous images, all involving what Mancini might do to them, Jackie's hatred for this short Italian man quickly surpassed what she felt under the light station watching a barracuda swim away crunching half of Charlie in his mouth. She was losing control, and wanted very much to kill both men with her bare hands, or at the very least kick each of them one good time in the balls like she had Ronnie back at school. She tried to move to do all of those things, but some invisible force immobilized her. The instructions Hoyt telegraphed her came to her again, and she regained some semblance of control.

Jeeze Louise, Jackie, it's the freakin' Mafia standing up there.

It was a harsh reality, but the cool wind from the helicopter's rotors seemed to drive the point home. This was really happening, and unless the water somehow gave her superpowers that hadn't been revealed yet, she knew that there was absolutely nothing she could do. Her grandfather was right. Geno Mancini didn't need any extra bargaining power with her stumbling into the fray. Hoyt's pleas for the air ducts were the right thing to do—the only thing to do.

Jackie ducked low again as all four of them started towards the stairs. The short guy, who she assumed was Geno, was doing all the talking. Some of it she could hear and some she couldn't. Approaching, he was yelling over the last of the rotor wash something about it being a beautiful day and that he had a surprise for them all arriving in a bit, but first they needed to go inside and have a nice little chat.

Jackie turned and ran down the stairs and when she hit the short steel catwalk that led to the main door to the light station, she looked out across the ocean. The bow of a big fishing boat was rising and falling, plowing across the sea. It was no more than a mile and a half out, and taking dead aim at the structure. It had to be Geno's surprise.

Chapter 26

It had always been quiet on the light station. When the generator
wasn't running or the wind wasn't howling outside, whispers carried
down the hallway like a mountain echo. And those few times when
conditions were absolutely pristine, normal sounds within the
structure seemed to be strangely amplified. Setting a plate down on
the galley table, unzipping a small suitcase, or something as quiet as
gently closing a door could easily be heard from one end to the
other, as if it had happened within arm's reach. Jackie had noticed
its peculiar acoustics before, but it wasn't until she pried off the grate
to the air duct in her room that she was abruptly reminded of just
how well sounds traveled there. She was looking over her shoulder
at the door, not paying attention, when the grate slipped from her
nervous, sweat-damp hands. It fell only a few inches, landing against
the steel bedframe, but the resulting *bang* echoed loudly down the
air duct, finding its way to every corner of the old light station. She
held her breath, hoping the combination of the slowing helicopter
rotors on the roof, and the fact that Geno Mancini hadn't shut up
since they'd landed, had produced enough background noise to
hide her blunder. The murmuring voices outside on the catwalk
never ceased, and Jackie blew a silent breath of relief. She paused
for another moment, just to be sure, then satisfied that her secret
was still intact, she crawled into the main air vent.

The vent was filled with dust and rust, and twice she caught her
t-shirt on exposed screws. As she carefully negotiated the rest of the
distance towards the galley, the footsteps and voices went right by
her on the other side of the wall in the hallway. As far as she could
tell, her mother and grandfather hadn't spoken. It had only been
the short Italian rambling on constantly about this and that—the

weather, the fishing, how quiet it was there, and how well Hoyt and his 'fixer-upper parties' of free labor had transformed the structure. When she finally made it to the edge of the galley vent and peered into the room, everyone but Hoyt was sitting at the small table. The short one was leaning forward, resting both palms on the table, still talking, while the tall one sat across from everyone still holding the pistol. Hoyt was busy clearing the last of breakfast's leftovers, carrying the dishes to the sink. It took multiple trips, and once, when he lingered a little too long there at the window, the tall one whistled and waggled the gun, inviting him to join them again at the table.

The short guy reached for a briefcase on the floor, sat it on the table, fumbled with something at the handle, then unlocked the two latches on the sides. There was a slight sound of air discharging, and a thin flow of white vapor breached from the cracks. Jackie's brow wrinkled. From her low angle, she couldn't see into the briefcase, but what she did see was Caroline and Hoyt's faces react. To Jackie, they were looks of staggering disbelief.

Geno slowly reached into the case, producing two slim champagne flutes. He sat them on the table, smiled at his two hosts who were still too shocked for words, and pulled out four more. Before he sat the last one down, he stopped, and closely examined it. Shaking his head, he reached for his handkerchief, hazed over a portion of the flute with hot breath, and polished the glass. Geno re-examined it, appeared to be satisfied, and sat it on the table with the others. Everything came to a halt while he thoroughly scrutinized the other glasses again. One more was hazed and polished before Geno pulled two full size bottles of champagne from the briefcase. He shook his head and softly clucked disappointment. "I've never seen such incompetence." He turned to the guy with the gun. "Can you believe it, Pauley? Smudges. Pay top dollar, and you wind up with crap. Additional dry ice or not, Sabastian's Fine Spirits is dead to me."

Geno cleared his throat and turned to Hoyt. "Wouldn't you agree, Mister Bennett? I mean, for businessmen such as you and me, when we pay good money for something, we usually have high expectations for services or products rendered. Same goes for when we are the ones rendering. I bet you set the bar high, trying to deliver the best fishing trips possible for your clients. And why wouldn't you? Good business is, well, just good business."

Hoyt stared, slack jawed, at the bottles and flutes on the table. It was as if he hadn't heard a thing Geno was saying. Geno looked back and forth between Hoyt and the glasses, then snapped his fingers twice along the path of his stare. Hoyt blinked and lightly shook his head. Down below on the water, the boat engine that had been getting louder and louder, slowed to an idle. Geno cocked his ear towards the window, nodded approvingly, then turned back to Hoyt who was still staring blankly at the briefcase.

"What were you expecting, Mister Bennett? A bomb? A gun? Some kind of torture device?" He shook his head. "My reputation sometimes precedes me, and you probably have heard stories from my less refined years that may or may not be true. But on an occasion such as this, one doesn't bring items of pain and torture. No, no. Quite the contrary. This sir, is a joyous occasion. And on such occasions, any civilized person knows that celebratory items are needed."

Hoyt and Caroline said in unison, "Joyous?"

Father and daughter looked again at each other. Hoyt ran a calloused but tender hand across Caroline's bruised cheek and said, "You hit my daughter, force her out here against her will, then hold a gun on both of us?" Hoyt's head snapped back to Geno. "Tell me how this qualifies as joyous."

Geno quietly peeled away the metallic foil wound around the top of a bottle and began working the cork with his thumb. "I admit this whole ordeal has become cumbersome. Miss Bennett was a bit higher strung than expected." The cork gave, popping loudly, and

Geno began pouring the first glass. "It took a little more persuasion than I'd hoped, and trust me, Mister Bennett, her few bruises in no way make up for half of one of my guy's ear she bit off." He sighed and made a big circular gesture with his free hand, "But the end result is that we are all here, all accounted for, and all about to raise a toast to good health, good fortune, and good business."

Geno poured more champagne, filling each glass.

Hoyt said, "Now look here. We own this rig and I demand—"

Heavy footsteps in the hallway stopped him. Hoyt and Caroline turned just in time to watch two men walk through the door.

Geno, who hadn't looked up yet, carefully stood, holding two filled glasses. "Well, well, I see the others have finally arrived."

At the door stood a much paler version of his mountainous bodyguard. Frankie Russo looked half dead—his right hand wrapped with what used to be a white terry cloth towel. It was a deep red now, soaked through with blood. Slightly behind him, stood a badly beat up and sunburnt, but smiling Mason LaRue. He was holding Sal's big Springfield, and his eyes seemed to bounce wildly back and forth between his former family and the man who was toasting them.

Pauley knocked his chair over coming to his feet, but Geno quickly raised his hand.

"Hold on," he said in a surprisingly calm voice.

Pauley complied and slowly righted the chair and sat back down—his pistol now trained on Mason. Neither Hoyt nor Caroline could say or do anything. Surprise and terror bound them tighter than any ropes could have.

Geno carefully sat the glasses down, making sure not to spill a drop. "I wasn't sure which one of you bought it back there. I assumed it was you, Mister LaRue." He shook his head. "I can't imagine how you managed to turn one of my best men into a permanent snorkeler."

Pauley suddenly stood up again, pointing the pistol at Mason. "When the boss gets finished with you, I hope you're still alive. I'm going to shove this pistol—"

Geno raised his hand again and said in a commanding voice, "Would you sit down and shut up."

Mason pushed Frankie out ahead of him. A rather large human shield. They took a few steps in the room, careful not to come too far.

Geno said, "Sal was probably the smartest guy I had. Cornell graduate, I believe, wasn't he Pauley? Oh well. You know what they say about book smarts and street smarts."

It didn't look like it, but the short Italian was still projecting control over the situation. He propped his elbow on the table and rubbed his forehead. "Well, I guess this changes things, doesn't it, Mister LaRue?" He glanced at Hoyt and Caroline, who were still staring stupidly at the man who had ruined numerous years of their lives. "Mister and Miss Bennett, I give you your big surprise, but I beg your pardon, this isn't how I wished to deliver him."

* * *

Jackie peered from the air duct grate into a room so full of tension, it shimmered like a mirage in the desert. She was confused by what Geno had just said, and it appeared that she wasn't alone. She could see it on her mother's and grandfather's faces, but it was particularly obvious on the man whose last name she shared.

For just a moment, a queer silence engulfed the room. The wind whispered through the open window above the sink, and outside, a tern squawked angrily at the new metallic bird perched on the roof. It was as quiet as Jackie had ever remembered it being. But when that brief moment of contemplation was over, the man holding the gun at the door who was using the fat guy as a shield completely lost his mind. His voice sliced through the silence, escalating quickly from loud murmur to irate screaming.

"What the hell did you just say? I was to be somebody's . . . surprise?"

A smile spread across Geno's lips, and somewhere in an imaginary universe, a bishop slid diagonally across a chess board, pinning Mason LaRue's king into a corner.

Mason stuttered, "You . . . you . . . you were using me? All that talk about being a philanthropist and keeping me around for the future. You were just conning me?"

Geno's eyes moved from Mason's face to Frankie's. He nodded towards the bandaged hand and said, "How bad is it?"

Frankie shrugged his shoulders, "Not good. Probably going to lose my—"

Mason suddenly swung his hand, cracking Frankie in the back of the head with the pistol, then pointed it at Geno and yelled, "Quit talking to him. That thumb isn't going to matter in a few minutes anyway." He punched the pistol into Frankie's back. "Ain't that right fatso. You and me—we've already had our come to Jesus meeting. Except Jesus had the good sense not to show." Mason's bloodshot and panicky eyes swept across the room. Pauley, Hoyt, Caroline, and then finally back to Geno. "You're dealing with me now. Not him." Those same bloodshot eyes looked at the table at the bottles and the filled glasses. "What the? You brought champagne?"

Geno ignored the tirade, and spoke calmly to Frankie. "You'll have to tell me when this is over how he managed to get the drop on you and Sal. Quite frankly, I'm a bit disappointed."

Mason's face erupted into a deep shade of red. His wild, unbelieving eyes bugged from their sockets. "Dammit, Geno, didn't you hear me?" He waved the big .45 in the air and said, "Tell string bean over there to drop his gun on the floor and kick it over to me, or else I'm going to shoot this fat bastard in the head."

Geno, still looking at Frankie, calmly said, "Think you can take care of this?"

The big man nodded.

Geno slowly raised his left hand over his shoulder. From his fist extended a short index finger. It was if he was saying to Pauley: *just one more minute.*

"Well then Mr. LaRue," Geno said almost too casually. "Congratulations are in order. I see you've finally figured it out." He reached for a champagne flute and took a long sip. "One must be ready for almost anything when it comes to the type of untidy business we conduct. You see, much like you suggested to me back at the motel, I didn't figure you to swing the deal immediately with just your purchased looks. What I really needed was for somebody just to plant the seed, whether they swung the deal or not. And how pleased I was when I learned that the new owners of the Frying Pan Shoals Light Station and you had a past. It was at that very moment I knew you and I were going to be partners again. And if that wasn't enough, what a brilliant stroke of luck it was that you and Caroline's marriage ended in a messy divorce. I must admit I was greatly impressed with how far you were able to coerce her in just one short meeting."

Caroline, who had been staring at Frankie, turned to Geno and huffed.

Mason began to speak, but Geno stopped him. "You've had your speech, now I'm going to finish mine." He sat the flute back on the table and smacked his lips. "You are indeed part of the bargain, Mister LaRue. You see, in order to gain favor with them," he hooked his thumb towards Hoyt and Caroline, "I had to make things interesting. I needed something that would, for a lack of a better term, serve as a gift. I had you in the loop from the beginning, and kept you there, but it wasn't for the same purpose you so eagerly assumed."

Mason stood there breathless. A string of spittle hung from his bottom lip.

Geno turned to Hoyt. "My apologies. I had planned to ease you into this, but it appears that all of our cards are now on the table."

He pointed at the closed briefcase by Pauley. "I've brought a sum of money with me that I'm prepared to offer—title, deed, and all considerations. I'm afraid it isn't going to cover your purchase price, but it should suffice to cover your time, materials, and travel you've put into fixing it up. You may not like the shortage, but I think you'll find that my complete offer is quite better than what I could have demanded." He laughed then said, "I seem to have acquired a rather interesting reputation over the years, but I'll argue that most of it is unwarranted. Why just look at the deal I'm offering you . . . money for expenses, along with an incentive that I'm quite certain at some point in the past, you'd happily paid a million dollars just for the pleasure to kill. Mister and Miss Bennett, I'm offering you the man you despise the most to do with what you please. Who else but yours truly would have had the forethought to bring this tantalizing morsel to the bargaining table?"

Hoyt reeled in his chair. "What would we do with *him*?"

"Use your imagination. After all, we are on a glorified oil rig, twenty miles offshore. No cameras, no witnesses, plenty of water and sharks, rope, boats, knives, and if you don't have any firearms, I'd probably lend you one or two of ours." He reached for the champagne flute and raised it towards them in a makeshift toast. "Despite my reputation, I'm really a nice guy. I try my best to offer fair compensation in return for what I want, all the while not hurting the people I'm dealing with. Just like I didn't want to hurt that little girl of yours. What's her name? Jackie?" Geno paused and took a heavy breath. "Ah yes, young Jackie. I nearly forgot about her. Where do you have her hidden, Mister Bennett? I'd like to meet her if you please, but before you summon her, I think we need to attend to a little unfinished business here."

Geno turned back to the two men. Mason's entire body trembled. He babbled something to himself, thumbing back the hammer on Sal's Springfield. The light station shifted with a wave, and the resulting metallic whine seemed to last forever. A short salvo of eerie pops and creaks followed. The timing couldn't have been more perfect. It was like the structure itself understood that a line in the sand had been drawn. Mason set his jaw, flexed his fingers around the Springfield's handle, and began raising the big pistol towards the fat man's head.

Geno said only two words, "Okay, Frankie."

Chapter 27

It was hard to tell exactly what happened next. Through the grate, Jackie saw a blur of movement and the man holding the gun went flying backwards into the hallway. The Springfield spit fire as he disappeared through the door. Not aimed, the bullet caromed harmlessly off the ceiling and broke through the upper pane of the window over the sink, whining into the endless sky. The explosion echoed within the confines of the room, then careened down the air duct, producing an ear-splitting pressure wave that Jackie absorbed.

For an instant, nothing else mattered except the pain. Fireworks went off inside her skull and she covered her ears, but quickly discovered they weren't the only thing that hurt. The ringing in her ears was soon accompanied by what felt like dull electric pulses spider-webbing across the top of her head. She ran her fingers through her hair, and the upper-side of the duct brushed against the back of her hand—then it made sense.

Way to go Jackie! Why don't you just knock yourself out?

The pain ran down her jaw bones and met underneath her chin, tying themselves together in a hopeless knot. When the stars faded and she looked back into the room, everyone at the table had fallen to a prostrate position on the floor—everyone except Geno Mancini. Geno still sat tall in his chair, gazing at the glass in his hand. In a graceful movement, he slowly raised the flute, swirling the contents in the light. After the short inspection, he drained the glass, smacked his lips, and ran a finger around the rim. He could have been a judge at the world's most civilized wine tasting contest, while just outside the door two men savagely fought for their lives.

Pauley swallowed hard and said, "Dontcha think he needs some help, Boss?"

"I don't believe so. In fact, if he wasn't injured, I'd say it take him twenty seconds or less. But he's lost some blood and in some pain— I don't think I'll gamble on time, but I do think he's still going to take him."

Watching Hoyt and Caroline pick themselves off the floor, Geno produced his wallet from an interior coat pocket, and pulled several green bills from it. "Does anyone care to make this little scuffle more interesting? I've got an even hundred that says Frank Russo is going to walk back through that door."

Caroline said, brushing the hair out of her eyes, "You're betting on this?"

Geno thumbed through the crisp bills, "Sometimes life is interesting on its own. And sometimes it needs a little help."

Outside in the hallway, two rampaging men were tearing each other apart. Grunts, thuds, falls, cursing, and the sounds of ripping fabric filled the room. And then a moment of silence fell, followed by a stifling laugh. Mason LaRue's throaty voice came through loud and clear. "I told you I was going to saw your head off with dental floss, but I've changed my mind. I'm going to blow it off, just like I did your thumb."

Pauley quickly reached for his wallet, but Geno waved his hand. "It's too late to bet now." Geno trained his eyes back at the doorway. "We are about to find out whether Frankie earns his pay this week or not."

An evil laugh came just before another ear-splitting gunshot erupted down the hallway. A moment passed, then three more shots exploded in rapid succession. Caroline covered her mouth with her hand, as a sickening cry of pain drifted into the galley. Heavy steps muffled the groans, going away from them, further down the hallway. There was a mighty heave, then a fading cry that ended in a distant splash.

Heavy footsteps sounded down the hallway again, and before Geno could put his wallet back into his coat pocket, Frankie stumbled through the door. Hoyt and Caroline gasped at the heavy man, heaving and wheezing and bleeding again from his injured hand. The towel had been ripped away, and the bloody stump was plainly visible against the lighter colored wall behind him—his thumb was completely gone. Red puddles began to form on the floor beside him.

Caroline jumped from the table. "You're losing blood! You need to sit down before you fall down."

Hoyt and Caroline helped Frankie to the chair and carefully began wrapping his hand again.

Geno looked amused. "Looks like we really are dealing with a lady and a gentleman here after all."

Hoyt cut his eyes to Geno. "For the record, I'm glad that miserable bastard is dead. But I don't think he was worth losing a thumb or possibly a man over."

Unattached and seemingly uncaring, Geno watched them work, while Frankie kept growing paler and paler. When the fat man's hand was wrapped, Caroline looked up and saw fresh blood running down the front of Frankie's shirt.

"Oh no," she cried, "You've been shot, too!"

Frankie gave Caroline a funny look. Caroline said it again, slower and louder this time, and the fat man nodded. His words slurred together into a barely audible string of syllables. "Nicked me with that first one before I could take the gun from him. But I made him pay for it."

Caroline pressed another towel against his shoulder, and said to herself more so to any one in particular, "This is more than a nick. We need to get the Coast Guard on the radio. He needs a doctor."

Geno grunted and walked over and handed Frankie the open bottle of champagne. Frankie tipped the bottle, and drank down several massive gulps.

"Easy. Don't finish it all at one time, you're going to ruin the aftertaste." Geno turned to Hoyt. "You don't happen to have any antibiotics or pain meds on this rig, do you?"

Hoyt rubbed his chin, and glanced at the air duct grate and smiled. He snapped his fingers and said, "As a matter of fact, I do."

Jackie saw the smile, but didn't know what he meant. Hoyt walked to the cupboard, sifted through a few things and picked up a small brown prescription bottle. It looked strangely familiar, and Jackie finally realized it was the same bottle that held the sleeping pills. Hoyt walked back to Frankie, opened the bottle, and picked out the other half of the one he cut for Jackie and popped it in his mouth. He swallowed it dry and shot a glance back towards the grate. "Needed one myself. My head is still ringing from those damn shots."

Hoyt shook the remainder out in the big man's uninjured hand and casually sat back down.

Frankie said, "What are these? All five of them?"

The old man shrugged his shoulders, "I usually take one for my back when I've been at it for a while out here. Sometimes two. You've got me by probably two hundred pounds. I didn't do the math, but I'm certain that five of them aren't too much. For a torn off thumb, and a gunshot wound, ten might not be too many."

Frankie stared at the pills in his hand, like they were going to magically tell him they were all right to take.

Hoyt said, "You need some relief, don't you? Well, it ain't poison. You saw me take one."

Frankie looked at Geno. Geno shrugged his shoulders. Frankie looked at them again, popped all five in his mouth, and washed it down with another swallow of champagne.

* * *

That spooky fading cry of pain and desperation just before Mason hit the water would haunt Jackie for a long time, but Frank Russo's bloody hand was absolutely terrifying. Blood had never bothered her that way before, but she'd never seen so much at one time. When he came back through the door, his blood-soaked shirt and pants looked like they'd been dipped in red paint, and the spurts pumping from the stump splattering on the floor was enough to make her sick. She didn't want to look, but at the same time, couldn't make herself look away. A wave of nausea enveloped her, but somehow, she'd managed to hold everything down until Caroline and Hoyt had gotten it wrapped again. Safely out of sight Jackie could feel herself returning to normal, and then Geno cleared his throat and asked Hoyt again where she was hidden. Suddenly, that cramping, miserable feeling deep in her gut was back.

Hoyt ignored the question while he and Caroline did their best to comfort Frankie. Geno inspected the makeshift bandage, and peeked under the towel Caroline was holding tight to Frankie's shoulder. He huffed disgustedly at the big man, and took the bottle of champagne away from him.

"Don't want to give away all your secrets Mister Bennett? Can't blame you there." He sighed and seemed to relax. "I never dreamed it would have been this difficult. The trouble getting Miss Bennett here, Mister LaRue not knowing when to give up," Geno poured the last of the bottle into his flute, and stared at his pale body guard, "And Frankie here, sticking out like a sore thumb. I just can't believe it took all this to convince a few folks to sell me something." Geno sipped from the flute. "And what's really a shame is that we didn't get to see the moment of truth. I was so looking forward to the look on his face."

"Look on whose face?" Hoyt said, making final adjustments to the bandage covering the mangled stump where Frankie's thumb used to be.

Geno looked annoyed. "I had him believing that we were in it together. I had him right where I wanted him, but never got to see it happen."

Hoyt said, "What happen?"

Geno huffed again, and a color rose in his cheeks. "The moment of truth, of course. That glorious moment when Mister LaRue realized that no matter how good he thought he was, he'd been bested." Geno chinned towards the window. "Sadly, most of that moment happened somewhere between here and Wilmington, and it cost Sal his life. But the entire revelation should have happened right here."

Caroline said, "I think you still got him. He looked pretty shook up when he realized he was part of the deal."

Geno stared at the empty bottle in his hand. "Perhaps, but if you thought that was impressive, seeing him fall like a wall full of precariously laid bricks all at once would have been simply magnificent. Standing here face to face with his ultimate destiny—a pawn being commanded into position of sacrifice by the king for the betterment of the kingdom." Geno sat the empty bottle on the table and fished around in his coat pocket, producing a cigar. "Shitty life these pawns lead. Don't you agree, Mister Bennett?"

Hoyt said nothing, as Geno struck a match and waved it under the end of the cigar, then snapped his fingers at Pauley. Immediately, crazy eyes lifted the pistol, pointing it at Hoyt and Caroline.

"Speaking of pawns," Geno said, slowly exhaling a mouthful of blue smoke, "I believe it's still my move. If you would, please call for your granddaughter. Pauley and I don't want to miss the opportunity to meet the ill-advised spawn of the LaRues."

Hoyt gritted his teeth, and unconsciously cut an eye towards the air duct grate. Geno saw it, and leaned, following Hoyt's line of sight. Jackie felt her heart tighten in her chest.

"Is our dear girl eavesdropping from the ventilation system?" Geno motioned to Pauley and quickly he covered the distance, pried back the grate, and grabbed a handful of strawberry blonde hair.

Chapter 28

Jackie resisted, spreading her shoulders and thighs outward against the duct walls, but the man with crazy eyes easily pulled her through the opening. It was nothing short of mayhem in the room now. Hoyt and Caroline were screaming at Pauley and Geno. Geno was yelling orders to Pauley. Jackie was screaming and kicking, trying to break free. It may have been simple luck, but at some point, she managed to land a solid kick square into Pauley's groin. The skinny Italian's crazy eyes momentarily straightened, and cursing with what little breath remained in his lungs, he savagely shook Jackie by the shoulders. It only lasted a second before his grip slipped, and with her arms freed for a moment, she raked her fingernails across the right side of his face. Pauley squealed as blood seeped into the red streaks. Jackie wiggled completely free and tried to run, but somehow the Italian managed to grab a fistful of hair. He snatched hard, bringing her to her tiptoes, then off the ground. He held her up, face to face, and Jackie almost gagged as blood slowly oozed into his crossed eyes.

"You little bitch," he groaned, and reached back across his chest, poised to deliver a hard backhand when something flew through the window. Whatever it was landed on the floor and exploded with a blinding flash of light. Almost immediately, the room was completely engulfed with a thick white smoke. Everyone was coughing, choking, reeling, when the SEALs stormed into the room. Pauley dropped Jackie and retreated back towards Geno, but was tackled before he could get there. Jackie rubbed her eyes, and through the smoke could see several black wetsuits swarming on the three men. Instantly, they were face down on the floor, hands cuffed behind their backs.

Jackie felt herself being lifted from the floor into somebody's arms, and quickly they were all whisked from the room and up the stairs onto the roof where the air was clean. Down on the water, a small inflatable boat holding several men buzzed towards them from the surfaced submarine. Even at a distance through watering eyes, Jackie easily recognized Captain McClendon's hat. Special Agents Cooper and Grier were standing beside him.

Caroline coughed and wheezed, pointing out at the water. "Am I seeing what I think I'm seeing?"

* * *

Jackie had her arms around Caroline's waist when the three men appeared on the staircase. McClendon walked straight towards Jackie, while Cooper and Grier, all business, quickly made their way to Geno.

The captain tipped his hat. The shiny insignia on his uniform shirt glistened in the sunlight like a disco ball. "Good to see you again, Miss LaRue." His warm, familiar voice made Jackie smile.

Hoyt looked confused. "See you *again?*"

Before he could say anything else, the captain turned to them and said, "I see that everyone came through this relatively uninjured. We are sorry that our abrupt entry has caused you a little respiratory distress, but decades of testing and practical application tell us it's the best way to make sudden entries. Don't worry, the effects of the smoke are only temporary."

Hoyt coughed loudly, still clearing his lungs. "What took you so long? Y'all need a written invitation? And what do you mean, good to see you *again?*"

Caroline took a ragged breath and said, "You knew about this?

"Yeah, it's a long story. I'll tell you about it later."

Caroline's stare intensified. Her voice was demanding. "How about right now?"

168

"In a minute, Caroline," Hoyt said pumping his open palm downward a few times. He looked at Jackie, and then back to the captain. "How about telling me how you two know each other first."

McClendon looked apologetic. "Miss LaRue visited with us this afternoon for a bit. One of our guys saw her in the water, bleeding. He thought there had been an accident. He escorted her back to the sub to have our doctor look her over." McClendon cleared his voice, changing the subject. "Now, storming the light station . . . I know we were supposed to get in there before anything happened, but we weren't expecting the boat and the other two men." He chinned towards Cooper and Grier. "We all agreed to wait to see who the other party was. We wanted to make sure it wasn't one of the bigger fish. I hope you can appreciate the predicament we were in."

Hoyt's look was anything but satisfied. He tried to smile and with a forced calm said, "What kind of accident did you have, beach girl?"

Jackie glanced at the fading red line on her hand, but when she looked up, Hoyt impatiently growled back at McClendon, "And you just let them shoot up the place while your guys waited outside?" He pointed at Frankie, white as a ghost and nearly unconscious. "That could have been one of us."

The captain removed his hat and ran his fingers through his hair, "We had eyes in the room, and rifles ready. We were trying to determine who the guy was. If we needed to protect him, or consider him a threat. The delay was a risk we had to take. They started fighting and shooting before our guys had clearance to do anything. It caught us off guard."

Hoyt flashed concerned eyes back at Jackie. "You gonna tell me what kind of accident you had or not?"

Jackie almost laughed at her Granddad. "It wasn't an accident. I'll tell you about it later."

Hoyt muttered, "Yeah, well, you need to quit being such a smarty-pants." He looked at the captain again. "Well, McClendon, however it went down, it's over now. But I want you to tell those two suit-wearing monkeys the next time they make a deal with someone, they should allow the good guys more courtesy. That little stunt wasn't in the bargain."

The captain nodded and said, "Who was that guy anyway? Two of our guys saw him fall. Looked to have a few terminal gunshots to the chest. He wasn't any of you, and since they had more pressing business up here, they just let him go. We're trying to find the body now."

Jackie blurted out, "It was crazy that he and I had the same last name, huh?"

Hoyt and Caroline looked at each other, then back to Jackie. Caroline nodded blankly at Jackie. "Guess it was just a coincidence."

Jackie saw the same look on her mother's face that she saw on her grandfather's when he lied to her about how bad the burn was. And somewhere down inside, she had a good idea of exactly who this mystery man was.

From behind them, a ragged laugh echoed across the platform. Geno peeked around one of the SEALs and said, "You mean she didn't know? She didn't recognize her own—"

McClendon hollered, "Shut him up!" and one of the SEALs slammed a fist into Geno's belly.

Jackie felt a pang again in her guts. Geno didn't finish the sentence, but that queer feeling intensified. She knew what he was about to say. Masking her emotions, she hugged her mother a little tighter and said in a low voice, "He was just one of the bad guys, huh?"

She felt the hug return to her, and looked up at her mom's battered face.

"Yes, sweetie. Just one of the bad guys." Caroline took a breath, then slowly exhaled it. "Wait here with your grandfather, there's something I need to do."

Caroline pulled away from Jackie and walked with purpose towards the group of SEALs. "Wait, wait. Before you take them away, I'd like to say something to him."

Jackie and Hoyt watched in amazement as Caroline walked straight to Geno—a man who'd broken hundreds of fingers, arms, and legs, ordered hits and personally executed untold numbers of men. All of that didn't matter, as she coiled her right arm, and buried her fist squarely into his mouth. Geno's head seemed to corkscrew before he went down to his knees. Caroline winced and shook her hand, but wasn't finished. While he was down she said, "And I recently learned this one from my daughter." She shuffled her feet and landed a swift kick squarely into his groin. The entire SEAL team said, '*ohh*' in unison.

Caroline said, "That's what you get for treating us like dirt, scum bag. Do us all a favor and rot in hell."

Hoyt bumped Jackie with his elbow and whispered, "Would you look at that!" He whistled through his teeth "How do you like your mama now, beach girl?"

Jackie beamed. Her mom was something else, all right. But the smile wasn't just for her. The loud-mouth mobster tried to get to his knees, but gave up. She giggled to herself. It was ironic that he'd referenced the game of chess while she was still in the air duct. The mighty Geno Mancini looked like a king that had been check-mated.

Chapter 29

Jackie and Caroline stood at the rail letting the warm breeze tease and tangle their hair. Down below, what was left of the flash bomb escaped from the open windows, but neither mother nor daughter saw the white wisps. They were too busy looking out at the water at something that Lieutenant Commander Thompson longed to see some thirty-five years ago. Just three hundred yards away was the submarine that the cavalry had arrived in. It wasn't as big as Jackie first thought seeing it under water, but it definitely wasn't small either. The fishing boats moored below rocked and swayed in the swells, but the sub was rock-solid in the water. Neither Jackie nor Caroline spoke for a long time, while the mop-up operation continued around them. The small inflatable boat that had shuffled men to and from the sub sped across the sea and disappeared under the light station. A few moments later, it appeared again, this time carrying Geno, his two goons, and three SEALs.

Caroline rubbed Jackie's back as only a mother could. "I still don't believe it. It could have been something from a James Bond movie." She gazed at the submarine again. "I don't like it when your grandfather keeps secrets from me. When this is over, we're all going to have a little chat."

Jackie looked at the scar on her hand. She didn't want to keep secrets either, but there were still too many ears listening for that kind of talk. And after how quickly all of it had happened, she wasn't really sure that she remembered everything well enough to make sense of it. It had been a big day—the biggest day in her life. Yet, amid all the uncertainty, there were two things that she was absolutely sure of: the hideous burn had completely healed, not leaving so much as a blemish on her skin, and the self-inflicted cut on her hand was gone now—only the thin line of a scar remained. Jackie rubbed a finger across the back of her hand. Even the scar seemed to be fading. Whatever Lieutenant Brooks wrote about in his diary was still out there, and still working its magic.

Out on the water, the small boat pulled alongside the sub. Two sailors held the boat steady, while four more heaved an unconscious Frankie Russo into the sub. Two more sailors accompanied Geno and Pauley across the deck, but before disappearing into the hatch, Geno stopped and took one last look around. Jackie thought about what McClendon said during her impromptu visit earlier. Geno was no dummy—he knew that this was the last time he was going to see the light of day for a while.

"Don't worry mom," Jackie heard herself say. "It's over now, and maybe we can get back to something closer to normal around here." Jackie surprised herself with the cool, even response.

Caroline smiled and squeezed her daughter. "You're sounding more grown up every day. When did you get so smart?"

Jackie shrugged her shoulders. "Hanging out with granddad helps."

Caroline laughed and kissed the top of Jackie's head. "You look okay, but how do you feel? It broke my heart when that guy jerked you around. And you're going to have to tell me how you managed to get that good kick in."

"I got lucky with the kick, I guess. And my head is okay. It didn't hurt too bad," Jackie paused, thinking, "but I didn't want him to know that. That's why I screamed like I did."

The look on Caroline's face was a combination of surprise and admiration. "You were sandbagging?"

Jackie shrugged her shoulders.

"You really are becoming a heckuva young woman, aren't you? I doubt I would've had the coolness in the moment to do that."

The small boat disengaged from the sub and headed back towards the tower. The only ones left to ferry back now were the good guys, then all of it would be over.

A voice came from behind them. "Miss Bennett, Miss LaRue."

They turned and Ethan Wade was standing there. The afternoon sun shined off his sandy-blonde hair, the wetsuit was a second skin. Every muscle seemed to ripple as he shifted his glance back and forth between them. Ice blue eyes captured Jackie's for a moment of sheer pleasure, and immediately she felt the power leave her legs.

"Remember me?" he said with that same baritone voice.

Jackie regained control, but her body tingled as she lightly swallowed and managed a nod.

"I heard about what you did just before we stormed the room. That took courage, and well I just had to tell you that the whole team admires you." He looked at Caroline, a smile broke across his full lips. "And ma'am, that punch. That punch just blew us all away. We train for situations like these all the time. Hand to hand combat is no big deal to us. In fact, most of the time when things get boring, we start looking for things to fight about. Civilians usually go out of their way to avoid fights. But we occasionally hear stories about people like you—people who aren't scared to fight back. I'm not sure all of them are true. Stories are just that . . . stories. And God knows the SEALs have their fair share of liars, but what you just did was worth its weight in gold. You're going to be a legend when word gets out."

Jackie blushed. Just the sound of his voice made her heart do funny things.

"It was a real pleasure meeting both of you. Especially you, Miss LaRue." His blue eyes captured Jackie's again, and immediately she was paralyzed. She somehow managed a shy smile.

Caroline said, "Thank you, Mister Wade. I'm not sure how well we did at fighting back, but we greatly appreciate you and your team for helping us."

"Our pleasure, ma'am."

Jackie's eyes were a sponge, soaking up every square inch of him. She'd never felt such an array of feelings before, but one desire was stronger than the rest of all of them put together. She desperately wanted to kiss him. She tried to move forward, but her feet were concrete. She screamed inside her head, begging them to move, but nothing happened. This young man was about to walk out of her life forever, and she couldn't do anything but make a goofy smile. Before she could convince her body to move, somebody called from the catwalk.

"I've got to go," Ethan Wade said. "Please take care of yourselves, but maybe I should save that for whoever comes up against you next." He flashed a handsome smile, then snapped to attention, offering a genuine salute. "Consider this from our entire team, ladies."

When the propriety was over, he relaxed and shook Caroline's hand. Jackie knew that she was next.

I can't . . . or can I?

The answer came quickly from somewhere deep in her own mind.

Nope, never in a million years.

And just as Ethan Wade's hand met hers, a hot rush of blood ran up her arm, and something inside her head popped. In one shining moment of victory, Jackie finally moved. She aimed for the center of his cheek, but he moved slightly, not realizing the intent, and her lips ever so gently brushed his, before settling on the dimple near his mouth. For that one instant, Jackie's world spun out of control. Seconds, minutes, hours could have passed and she was content right there feeling the distinct electric pulse of love for the first time. The young SEAL began to pull away, and Jackie's heart began to beat again.

That easy smile came to his lips as he rubbed the wet spot on his cheek where eager fourteen-year-old lips had just been. "I believe you are going to have your hands full with this one, Miss Bennett. She's going to be a heartbreaker." He gave Jackie one last smile and said, "Talk your mom into letting you come to Pensacola on spring break in a year or two. Look me up, and we'll go for another swim."

Another command volleyed from behind him, and he turned and jogged back across the platform and disappeared down the stairway. The wetsuit hid nothing, and they both admired the view until he was out of sight. Jackie could still taste him on her lips, and a fresh dose of teenage hormones coursed throughout her body. Her first kiss was an older man—a Navy SEAL—that was six feet of rippling honed muscle.

Caroline brought her out of the trance. "Just what are *you* thinking about, young lady?"

Jackie blushed again, and they both laughed, as Hoyt and Captain McClendon appeared on the staircase. Caroline leaned and whispered. "Remind me you tell you sometime about the benefits of being a damsel in distress. You'll learn there are some guys you'd like to be rescued by, over and over and over again. I think Ethan Wade fits nicely into that category."

Chapter 30

They all made small talk for a few minutes, and another SEAL
appeared at the staircase and told them that agents Cooper and
Grier wanted to see them. The air in the hallway was still pungent.
Their eyes and sinuses watered, but it was getting better with each
passing minute. When they walked into the galley, the two agents
were sitting at the table, a single and rather large SEAL stood near
them. Both men were writing in notebooks, and as the group
approached the table, they looked up in unison.

Grier said, "I'm terribly sorry again for how this went down."
Calculating eyes went to McClendon then back to Hoyt. "I think the
captain has explained why we waited like we did. We regret any
discomfort that small delay may have caused you."

Hoyt shrugged. "The big guy and that Mister LaRue fellow
seemed to get the worst of it. What's done is done. We're well on
the way to forgetting about this whole ugly business."

Grier cleared his throat and said, "The US Government
appreciates your willingness to assist with this operation. You very
well may have just saved countless American lives."

Hoyt smiled a fake smile and said, "No trouble."

Both agents looked pleased and returned to their notebooks—
their pens seemed to be synchronized as they jotted down several
more notes before they stood, and both stuck the pens inside the
jacket pockets. It looked rehearsed.

Agent Cooper said, "We have all we need here. Captain, since
you've done such a good job of handling this, we'll leave the final
instructions and good-byes to you. We'll be waiting in the boat."

McClendon nodded, and both agents shook Hoyt's, Caroline's,
and Jackie's hands on the way out of the room. The SEAL who had

moved step for step with Cooper and Grier looked at the captain. McClendon nodded and chinned towards the door, and he quickly caught up with and continued following the agents. Their footsteps made it all the way down the hall before McClendon finally spoke. "I understand that some champagne was brought to this little party." He walked to the table that still held forgotten glasses Geno had filled earlier and the unopened bottle. "If I had the time, I'd sit down and finish off this one with you." He picked up the bottle and looked at the label. "It's still cold."

Hoyt said matter-of-factly, "I think I'd rather just have a beer."

Everyone's eyes seemed to gravitate to Geno's second briefcase. McClendon retrieved it from the counter and sat it on the table in front of them. He ran his finger down the gold embroidered letters 'GBM', then across the four little brass combination wheels partly exposed near the clasps. Jackie looked the expensive case over again, then noticed a small hole in its side. It was about the diameter of a pencil, and a thin ribbon of white vapor rose from it. She was surprised that she hadn't noticed it sooner.

McClendon saw her staring at it. "We didn't have the combination for this one, and Geno wasn't being too accommodating during our initial questioning here. But he didn't figure on us having this little doohickey." A thin black coil of tubing appeared from his uniform pocket and McClendon unrolled it to its full length. He pressed a button on what looked like a small black box attached to one end, and a small light came on at the other. It looked like a long, flexible black straw.

"Have you ever seen a bore scope? They're fairly common in gunsmith shops, and our snipers use them to keep an eye on barrel wear on their long-range rifles. Luckily, we had a sniper trained SEAL on board last year who left us one of these. They are handy for trouble-shooting various things on subs. Pipes, conduits, valves, nooks and crannies—there's nothing on those blasted boats that are easy to get to, and you never know when you might need to scope out a tight area. And in this case," McClendon laughed a little, "it also helps with checking the contents of unopened briefcases."

He began feeding the lighted end into the small hole in its side, and Hoyt asked, "Why didn't you just bust the locks with a screwdriver or something?"

McClendon looked at the small LED screen that was built in the small box—the display end of the tube. "The company that makes these cases cater to the more, oh how do I put this, risqué business operators. Our research told us that there are some models of this case that have anti-theft devices built into them. In some cases, there are small amounts of explosives linked to the locking system. Bust open the lock, and boom! It's usually not enough to kill, but you might easily lose a finger or two if it's triggered. We weren't sure of the model, but we decided to play it safe and use the bore scope. A small hole is all we needed, as long as we stayed away from the locking clasp."

While Jackie and Caroline peered at the miniature screen at champagne labels, McClendon said, "This case turned out not to be one of those models, and it looks like you have two more bottles for later tonight—that is, if you can pry this thing open. Regrettably, the drill that was brought over with this scope has already been returned. A well-placed hole through the locks would probably do the trick. I assume you have a drill or a hacksaw or something that can do the job without busting the bottles?"

Hoyt said, "I've got some tools that'll do the job. I hate that Geno wasn't a Pabst man, but hey, I guess everyone can't be as refined as me."

"Very good," McClendon said trying not to laugh. "Our two agents have advised me that whatever they couldn't use of Geno's as evidence was considered dead weight. And according to maritime law, as I understand it, if someone abandons something at sea, it becomes the property of whoever finds it. Kind of like shipwrecked treasure. This is your light station, so we just figured that you two would claim it and put it to good use."

Caroline said cheerfully, "Don't worry, it'll be put to good use."

Outside, on top of the platform, the helicopter engines began to whine. All four of them turned their heads towards the window.

Hoyt said, "What are y'all going to do with the whirly-bird?"

"That's a very good question. Even though it fits in the same category as the briefcases, unfortunately we cannot let you have it. Cooper and Grier say it's linked to a subsidiary company that's operated by some of those medium-sized fish we're after up in Jersey. This kind of thing could blow our cover if it shows up somewhere it isn't supposed to, so we are going to cover up this fun little outing. We have a few SEALs on board that can fly those things, and one of them is going to fly it back to Wilmington, literally under the radar, so our friends at the FAA can't track us." McClendon closed his eyes and rubbed his temple with two fingers. "And this is the part of my speech that gets very serious and very important, so listen carefully. We'll need your full cooperation with this, or we'll likely lose whatever head start we have. All of Geno's dealings in North Carolina were on orders from Jersey, so we have to assume that they know he came out here to see you. And if they know that, they are probably not going to like him forgetting to check in with them later this evening. So, a mile or so offshore, we are going to ditch the bird in the drink. The beaches and the fishing piers will be covered with vacationers, so it's going to be nice and public. Just an everyday, run-of-the-mill helicopter crash."

Jackie and Caroline shared concerned looks.

"Now don't you worry about our pilot. He's going to bail out well before the crash, so it'll just be a high-dive act for him. Believe it or not, our guys jump out of planes and helicopters all the time. They train for stuff you couldn't begin to think of. And don't forget, he swims like a fish, and we'll be there with the sub to pick him up, the same way we picked up Miss LaRue earlier today.

"The Coast Guard base in Wilmington will be called to help look for the wreckage, but they'll make sure it's tomorrow before it's found. They'll spend the required time looking for bodies that aren't there, but the moment that time is up, it will be assumed that sharks have had a free meal, and with no remains, they'll just be considered lost at sea. The news will be all over it, the helicopter will be identified a day or so later, and if they don't know about it from their own people, word will quickly make it back to Jersey that Geno and a couple of his guys made the ultimate sacrifice. Jersey will have to scramble, lining up replacements to work the coastal region down here. That should take a little wind out of their sails, and get them thinking about other stuff, rather than continuing to harass you. Hopefully by then, if we do our jobs efficiently, Geno will have implemented the bigger players, giving Cooper's and Grier's outfits a chance to nab the lot of them.

"Now, if we are wrong and Geno was doing all of this on his own, Jersey will still hear about the crash, but won't know what they were up to. Either way, they'll have to start the process of shifting power to somebody new. Everything else will play out identically, and when Geno sings, it will effectively take you off the hot-seat."

Hoyt said, "Geno sings? How sure are you about that?"

The Captain winked at Jackie. "Why don't you tell your granddad what happens in rat nests when the door is kicked open and people with badges and guns start shining flashlights."

Hoyt and Caroline both looked at Jackie. She shrugged her shoulders and said, "They try to save their own bacon."

Captain McClendon smiled approvingly. "Don't worry, Mister Bennett. Geno will sing, probably louder than anyone has ever sang before. Never known one not to. But for all of this to work, we need absolute silence on your end. And before you say no sweat, believe me, the temptation will be monumental. You can't tell a soul about what happened out here this evening. Fishing buddies, pals at the bars," he looked at Jackie, "friends at school. Ears are in every bush and behind every lamppost. If the right people hear it, or if the news somehow gets their hands on this, our chance with the bigger fish in Jersey and beyond will go away, likely forever. Then we will be back to square one, and New Jersey will still have all of you in their sights. In short, you must never speak of this to anyone. Geno, his men, nor the helicopter were ever here, and neither was the US Navy. Understand?"

They all nodded, but Hoyt quickly spoke up. "But what about radar? Doesn't the FAA know the helicopter came out here?"

"Did you see it approach?"

"Sure. I was on the roof when it was probably a quarter of a mile from us."

"When you first saw it, was it high up, or was it down *low* . . . like under one hundred feet *low*?"

By the way the Captain stressed the words low, even Jackie knew what the answer was. She looked at her grandfather and his face changed. The lightbulb seemed to come on.

"I'll be damned." Hoyt said, as if he'd just solved an unsolvable puzzle. "They were under the radar the whole time? The air traffic guys have no clue that Geno ever came out here?"

"Doubtful. I'd bet my pension that nobody, short of a few rats in Jersey, knows anything about their little trip. And when the FAA learns of the crash, they'll scratch their heads and curse under their breaths, but most likely they'll chalk it up to a stupid individual in a privately-owned helicopter playing around off the beach, not following protocol. The penalty for such things is heavy fines and revoked pilot's licenses, but you can't punish a dead man."

Caroline said, "So just like that, you get Geno, the bosses up in Jersey think their guys crashed the helicopter, no one is recovered, alive or dead, and we are off the hook?"

McClendon smiled, "That's how Cooper and Grier drew it up, and other than that second boat showing up, it was all working beautifully. But even that loose end has been tied up, thanks to Frank Russo, so technically, we should still be in the clear."

Jackie shook her head and said, "What about the other boat? Are you going to take that too?"

"I'm glad you brought that up. That was the only thing that our two masterminds couldn't agree on. We ran the numbers, and it came back registered to some bogus real estate company that's based in Virginia Beach. Other than phony licenses, would you believe that the owners of that company have no record anywhere within the US? Zero history or records for any school anywhere, no driver's licenses, no visits to the dentist, no vaccinations, they don't own homes, or have credit cards, or have even so much as a simple traffic citation. In other words, the folks that own that boat are as fictional as good food on submarines." The captain shook his head, "I guess that as long as the State of Virginia kept getting cash through the mail in envelopes that I'd also bet held no return address, they didn't mind keeping a fairly expensive registration current on a very nice fishing boat.

"We thought about ditching it in out in deeper water, but Miss LaRue's SEAL friend had a very good idea. In fact, it was such a good idea, we all agreed on it immediately. So, I'm going to make a deal with you." McClendon reached for the unopened bottle of champagne on the table. He ran his fingers over the foil around the bottle's neck and examined the label. "Speaking on behalf of the non-existent real estate company owners, I would like to propose a trade. You see, I've got a crew member down there on that submersible cigar that's a very special person. She and I get along just fabulously, but she's scheduled to transfer off the boat in a few months. I would like it very much to share a bottle of fine champagne with her before that happens. And coincidentally, you've got this bottle just lying around, and two extras in a briefcase that Hoyt here just told me he'd have no problem freeing. Now, I just happen to have a very nice fishing vessel moored below that I really don't have a use for. So how about I trade you that nice fishing boat for one of these bottles?"

All three of them stood there staring blankly at McClendon.

"Say something before I have to scuttle a very nice boat out in the Gulf Stream somewhere. All you have to do is nod your head, and it's yours.

Caroline said, "How would it transfer? Legally, I mean?"

"We're in the process of producing transfer of property documentation clearly identifying you as the recent purchaser. It's a shame that the real estate company and its two apparitional owners have fallen on hard times. It seems they've recently resorted to liquidating their assets to pay off years of back taxes that the IRS is, at this very moment, developing and backdating inquiries about. And what a nice gesture it was for the owners to deliver the boat to you out here today. Long story short, you now have a second vessel in your sport fishing fleet, Mister Bennett. You have been promoted from captain to commodore. I'll assume you'll choose this beauty over the Grady White as your flagship?"

There was a moment of silence, then Caroline and Jackie both began to cheer. Hoyt finally managed to speak, but all he could get out were a series of choppy wheezes that sounded like a stuttering toddler saying "but . . . but . . . but . . . but" over and over again.

"I assure you, commodore, the correct paperwork will be in place by tomorrow morning. There will be no disputes from anyone on this—and how could there be? The man who 'shadow' owned the boat for all intents and purposes doesn't exist."

Hoyt still blubbered.

"Remember the lag time before the SEALs stormed the room that you were so upset about. Well, let's just say that the FBI and CIA both extend their deepest sympathies for the mental anguish you and your family suffered during those few minutes. Hopefully this gift will help overcome any hard feelings."

Hoyt finally said, "I can't . . . believe it!"

McClendon shook each of their hands and cradling the bottle like a newborn baby, he made his way to the galley door. "Thanks for your help with all this. I really enjoyed meeting all of you, but I'm afraid I have to go now. I believe we will soon be needed at the scene of a small helicopter crash near the coast, then I suspect we'll be off to the Mediterranean. If things go as planned, we'll drop Geno off somewhere over there for an extended vacation. I understand he has some ex-business contacts in that region that would love to discuss some prior dealings they had together after we're done with him." He smiled one last time, "Now if you will excuse me, I've got a boat to catch."

The helicopter's engines sounded like they were at full power, and he'd only made it a couple of steps down the hallway when the captain quickly turned back to them. He pulled a plastic baggie from his pants pocket and held it out in plain view. Jackie's heart nearly stopped. She recognized it immediately . . . the one from her backpack. The two crudely rolled marijuana cigarettes were still in it.

McClendon yelled over the engines, "One of our guys found this hung in the support structure down near the water." Quickly and without Hoyt or Caroline noticing, McClendon cut scolding eyes at Jackie. "We've been so busy with apprehending people, drilling holes in briefcases, searching helicopters, and brokering boat sales, we haven't tracked down the owner, but we feel fairly certain that it belonged to one of Geno's men. Or maybe it came off the guy who was shot?"

Caroline squinted at the baggie, "Are those joints?"

"You have good eyes, Miss Bennett. I just wanted to tell you in case more of it turns up. I know this place is outside of regular police jurisdiction, but it never hurts to be reminded about how quickly lives can be ruined by drugs."

Jackie could feel the captain's eyes pressing down on her. Somehow McClendon knew it was hers, but he was letting her off the hook. She had to concentrate just to breathe, and to her left and right, Hoyt and Caroline both nodded and reassured the captain that if any more was found they'd pitch it off the platform and let the fish get high.

* * *

They stood against the rail and watched the submarine slowly back away from the tower. In the deeper water off the shoals, it turned and headed south, then quickly turned east, paralleling the southern edge of the shoals on its way to Wilmington. The boat picked up speed, and the conning tower slowly sank in the water until there was nothing left but a white foamy swirl.

Hoyt took a deep breath and said, "I wonder what they're going to do to Geno to make him talk?"

Neither Jackie nor Caroline answered. Both still gazed blankly at the foam where they'd last seen the sub.

"I can't imagine it being too pleasant," he said shaking his head. "I sure would hate to be in his shoes whenever the shit hits the fan down there."

Hoyt and Caroline turned towards the walkway that lead to the catwalk, but Jackie didn't follow. She leaned against the chain rail, watching the waves roll by and enjoying the warm summer breeze kissing her cheeks. The darkening eastern sky was ushering in the night, and still bathed in the sunlight thousands of feet above, the fair-weather cirrus clouds strangely glowed, making grotesque figures that all seemed to point menacingly at the light station. Jackie shivered. It was a sky that could have been in any horror move, and she wished it was the last thing Geno had seen before disappearing into the submarine.

Chapter 31

In the quiet they made their supper on peanut butter and jelly sandwiches, Vienna sausages, and dried fruit. While they ate, each relived what happened many times over, eagerly telling the stories from their own perspectives. But once the food began to settle in their stomachs, the conversation waned as the enormity of it all hit home. Digesting the meager meal proved to be much easier than trying digest the terrifying drama they'd just lived through, and before they'd finished, none of them were talking at all. Jackie rolled a Vienna around on her plate, and stole a glance at her mother and grandfather. Both were simply staring into their paper plates, chewing and swallowing, chewing and swallowing. Eye contact with anyone would have been a sin worse than murder. It was strange and abrupt change of mood, but somehow, she understood. They were all simply coping.

Caroline finished off her less-than-delicatessen sandwich and picked up the empty bottle. A delicate finger ran across the label's intricate embossing. "There's no telling how much these cost. It's all French. I can't read a single word of it." She took another sip from her glass. "It's almost shameful, wasting such a fine spirit on a supper like this. I bet somewhere fine French grapes are turning over in their graves."

All three of them laughed, then Hoyt popped a Vienna in his mouth, stood, and walked out of the galley down the hallway. There were rummaging noises, and then he reappeared, holding a cordless drill, a ball-peen hammer, and a chisel. "These glasses still have a hint of gas in them. Let's see what the real thing tastes like. Keep your fingers crossed, maybe I can get this case open without busting one or both."

He sat the case on the floor, and slowly drilled a small hole through the brass locking mechanism. He backed the bit out and sank three more holes through the lock, but the case still wouldn't budge. Not to be outdone by something as simple as a locked briefcase, the chisel's point found the crack near the handle, and gingerly, so not to damage the bottles, he tapped on it with the hammer.

Tink, Tink, Tink, Tink, *Pop!*

A large crack opened along the edge, emitting a small cloud of dry ice vapor. A couple of additional taps with the hammer and chisel opened the case completely.

* * *

It had been dark for nearly an hour. The clouds overhead were sparse and the climbing moon shone around and through them, sending winks of silver down on the water. The light was almost supernaturally amplified across the calm ocean, but underneath the structure, the shadows were deep and dark—a small pool of evil hidden from the universe. Hardly visible, small bubbles popped at the surface, originating from the cracks Jackie found the day before where the steel pilings had been driven into the shoals. If Jackie had been down there now, she could have easily seen a faint, but steady greenish glow escaping upward through the sea floor into the dark water.

The small bubbles continued to dance near the piling, but near the boat, a large bubble surfaced and popped. A moment later another, then another. Between the gentle waves, a white, wrinkled, clammy hand materialized from the blackness. Rivulets of seawater ran down the grotesque appendage as it groped at the air. It finally gripped the chrome ladder frame attached to the transom, then a second hand emerged, followed by Mason LaRue's head, free from what was once its watery grave.

The man was a portrait of death. His once full, dark hair now resembled a bowl of cotton. His tanned skin was white-washed a creamy pale, his tattered clothes seemed to be moth-eaten almost completely through in places. And his eyes that had once been a hard hazel, now shone powdery-blue against scleras that were no longer white, but a sickening yellow. Even though his vision was as clear as he ever remembered it being, they were a blind man's eyes.

At first, Mason had no idea where he was, or what had happened. Those spooky eyes, dilated and confused, focused on the back of the transom where the shallow, ambient light illuminated the block letters 'SHOW TIME.' It took a moment before it all started to come back to him: his first conversations with Geno Mancini in the restaurant, his rendezvous with Caroline at the cottage on Quarter Main Loop, the night with the hooker (what wasn't blurred by cheap bourbon and beer), the impromptu plan to take down both Frankie and Sal with the hidden .380, Sal's body going overboard during the ride out, and his maddening fight with Frankie after Geno had written him off in front of his ex-wife. There was a sudden tightness in his chest, followed by an involuntary, gurgled cough. A spray of florescent green sea water fanned from his nose and mouth. Twice more he coughed, twice more water sprayed. With his lungs almost clear, a great pain and a feeling of emptiness engulfed Mason's chest—a desperate feeling of needing to breathe.

He leaned into the crook of his elbow and muffled a final, strangling cough, then drew in a massive lungful of air—the first breath he'd taken in almost four hours. Mason remembered the gunshots, and was sure that both lungs had holes in them big enough to easily pass golf balls. The phantom pains still ravaged his chest, yet the cutting air somehow managed to stay in him. As his chest expanded, the pain began to ease, and after wheezing out that first big, panicked breath and inhaling two smaller, more controlled breaths, the pain he felt was little more than a stitch a runner would feel halfway through a sprint. Eyes blinked, legs kicked, toes wiggled, back flexed and arched, and fingers flexed around the chrome ladder frame. To his complete shock and surprise, after being shot three times in the chest, everything seemed to be working just fine. Mason peered into the darkness beneath his chin. He didn't know how long he'd been down there, but he distinctly remembered the sun was still up when he'd tangled with fatso. And just that small recognition was a catalyst for yet another avalanche of memories …

Frankie had been unbelievably fast—the fastest big man he'd ever seen—and the timing had been uncannily perfect. Through what could only be described as pure dumb luck, Frankie had managed to dip at just the right moment, forcing the bullet into his outer shoulder, avoiding what was to be a mortal injury. The blast at close range must have caused a surge of adrenaline because before he could pull the trigger again, the big man bristled then sprang on him with all the quickness and tenacity of a cornered jaguar. A powerful fist knocked the gun away, along with most of his wits, and somehow the fat bastard managed to do it all with a fresh bullet hole through the meaty part of his shoulder and a badly wounded hand.

There was a short scuffle for the gun, but Frankie stood first, the Springfield solidly in his good hand. Mason's chest tightened. He'd dodged his fair share of bullets over the years, but it had always been on the run and at some distance, hardly what would be considered high percentage shots. This time was different. This time he was close enough to see the rifling in the end of the barrel of that .45. There was no doubt in either of their minds—Mason LaRue was about to die. And with that realization, Mason's bladder all at once let go. He stood there smelling his own piss and blubbering like a lost child, waiting for the ear-splitting noise and the pain and bleeding to start.

It all happened in slow-motion. Frankie's fat finger slowly flexed against the trigger, followed closely by an audible click . . . the faint sound of the firing pin striking the round. Then there was nothing but a screaming explosion and a flash of bright light. He could actually see the bullet being pushed from the gun. It had a tail like a comet as it slowly covered the short five feet between them.

Two more gunshots exploded. To Mason, they seemed to happen even before the first bullet struck—three hot pieces of lead, the size of large marbles, tore holes completely through his chest—and my God, it was loud. An exquisite pain exploded in his head as the concussions forced both eardrums to simultaneously burst. He staggered backwards, and the last thing he saw before going over the rail was Frankie Russo's fat face, peeled back into a satisfying sneer.

Although Mason was quite certain he was screaming, he fell in a queer silence. Each time he attempted to breathe, blood sprayed from his nose, and painted the inside of his shirt. Seventy-five long and twirling feet straight down from the rail—the fall, itself, should have killed him, but luckily he entered the sea feet first, almost in a standing position. What came after that was nothing but a dream of death. He was a helpless, drifting, dying jellyfish engulfed in a massive, world-ending pain. His brain gave the command to swim for the surface—to live—but nothing responded, and as he slowly sank, he was sure that Satan himself had him by the testicles, dragging him down to the bottom. Before everything went black, deep within the recesses of his short-circuiting brain came one final realization: *nobody walks (or swims) away from three .45's to the chest . . . nobody.*

The memory reminded him that he had every right to be dead, yet somehow, someway, he was alive. A warm wave slapped him in the face, and for the first time in a long time, Mason LaRue was swallowed by a feeling so alien to him, he scarcely knew what it was. He'd not felt regret since he was a small boy, but now it consumed him from the top of his strangely white hair to the very bottoms of his wrinkled toes. In that brief moment of clarity he saw himself as he really was, and it was disgusting. Swimming against the current, he slipped partway from under the tower and looked up at the sky. It was no longer just a two-dimensional dark canvas scattered with diamond chips. He could actually feel the depth of it all expanding in every direction—the heavens were beginning to open up to him.

Mason cleared his throat to begin a long overdue conversation with God, but somewhere in the watery darkness below came another tug on his balls. The battlefield inside his head raged again, as his thoughts were now mixed with strange voices. They demanded to be heard, and in a blinding confusion, whatever honorable and wholesome thoughts that were beginning to occupy his consciousness vanished, and hatred, again, gripped his guts.

Glaring at the sky, he noticed a large cluster of clouds straight overhead. After a double take, Mason thought he saw something embedded in it. A hallucination, perhaps, but after a couple of hard blinks, the image actually became clearer. What he saw enraged him even more. It had to be Heaven's gate eerily illuminated within that glowing bank of clouds, and there looked to be a single file line of glowing people emerging from the depths of space. The people or souls or whatever they were came out of the empty sky, walking or floating on nothing but the white water vapor. And just inside, sitting behind an elevated, stately podium was a faceless apparition dressed in a long white robe.

Mason's eyes became slits. The edges of his teeth ground together. Could it really be?

The white robe moved, revealing an arm and a hand holding a quill pen. Whatever he or it was seemed to be checking names as the line moved steadily towards him. Few entered, while the rest were turned away and just simply vanished. Mason thought he could hear faraway screams each time one was rejected. He shook his head, trying to make it all go away, but the more he tried to erase it, the more real it seemed.

Mason said aloud, "He ain't God, but he's close enough. Saint Pete, if you've never heard me before, hear me now." A dirty smile crawled across his lips, as the man in the white gown halted the line, as if someone had whispered in his ear. "You tell God that he didn't get the job done. I'm still very much here, and very much alive."

The current seemed to strengthen, pushing him back under the platform, and Mason kicked with his legs, keeping eye contact with what he thought he saw. Something bulky, cold, and metallic rubbed both of his inner thighs.

The Ruger!

His sickening smile widened. "And you tell him that unless he sends someone better than Frankie Russo to stop me, I'm going to be sending Hoyt Bennett and his daughter up for a visit before the sun shines again on this god—" He blinked, thinking, "Before the sun shines on *His* damned hunk of steel again."

Chapter 32

Jackie smacked her lips and made a face. The lingering taste of beige, bubbly adulthood lingered on her tongue while the big swallow warmed her throat. She didn't quite know what to expect, but what she just experienced wasn't even close to what she'd envisioned alcohol to be like. It was horrible. She was reaching for the soft drink to wash it down when something about the opened briefcase caught her eye. It seemed like nothing at first—a twist of thread, perhaps a frayed lining, and she leaned in for a closer look.

Hoyt was pouring a second glass and noticed Jackie staring at the briefcase. "Whatcha got there, beach girl? Tell me you found a porterhouse or a ribeye hiding in there too."

Jackie stuck her pinky finger in what she saw—a small hole in the lining—and the sensitive fingertip relayed to her brain that it had encountered something cold and flexible. Hoyt quickly had his pocket knife out, and ran the blade against the smooth lining. He folded the fabric back and neatly situated in the cavity between the hard shell case and the liner was a large sealable plastic bag holding several stacks of money.

Caroline almost spit champagne out of her mouth. "You're kidding me?" She wiped the remnants from her chin, picked up the baggie, excised a bundle from it, and thumbed through the bills. "Hundred-dollar bills. A fifty stack. That's five thousand a bundle!" She ran her eyes over the four bundles still left in the case mentally calculating the sum. "That's twenty-five thousand."

Hoyt ran his finger over the small hole in the side of the case. "They drilled from the side, instead of through the top. That's how they missed it." He looked at Jackie then to Caroline, then back at the case. "A new boat, and twenty-five grand to boot! Looks like this is our month!" They all shared a jubilant glance before Hoyt said, "I wonder if there's more?" He moved to the other side of the counter, and ran a finger along the liner and pressed his hand against the interior. He shook his head, and all eyes moved to the other briefcase—the one that Geno opened first. Hoyt felt something inside the hidden compartment, and the blade quickly moved. Inside, there was another plastic bag that held some papers. A quick tug freed a real estate contract, already filled out, that was to transfer the light station from him and Caroline to Geno Mancini. The only thing missing was Hoyt's and Caroline's signatures. It had already been notarized. There was another envelope in the plastic bag—customized printing said it was from Oberlin Laboratories, Trenton, New Jersey. The first page was all charts and graphs, but the second page was a written report that seemed to be a summation of the numbers and symbols on the first page. He scanned over the gibberish, and handed it to Caroline.

Caroline took a long look at the paper. "I'm not real sure, but I think this is a water analysis report. It says that two previously unknown elements were found." Her arms dropped a bit and looked at Hoyt over the report. He was running his thumb through a stack of cash. "Did you hear me, Dad? Two unidentified elements! I didn't make straight A's in chemistry, but I don't think this happens. That's like, Nobel Prize stuff." She continued reading. "It says here that oxygen levels are nearly twenty times greater than what's usually found in any fresh or salt water on the planet."

While Caroline continued to read the report and Hoyt busied himself counting the money, a tern flushed from the catwalk just outside the galley window. It squawked angrily as it disappeared into the darkness. Jackie was the only one who noticed.

Chapter 33

The half-moon dominated the sky. Its silvery glow transformed the structure's hard steel and sharp lines into a ghostly pale image. The moonlight fought its way through the windows, but inside it was still and dark. It was as if the entire light station was exhausted from the day's unusual excitement and was enjoying a deep sleep. There was one small exception—a small, soft incandescence coming from a single room. Jackie LaRue sat on her bed in a familiar position, back against the wall, knees drawn towards her chest. On the table next to her bed, a small flashlight glowed warmly, casting its small beam across the room. The sips of champagne that her mother gave her softened her mood, but Jackie's mind was far from sleep. She thought of the submarine. She thought of the intense fight between Frankie and the stranger with the same last name. She thought of the money and the boat. She thought of Ethan Wade—a young man who was her first kiss, and who, without hesitation, would die for them. Die for her.

Three rooms over, her grandfather's snores were loud and constant. Jackie wondered how anyone could sleep making that much noise, and then the metal below her began to creak and pop loudly, doubtless fighting its way through a series of large swells. The structure swayed, and realizing that sleep wasn't coming anytime soon, she reached for Lieutenant Brooks' command journal. She situated herself and the flashlight so that the beam fell across her lap, and with better light, she peeled back the bound leather cover. The journal actually creaked as she opened it, and even though she had read from it several times, this was the first time she noticed its condition. The aged paper looked like the archived newspapers displayed under glass at the Wilmington City Library . . . the historic ones, whose headlines included the bombing of Pearl Harbor, the dropping of the atomic bomb on Hiroshima, and the one whose headlines read, *Tragedy in Dallas: Kennedy Assassinated.*

She flipped through the yellowed pages, skimming through years of Coast Guard living as a junior officer in the early 1980s. Most of what Lieutenant Brian Brooks wrote about was far from historic. In fact, most of it read like a class assignment that students usually groaned over. But occasionally there were gems hidden amid the boring stuff—talks of disagreements and fist-fights, and there was even a significant galley fire in August of 1980 that the junior officer suspected was purposefully set by someone, just to escape the monotonous doldrums of life on the light station. Jackie's eager eyes found another entry where one of the men had received a Dear John letter. This poor, heart-broken guy paced around the platform for three hours in the January cold in nothing but boxer shorts, holding a pistol to his head, while reciting his marriage vows over and over aloud. Lieutenant Brooks' notes were meticulous. Every entry recorded everything down to the smallest detail, but the story of the Dear John letter was left without a finale. The bottom half of the page was ripped clean from the journal, erasing what had happened from history forever.

Jackie thumbed through more pages, and in her mind's eye, it was like watching a documentary unfold on television. The thought of recording everyday life in its totality was something that she'd never considered. Sure, she knew several girls in school who kept a diary, but they were the type that seemed to overly-dramatize everything. The stuff they were writing down was probably closer to dreamy fiction than what was actually the truth. They were all charter members of the selfie generation—girls who would probably love to have a Hollywood film crew follow them around all day. Jackie LaRue didn't have the time nor the desire to turn her life into some over-emphasized soap opera.

It's probably a good thing, anyway. How boring would that be?

Her simple world began and ended with her mother, grandfather, and just a couple of distant friends at East Wilmington middle—a fairly small circle, most would agree. But reading through more of Brooks' less-than-exciting entries, she began to sense her world expanding. In just a handful of trips to the Frying Pan, she'd taken part in an FBI undercover sting operation, been held captive and nearly tortured by some mobster's henchmen, and then rescued from it all by a handsome Navy SEAL. Jackie's meager borders were indeed broadening. And then her mind settled solidly on the guy that saved her life. The Navy SEAL named Ethan Wade. Just thinking about him sent electric pulses through her body, intensifying the champagne-encouraged tingling.

Maybe I should have pinched his ass when I gave him that kiss?

She giggled then remembered something the older girls at school did. Jackie made a fist and turning her knuckles toward the ceiling, her thumb naturally fell across the curled index finger. A crumpled mouth with a pronounced under-bite now stared back at her in the soft light. It wasn't exactly like his mouth, but it would have to do. She closed her eyes, then opened them again; a regal nose and two blue eyes were there—Ethan Wade's eyes. Embracing every ounce of imagination she could muster, the thumb moved up and down and a faint voice came from within her fist—Ethan Wade's voice.

"There's no way I was going to let a pretty one like you drown in the ocean. I'd a swam a thousand miles, through schools of sharks to save you."

Jackie's eyes fluttered. That same flush of warmth she'd felt on the platform when the real Ethan Wade complimented her suddenly gripped her torso.

The fist spoke again, this time with a stronger and more masculine voice. "Braving a school of sharks is nothing to get to talk to a pretty thing like you. A knockout, with beautiful strawberry blond hair . . . what have you got? Just a few more years before you go to college? You're a heartbreaker in the making."

Assisted by the alcohol, it all began to feel very real. Jackie's cheeks reddened. The warmth building in her chest quickly worked its way to her belly, then crept ever so slowly into places that embarrassed her. The feeling was exquisite.

The tingly thumb that looked more and more like Ethan's lower lip moved again. "I wish I could have seen you fight. So pretty. So brave. You probably don't know, but that's just what SEALs like. Pretty and brave girls—"

Jackie came back to reality. Deep furrows carved their way into her brow, and in her own voice she said, "No, no, no. That's not right."

A deep breath cleared her thoughts, and Jackie replayed the conversation in her mind. When the right moment came, magically, Ethan Wade's voice started again, correcting that horrible word. "You probably don't know, but that's just what SEALs like. Pretty and brave *women*."

That one little word pressed the right button. Jackie squeezed her legs together. Her inner thighs were hot and slick with desire. Seductively, she said, "I'm glad you were there to save me. Momma said there were people like you. People that were good and nice. I've never met anyone like you Ethan. Strong, handsome—I wouldn't mind you saving me every day for the rest of my life."

Jackie clearly saw every bit of him now. It was if he was actually there, kneeling by her bed.

"Oh Ethan!" she whispered, "I think I . . . I think I love you."

His blonde hair, ice-blue eyes, and pursed lips moved towards hers. It wasn't real, but somehow it was. She felt his warm breath, teasingly close. Every square inch of his arm was pure muscle as Jackie's left hand ran up his flexed forearm to a bulging bicep. A strong hand moved to the small of her back gently lifting her from the bed, and then his smooth cheek brushed against hers. A lingering pause heightened the anticipation, and then, for just a moment—a glorious moment—her lips touched Ethan Wade's.

Totally lost in a world all her own, a little moan escaped her parted lips. The air around her was thick with his essence, as the lingering kiss totally paralyzed her still tingling body.

Ethan Wade *was* there. He *was* real. He *was* kissing her. And lying there alone in her bed, the room lit only with a cheap flashlight and the vividness of her imagination, he was hers and she was his.

Chapter 34

Mason LaRue slowly walked down the hallway towards the galley, his tattered clothes still dripping sea water. His eyes—eyes that had seen death's inky blackness—worked surprisingly well in the dimness. He moved effortlessly, picking his steps, avoiding the supply boxes and odd cans of paint that were stowed haphazardly against the walls. His socks squished out puddles of the Atlantic behind him; the .380 firmly in his hand. There were rooms to his left and right, and he peered into each he came to, knowing that sooner or later he'd find what he was looking for. The first three rooms were empty, and he was peering into the fourth when a heavy volley of snores echoed from up the hall.

Mason's fingers flexed around the pistol. His heart thumped heavily in his chest and a feeling of invincibility came over him. This was it. Mason LaRue was about to right every wrong that he's suffered with this worthless family. He tiptoed forward and was almost there when a faint sound met his ears. He turned towards a half-open door, and he heard it again—the soft sound of a blanket rustling, perhaps someone rolling over in bed. The snoring continued from a couple of rooms down, and his head swiveled from the door beside him, to the snoring, then back to the door.

Well, well. Could this be the best-looking legs in Greenville hidden all nice and cozy in there? Snug as a bug in a rug?

A gameshow host's voice now filled his head. *Congratulations, Mister LaRue. You've just won our grand prize package. However, like in all good gameshows you have to choose. You can take everything you've won home with you now, or you can trade them for what's behind door number one.*

Another loud snore tumbled down the hallway, and Mason shook his head.

Damn fool nearly choked on that one.

He stood still long enough for the snores to start again. Satisfied, Mason turned to the door and slowly, millimeter by millimeter, opened it just enough to slip through. The room was darker than the hallway, but the moon outside the small window was still doing its job. Straining eyes found a blanket-covered outline on the bed— a smaller frame than Caroline would've made.

Jacqueline.

She was dead to the world, but oddly had a frightened look on her face. His cupped hand moved to her mouth, but stopped short. Something else in the room caught his attention. A single chair stood in the corner and draped over its back was a white terrycloth towel. In the dimness, it shone like a beaming neon sign.

That could have been an ambush, stupid. I missed it completely. Come on Mason, you're getting sloppy.

He lifted the towel from the chair. It was at least twice as large as the one he used on Sal. If split down the middle, there'd be enough to silence the Ruger again, with more than enough left over to gag somebody. Maybe two somebodies. Whispering, he said, "I'll deal with you later, my dear. Right now, I've got a promise to keep."

Chapter 35

While Mason LaRue was leaving puddles of the Atlantic in the hallway, Jackie slept and dreamed.

Standing in her grandfather's boat in the full darkness of the night, she cursed at the sea. It was a raging squall, and the menacing waves all seemed to be alive—each one trying harder than the last to capsize her into the deep. She fought the controls, but the sputtering engines kept the boat from responding to her commands. There was something else though. Over the whine of the gale that forced whitecaps across the bow, there was a noticeable squeal that was accompanied by a series of pops and creaks. She blinked away the ocean spray and noticed that the bow cleat was now half-way to the cockpit. It couldn't be, but somehow it was. The boat was actually shrinking.

Shaking off another growling wave that winked at her as it went by, she had one last cognitive thought before switching totally to unrefined and untested instincts: if she was in the Atlantic anywhere near the light station, the coastline would be to the west.

Panicked eyes went to the GPS. The unit was clearly powered up, but the screen was blank. She hit it once with her bare fist, paused, then hit it again, splitting the skin on two of her knuckles. A thin red line of blood appeared on the screen, but it still failed to respond. Power or no power, it was useless.

Her world was crumbling around her, and she couldn't even save her own life. She wanted to quit, she wanted to scream, she wanted to fall down into the floor and cry until that next big wave toppled over what now seemed to be just a large rowboat, taking her down into the blackness, but something deep inside Jackie LaRue wouldn't let her give up. Searching for something—anything—her eyes finally dropped to the antiquated black ball compass sitting so neatly in the glass globe affixed to the console. For just a moment, there was a sense of relief, as the big 'N' danced happily a few degrees on either side of the white line on the housing. Her shrinking ship was facing north. Frantically, she whipped the wheel left and rammed the throttle home.

The engines belched a cloud of greasy smoke, and the boat sluggishly responded. She felt it turn under her, but the compass didn't move. She stared at it, mentally begging it to make sense, then something happened that drove her to the brink of insanity. As if demon possessed, it rapidly turned three full counter-clockwise revolutions, then it reversed, and spun clockwise three more revolutions, stopping abruptly where it had started. Her mouth dangled open as the black ball then spun forward on an axis that couldn't exist, completing three full front rotations, quickly followed by three full back rotations. When it had settled again on the big 'N', a thin, horizontal line opened across the compass' black face, curving into a terrible, toothless smile. In a low voice—a voice she recognized—it said, "I'll deal with you later my dear. Right now, I've got a promise to keep."

She screamed until the salty taste of blood came into her throat. And before her endless breath waned, the compass glass split a great jagged crack across its face. The fluid that floated the compass began to leak from the globe, but instead of it being thin and clear, what oozed from it was thick, clotting blood. The crimson streak poured down the white fiberglass console pooling at her feet. She recoiled, as the blood swirled and began to form a face on the floor. The face of Mister LaRue . . . the face of her father.

She came out of the nightmare, gasping for air, groping at the sheets, wet from her own sweat. Darkness was the only thing that met her bulging eyes, but the bloody scene on the shrinking boat was still tiptoeing down the thin line between what she knew was real and the land of dreams. It was as vivid as a newly minted memory.

All of it was simply too much for her fragile mind to bear. The only logical response was to scream, and she opened her mouth to do just that, but someone down the hallway beat her to it. Jackie's breath left her, as a shrill wail drowned out the light station's musical metallic creaking. It sounded like her mother, but she'd never heard her sound like this . . . utterly, desperately, terrified.

The scream ended abruptly, and then there was another loud metallic *pop*. Eerily similar to the glass breaking in her dream, the sound echoed down the hallway and came back to her ears as a solid *ping*. The circuits in her brain overloaded analyzing the sound.

Jackie's skin tightened. And suddenly, she knew.

Chapter 36

When Jackie LaRue saw her father for the first time (and was certain of his identity) he was standing in the galley, looming over her bleeding grandfather. Her mother was tied to a chair at the table, part of a white bath towel stuffed in her mouth, while another strip of it was tied around her head holding the gag in place. Caroline could manage no more than a whimper. Jackie blinked once, then twice, peering helplessly into a room that was as close to a living hell as you can get without getting burned.

She rubbed her eyes hoping that what she saw was just another nightmare, but nothing changed. Her mother's wide eyes pulsed, as her chest rose and fell sporadically, screaming only silent screams. Her father's silhouette pointed a gun at her grandfather who was sprawled on the floor. He looked hurt—how badly, she couldn't tell—and between the eerie metallic creaks, Jackie could hear labored wheezes. His shirt was torn, and two dark red holes were still leaking blood. One was on the right side of his chest just below his nipple, and another low in his belly.

Mason's voice was a low growl. "Old man, I've wanted to get rid of you for a long time, and that punch was the final straw. I thought about cutting you into little pieces, starting at your feet, but that would be too messy. A bullet through the head is too quick and too damn good for you. I thought about playing around with electricity, but I hate the smell of burning hair. But I've finally come up with something that may just do the trick." Mason waggled the gun at Hoyt. "Part one just happened. Those two bullets won't kill you, at least not right off, but while you are bleeding and hurting, I'm going to *really* hurt you—right where hurt hurts the worst."

Mason took a step towards Caroline. "I've got some catching up to do with the prettiest legs at East Carolina. And you're going to have a front-row seat. A proper send-off that you can spend forever in hell remembering."

Caroline's long hair whipped side to side. Her muffled screams transformed into low groans through the terrycloth. Mason reached for the back of her chair and heaved it and Caroline through the air. When it hit, the chair exploded, sending Caroline sprawling like a discarded rag doll. Before Hoyt could reach his daughter, Mason was already there, pulling her hair, separating the two. A pale hand blurred across her face, and blood began seeping from a newly formed split on her cheek. Caroline whimpered again.

"Now why did you have to go and break the chair like that? Keep it up and you're going to wake up the rest of the light station. And believe me, if you think this is bad, you don't want *her* stumbling into this right now. I've got some plans for me and *her* after you two are feeding the sharks. And just to keep it nice and simple, I'd just as soon not have to explain to *her* the real reason why she's going to have to come live with me from now on."

Mason loosened his belt and groped at Caroline's shorts, pulling them off her hips. Then Jackie heard her Grandfather's low voice. "Leave her . . . leave her alone you—" Hoyt choked on his words. He tried to breathe, but only managed what sounded like a wet gurgle.

Jackie brought her hand to her mouth just in time to cover a gasp. She tried to breathe for him, but it was no use. A tear rolled down her cheek. Was that the last thing she'd ever hear him say? He was still for only a moment before coughing violently, dislodging something in his chest. A ragged breath went in, and a wad of bloody phlegm was spat out.

Mason turned back towards the old man, and Jackie's eyes scanned the room searching for something or some way to help. Hoyt wiped the bloody spittle from his lips and saw Jackie. Both of their eyes widened, and the same mental connection she'd felt on the roof opened up again.

Hoyt's eyes moved back to Mason, and in a hoarse voice said, "I wish you'd *just go,* and let me die in peace and leave them alone. *The keys are in the boat,*" he pointed towards the table, "and you found the money in the briefcase. Just take it *and go. Just go.* Leave us alone, take the money, and *get the hell out of here.* You don't need them. You've done what you came here to do, so *just go.*"

Jackie understood the meaning of every emphasized word. But the urge to run never crossed her mind. They were in trouble, and she was their only chance. Quick eyes probed the room. At first there wasn't so much as a broom handle in sight. She took a deep breath and looked again. This time, things began to jump out at her.

The briefcases

Too flimsy and light.

Three chairs

But they're made of wood, and aren't stout enough to hurt him.

The two champagne bottles

Maybe I can break the end off like they do in the movies and cut him?

The glass flutes were on the counter next to the sink

No, no, no, Jackie. How's any of that going to help when he's got a gun?

Panic was beginning to set in when something lying on the counter against the left wall came into focus.

The speargun!

The thought had barely cleared her mind when Charlie suddenly appeared in front of her, a ghostly fish, swimming in midair. Jackie took a startled step back into the hallway, and the image moved with her. The fish's mouth opened, "Looks like you've gotten yourself in another pickle, huh?" It turned towards the counter, then turned back and winked. "Do you see what I see over there?"

Jackie inched forward peering into the room. She saw what the fish saw.

"Well, what are you waiting for? He's going to kill them if you don't hurry up and do something."

The speargun was barely visible in the dimness, but something else glistened in the weak light beside it—the barbed tridents from the end of the spear. She licked her lips, as her focus came back to her imaginary dead fish friend.

The fish nodded his ghostly head. "That's right. The spears are lying beside it—two of them. But as good as you were with that barracuda, I think one will do. You couldn't save me," the small fished turned towards Mason and instead of the whole fish, now there was ragged, torn meat behind the gills. Nothing was left past the pectoral fins except a thin trailing string of chewed intestines, "but if you hurry up, you can save them. If you're going to do it, you've got to do it now."

Charlie disappeared, but not before Jackie heard his voice trailing off into the beyond. "Get him in the water quickly."

Was any of that real?

Mason's voice came back to her from across the room. "—too easy, old man. Nobody can stop me, so I'm going to do it my way. And my way has always been the best way."

The phantom fish's voice came to her again. In a kind of garbled underwater scream, it said, "Do it NOW!"

Jackie's eyes narrowed and her back stiffened. The man holding the gun was in clear focus, while everything else in the room faded away. Charlie was right. He was going to kill them both.

A string of profanity cascaded through her mind, attempting to classify this low life. He was all those things and more, but there was one thing that she felt sure he wasn't. Her lips became two thin lines retreating from gleaming teeth. She said in a low whisper, "You aren't my father."

Jackie's eyes locked on the speargun and she bolted into the room.

Chapter 37

Mason LaRue stood over Caroline and Hoyt. A small trail of drool seeped from the corner of his mouth and ran to the tip of his chin. The feeling of power coursing up his arm from the small pistol calmed him, and in a moment of pure psychosis, he considered what was about to happen. The creaking and slight sway coming from the structure seemed soothing, as Caroline lay on the floor, crying, gagged, and almost naked. Just a few feet away, Hoyt was slumped against the wall, with two bullets in him. Mason couldn't help but smile. There was just something magical about pointing a gun at somebody. Holding another man's life in your hands and delivering the final verdict was the only thing that had ever topped sex, and here he was, about to accomplish both feats at the same time. A warm, electric pulse ran through his body. It settled around his groin, and an instant erection crowded his pants.

Hoyt's scruff, pleading voice brought Mason out of the fantasy. "Please don't . . . don't do it."

Mason stared down the short barrel of the gun, putting the front sight squarely between the old man's eyes. "Well ain't that something. Never seen you beg before."

Hoyt's stare was blank, almost looking past him. "You've never made a good decision in your life, and how you ever got Caroline to love you is beyond me. We took you in—"

"You took me in? Into what? We were as poor as church mice, living crumb to crumb, and whatever I could steal and hustle from bums. That shack we lived in . . . it was only a step above a cardboard box on the street."

Hoyt's tired eyes moved, his hand clutching the wound in his belly. He coughed once, and said, "Yeah, it was a shack, but it was our shack. Remind me again where you were calling home when you met Caroline?"

The tower creaked again, and outside, a cloud passed by the moon, dimming what little light was in the room. Something moved at the edge of his vision, but it wasn't enough to break the building rage that was focused at Hoyt. "I'm tired of hearing your voice, old man. I was going to make you watch what I'm about to do to your daughter, but I think I'm just going to put a bullet in your brain right now."

Hoyt seemed to focus on something else for an instant, then settled again on Mason. "I don't think you're going to have the chance, you son of a bitch."

Mason's right eye twitched. His lower lip quivered. The nerve!

Down below, a large wave rolled past the lighthouse, producing an eerie series of descending metallic pops. When the structure's rivets and bolts had overcome the lateral stress, there was a split second of unnatural, almost forced silence. It was in that silence that Mason's newly refurbished ears registered something. The sound was so faint, he wasn't sure that it was anything at all. Maybe it was his own body moving in damp clothes? He paused again, perfectly still, listening. There it was again—the soft *shooshing* sound of ruffling fabric—perhaps a curtain rustling against itself in a slight breeze? Mason's pale eyes went from window to window, then widened. There were no curtains in the galley.

Chapter 38

Jackie darted across the back of the room and gently lifted the gun and spear off the counter. Soundlessly, the bands came back to the latch and the spear went on the rail. She heard her grandfather say 'don't do it' and then Mister LaRue saying something about begging, and suddenly, her television screen fuzzed out again. Jackie leveled the loaded speargun at the man and began walking. With each step, her sanity stretched thinner and thinner. She wasn't completely out of her mind, at least not yet, but there was a question as to who or what was really in control.

In control or not, Jackie kept moving. She could tell they were still talking, but none of it made sense. Her bare feet were silent as the deliberate steps came—the only sound she was aware of was the almost imperceptible shuffle of clothes ruffling against her skin. She was no more than six steps from him when four words crescendoed loud and clear over the previous mumbling. Jackie had rarely heard her grandfather curse, but when the words 'son of a bitch' echoed low across the room in his slower-than-usual, labored drawl, she finally snapped. Her own internal compass began mimicking the possessed boat compass from her dream, turning the wrong way and doing front and back flips, snapping the few lingering mental tethers that so desperately connected her to the last semblance of reality. Those once soft green eyes, now filled with a blinding rage, looked at the man with the gun, then at her gagged mother, then finally at her bleeding grandfather.

If it takes crazy to kill crazy, then by God, let's do this!

The structure swayed against a wave, and instantly pops and moans rang out as the metal flexed out of, then back into position. The spooky sounds gave way to a deep quiet, and she took another step and prepared to shoot. As she raised her arm, the sleeve on her sleeping shirt caught something on the speargun. The flimsy fabric stretched for a moment, then snapped back along her wrist, making a light *swoosh* sound. It wasn't much, but she clearly heard it in the unnatural silence. The man with the gun froze, and a sliver of worry spread through her mind like heat lightening jumping from cloud to cloud.

He heard it too.

Chapter 39

Jackie felt nothing but the cold sting of hate when her father turned to face her. When she saw him through the ventilation grate, he hadn't seemed so big. Now, only steps apart, he was indeed an imposing figure, standing a foot and a half over her meager frame. The shadows intensified his frightening persona, and even with a body full of rage and determination, chills turned her arms into gooseflesh.

Jackie's steady eyes went to the small pistol in his right hand, and then came up again.

Why isn't he reacting?

The shadows couldn't hide his pale eyes and arrogant smile. The smile, alone, was enough to flip her mental switch, but like a bouquet of roses, somewhere nestled in that sea of red, there's always that one darling blossom that stands out over all the others. She hated this man with every ounce of her being and wanted nothing more than to bury that trident into those sickening eyes, but that one gentle blossom began to unfurl. This demon who had so savagely hurt her family, was projecting a feeling of calm and cool that could have extinguished the Hindenburg's flames. It was unmistakable, even to a fourteen-year-old girl. And those eyes. She'd never seen pale yellow eyes like that before—dead man's eyes.

* * *

Mason LaRue couldn't believe what he was seeing. If it hadn't been for that faint rustle of fabric, he wouldn't have known she was there until those three prongs had buried into whatever part of him she wanted. Was he losing his touch or was the screwed-up water affecting his senses that badly?

Regardless of how she'd gotten that close, she was there, and strangely, some small part of him was actually glad. He could smell her now. That strawberry blond hair disappearing behind her shoulders was straight and pretty, wafting a hint of citrus conditioner into the air. Pink and full lips almost shined, and her night shirt that smelled unmistakably like a woman cascaded across a taught stomach from firm, modest breasts that were well on their way to catching Caroline's. And if that wasn't enough, those toned legs had a tantalizingly familiar shape. The whole package transported him back to the fifty-yard line in Dowdy-Ficklen stadium—a clear reminder of her mother shaking a pair of purple and yellow pom-poms, among other things.

Hoyt wheezed loudly and Mason blinked. His daughter was still sneering, and still pointing a speargun at his chest. He tried to think of something to say, but what was tumbling around in his mind was more suited for adults than teenagers. He'd never attempted to work his magic on anyone this young since he, too, was that age. And given the situation, he was quite certain now was not the time for anything risky. She looked determined and angry and borderline crazy—looks you didn't mess with—and it all added up to one conclusion. If he couldn't smooth things out quickly, he'd have to kill her. He didn't want to do it, but if she was as crazy as she looked, he would have no choice.

Mason considered the situation. Could he cover the short distance before she shot? Disarming her would be easy, if he could just get there. Then he remembered how quickly Frankie fatso Russo moved. The speargun was a single-shot. If she didn't back down, then maybe he could make her miss? Mason shifted his weight ever-so-slightly, and almost as quickly Jackie responded by lowering herself into a crouch. The standoff was unmistakably similar to how Caroline reacted at 485 Quarter Main Loop, but instead of looking into the cylinder at pistol bullets, Mason now stared at three silver points of a fish spear. They seemed to wink at him in the dimness, daring him to move. Mason's mind shifted gears. Synapses fired in those strange places again, and immediately, another plan evolved.

First things first: he had to eliminate the tension. If she wasn't calm, or calmer than she currently was, it was never going to work. Mason, himself, was adrenalized far beyond his normal operating level, so he consciously sighed, releasing a tranquil breath into the void between them. At first it didn't work, and if the light had been better, Jackie would have easily seen a trickle of worry run down his forehead. He slowly breathed again, but Jackie's gaze only seemed to intensify. Realizing he was losing it (losing her), Mason made one last unbelievable amendment to his plan.

It was lunacy, pure and simple, and even his own evil brain didn't believe what it was attempting to make her believe. Dropping to a knee, in the most loving pose his corrupt brain could imagine, he spread his arms wide and somehow willed big tears down his cheeks.

"Jacqueline." The voice was filled with a shocking compassion. Those spooky eyes looked straight into hers. "It's me, sweetheart. It's your dear ole—"

Immediately he knew it was a mistake. He couldn't even finish the sentence. A fierce green eye stared at him, perfectly aligned above the silver shank of the spear. Behind the gun, the corners of her mouth slowly curled. His daughter—his fourteen- year-old strawberry-blonde, sweet-smelling, perky-titted daughter—revealed perfectly straight, gleaming white teeth in a sickening smile. It was a smile that could have turned fresh milk sour.

"It's Jackie, not Jacqueline, you son of a bitch."

He stared helplessly at the three sharp points and tried to swallow. Behind him, Hoyt's gravelly voice wheezed the last words Mason LaRue would ever hear.

"Would you look at that."

Chapter 40

Jackie tossed the speargun aside and ran past Mason quivering on the floor. "Granddad! Granddad!" she said in a panic, hovering over him, pumping fingers into and out of fists.

Hoyt's eyes opened, and in them Jackie could see only pain. He managed to raise his arm a little and pointed towards Caroline lying on her side, still gagged and tied to what was left of the chair. Quickly the knots were loosened, and both were standing over him. Jackie helped her mother lay him flat on the floor, and she held his hand while Caroline went to work on the gag towel. A big rip had it in two pieces, and she folded them into hand size squares and pressed them gently on the wounds. A gurgling sound came from behind them, and they both turned at the same time. Mason's spooky eyes stared lifelessly at the ceiling. The fish spear buried in his neck rose straight above him, Jackie's planted flagpole, without the flag. Caroline shook her head then turned back to Hoyt. "The radio. We need the Coast Guard—" She stopped mid-sentence, her voice fell into defeat. "But it'll take them an hour to get here."

Jackie saw her mother's face change. Concern and worry morphed into a look of total devastation. Hoyt grunted something inaudible and shook his head. He coughed, and a thin line of pink stained spittle ran across his lips. Desperately he groped for Jackie's arm and touched it where the blister had been. It looked like he wanted to say something, but before he could, the weakened old man slipped into unconsciousness.

Jackie's eyes blurred with tears. They were going to lose him. There was nothing either of them could do. She pressed clinched fists into her eyes and began to cry, and that's when she saw it. Even the dimness couldn't hide the small white line where the knife blade sliced into her hand.

Charlie!

"Mom," she said reaching for her grandfather's arms, "we can save him. The water. We've got to get him in the water."

Caroline wiped teary cheeks with the back of her hands. "What?"

"The water . . . it heals. Granddad was pointing at my burn. I burned myself on the grill and I cut myself, and the water fixed it." She thought about her father's ghostly reappearance, and it all started to make sense. "Jackie pointed over her shoulder at the dead man on the floor, "The big man they called Frankie shot him, and he went in the water. That's how he came back."

Caroline seemed swallowed by a confused silence.

Jackie let Hoyt's arms go and turned to her mother. Nose to nose, she pressed Caroline's cheeks with the palms of her hands and slowly said, "We've-got-to-get-him-in-the-water."

Her mother's eyes were still distant.

"I'll explain later. Just help me get him outside."

She reached for her grandfather's arms again and began to drag him across the floor. She'd moved him only a few feet when Caroline grabbed the other hand. Jackie could still see confusion in her mother's eyes, but it was confusion that trusted.

Both were out of breath when they made the catwalk. Between gasps Caroline said, "How do we . . . get him . . . down there?"

"Over the rail."

There was a pregnant pause, then Caroline said, "Are you crazy? The fall will kill him."

Jackie felt for a pulse in her grandfather's wrist. "No time. He's dead if we don't."

Reluctantly, Caroline reached from behind, running her arms under her father's blood-slick armpits. Jackie grabbed his feet, and together they managed to get him up to the rail. With one last push, Hoyt went over the side.

Caroline watched him fall, then disappear in the dark ocean below. In a type of serene finality, she said, "I can't believe we—" A sudden movement interrupted her. Caroline looked up and screamed, "Jackie, NO!"

* * *

Jackie hit the surface feet first. She covered the seventy feet in a little less than two seconds, but those two seconds seemed like an eternity. A few months later, in science class, she would calculate the speed of a falling object traveling seventy feet in a vacuum to be 20.4 meters per second. That didn't sound so bad, but when converted to standard units, she realized that if she'd landed on her head, or back, or anything other than straight in like a toothpick, 45 miles per hour could have killed her instantly. A small wonder.

What wasn't a small wonder was that ten feet below the surface, with only the moon above, there was very little light—something that she hadn't accounted for. The waters may have healed her, but it was very stingy with transmitting thin moonlight. She had no mask, and her eyes, fully dilated and stinging from the salt water, only managed to probe four or five feet though the murk. Hoyt entered the water only seconds before, but he was nowhere in sight. She didn't know how the water healed, but she knew that the funny bubbles coming from the bottom around the pilings had something to do with it. How far away from the tower would it work? What if he drifts away from it, out into 'normal' water? If he wasn't dead already, he'd drown.

She swam in a circle at first in a panicked frenzy. Realizing the folly, she slowed and allowed herself to sink in the currents, searching as a child might look for a toy in a dark room. Maybe twenty feet down, she turned two more complete circles before something came into view. Below her, against a solid darkening gray canvas, there was something that seemed odd. A dark ribbon with silver highlights was suspended in the water like an image in those crazy three-dimensional computer generated prints. She had never been able to see the images spring from the patterns, but judging from what her friends told her about them, this column of dark water was mimicking it pretty well. It wasn't much at first, but the more she stared at it, the more it stood out in the drabness. An almost black streak in dark water with a silvery edge? Nothing her mind could conjure made it a natural occurrence.

Pulling massive amounts of oxygen in through her skin, Jackie turned downward and kicked. The dark streak seemed to be dissipating, but the closer she got to it, the more she could see of it. It was like walking towards smoke from a fire on a windy day. Darkness was beginning to totally envelop her, when the silver highlight to the dark object scattered.

Fish . . . and blood. The fish were attracted to grandad's blood. Just like when I cut my hand.

Jackie kicked again towards the bottom. Her head and chest began to pop violently, a product of the mounting pressure. Blackness seemed to cloak everything, but frantic fingers finally found the bottom, and she crabbed blindly along, feeling for something familiar, hoping for anything. A big push of current pressed her against the muck, and a cloud of silt hit her in the face. She wiped the grit away, and when she looked up, maybe ten feet in front of her, she saw a faint green glow. She moved closer. There were fissures along the sea floor that looked like translucent blood vessels—each one pulsing with what looked like florescent green alien blood. Careful not to touch any of it, she rose off the bottom, trying to get a better view. The glow followed. She swept her hand through the water, and the pale light parted as if she'd fanned through a cloud of smoke. Jackie squinted. It wasn't just the cracks that were transmitting light, it was actually small glowing particles suspended in the water. Jackie was now surrounded by what looked like hundreds, if not thousands of miniscule points of light. They were everywhere . . . on her arms, flowing around her face, sticking to the hair on her arms and head, even filling the small open pores in the fabric of her shirt.

It was all quite mesmerizing, so much so, she nearly forgot what she'd risked her life to do. Staring inquisitively at the glowing particles stuck to her hand, something past her fingers moved. She glanced up just in time to see what she thought was a large caudal fin swoosh back and forth, fanning the drifting points of light.

Was that a—

Above the movement, something else caught her eye. It was at the very edge of her vision, but whatever it was seemed only to flutter rhythmically in the ocean currents. It reminded her of the sea anemone that the cartoon clownfish Nemo lived in. Past the fluttering, another big fin swooshed through the water. Jackie first imagined a big barracuda, but her mind quickly transformed it into a larger fish that had big jaws and lots of sharp teeth. Closer to her, the fluttering object still swayed in the currents, and beside it was the dull gray steel piling that supported the light station. It had literally come out of nowhere, standing tall in front of her like a monument to life itself. She swam closer, and through less and less murk, she realized that what she had seen was a piece of cloth caught on a rusting rivet head. Carefully avoiding the sharp barnacles, hand over hand, she moved up the steel.

When she grasped it, there was an immediate resistance. One tug had it moving, and suddenly her grandfather came out of the gloom. A big blast of air escaped her lungs in an underwater scream. She quickly regained control and gently worked open his shirt. The wounds were still there, red and raw, but they were closed and not leaking blood. Accumulated around each little red circle were doughnut shaped concentrations of the tiny light particles. The flesh rippled, and she knew that her grandfather's cells were slowly being spliced back together.

Jackie saw the massive column of air bubbles from her scream rising above her, and immediately realized that no amount of oxygen diffusing through her skin would fill empty lungs. She felt the crushing pressure of the Atlantic and a terrifying need to breathe seized her. One hand firmly grasped her grandfather's wrist, while the other pulled at the water. Both feet kicked with everything she had, and the mental countdown began.

With her grandfather in tow, every inch was a struggle. She forced herself upward and soon began to feel the swells making her sway side to side. Jackie was quickly running out of what little air she had left, and the view of her watery nightmare began to shrink into a small aperture. Above her, the waves on the surface lapped against the side of the boat and above that was air. Oh, what a grand thing it was to breathe. So natural, so easy, so free, but her screaming lungs could not be satisfied. Pulling inward with an ever-increasing force, they began to collapse on themselves, turning her windpipe into a thin thread. Weakening fingers began relinquishing their grip on her grandfather, and Jackie pleadingly looked up one last time. Oh God! She could almost touch the surface with her free hand. Fighting the fog that was engulfing her mind, she contemplated turning loose and quickly breaching the surface. A newspaper headline flashed in her mind, *Young Girl Drowns Trying To Save Grandfather.*

If they both died, would any of it matter? Jackie didn't want to lose Hoyt, but it was becoming painfully clear that one or the other was about to happen. Fuses began to blow, and one by one, areas of her brain flickered and started going out like the lights in Wilmington when a storm blew through. Struggling against the current and Hoyt's weight, every available molecule of air left in her lungs was exhausted, and her body convulsed.

Air, precious air!

It was right there, so close Jackie could taste it. Her collapsing lungs still didn't care how close she was to breathing, they just knew that they needed air, and they finally began to win the battle. The negative pressure was so great, water started to seep, then spray between her clinched lips, coating the inside of her mouth and throat with salt water. Finally, the right fuses blew, and the sea poured in with the force of a thousand firehoses. The surface of the sea, which had been right there, suddenly was gone. The last things Jackie LaRue felt was a brief brush of cool air and then a crushing pressure on her left hand. Drowning or not, dead or alive, or somewhere in between, if she could have screamed, she would.

Chapter 41

Jackie actually felt dead. Everything was black, still, and cold, and even though she couldn't feel anything definitive for a long time, she began to be aware of a heavy pressure on her chest. It was there, and then it wasn't, then back again, then gone again. The fuses were slowly being replaced and the lights were coming back on, but not enough at one time to allow her to understand what was happening. Her senses were still out of commission, but even in her severely handicapped state, the small part of her brain that was working imagined a scared little girl floating along in space, surrounded by pin-pricks of greenish light. There was nothing above or below, or side to side—just an endless empty black void where only a frail body, thanks to the thousands of tiny lights, took on a creepy green glow. The mind's capabilities are fantastic, and even operating at some minuscule capacity, somehow she knew that this little girl was her.

It was a terrifying and helpless feeling, only mitigated by a single memory: she was in the water saving her grandfather when she tried to inhale the ocean. A part of Jackie sensed that the girl floating on the strange green light wasn't breathing, and may never again, while another part of her, the part that seemed to be sprinting madly towards the end, knew better than trying. But wherever she was or whatever she was doing, that awful feeling of needing to breathe was still there.

The pressure came once more—on again, off again—and things began popping in her head. The lights flickered, as short bursts of electricity coursed through the miles of nerves encased within her skull. She was beginning to think they were coming back on for good, then everything went black. When the lights flickered again, more of them came on, and a dull, achy pain landed in her chest. Jackie felt pressure on her nose, then a great influx of air tried to push itself down her windpipe into her saturated lungs. She could feel and hear bubbles inside, and the part of her that was trying to live smiled.

Suddenly, the feeling of needing to breathe overcame everything. She opened her mouth and tried to suck air in, but nothing happened. Her head involuntarily turned to the side and a startling amount of green-tinted water sprayed across the deck of the boat. Her chest expanded as she inhaled a massive breath of air. Another spray of greenish water came with the exhale, and in went another deep breath. Jackie's eyes opened. The fuzzy form above her wobbled around the periphery of what little vision she had, then all at once it came into focus. Her mother was straddling her, hands clasped, poised to perform another round of chest compressions. Their eyes met, and in a brief moment of singularity, they both knew that life had filled the void that death once controlled.

Caroline's head fell to Jackie's chest, "Oh thank God! I'd thought I'd lost you."

Jackie stared at the underside of the light station. The sky was a dreary gray that seemed to brighten with every second. Above them, several terns flew from under the structure. They were once ugly to her, but now they were the most beautiful things she'd ever seen. Another great cough came, a gasp, a gag, before finally she drew in a solid breath of air and all the fuses were connected once again. She blinked wildly and tried to talk.

Caroline laid a finger over her daughter's lips. "No, no, sweetie. Just breathe."

* * *

Jackie was still recovering when she heard a clotted cough. She struggled to sit up, and in the bow, she saw Caroline leaning over a familiar form.

GRANDDDAD!

226

Getting to her hands and knees, she crawled to them and reached for his hand. A pulse was there . . . weak, but steady. His shirt was open, and the wounds were raw and inflamed, but both holes were half-way closed. She remembered the Lieutenant's log book. His description of Corbin's neck and what she saw on her grandfather's chest and belly were a perfect match.

Not really knowing what to say, Jackie rubbed his hand, then placed it gently on his chest. She looked at Caroline and finally said, "You think he's okay?"

"I dunno. He's not conscious, but at least the bleeding's stopped. He seems to be breathing okay." She ran her hand along his back. "No holes back here, so the bullets must be still in him."

Jackie's heart sank a little. He was alive, but the water couldn't remove the bullets. That would have to happen in an operating room. Despite that sober realization, she almost smiled, whispering, "The water. It helped him. Charlie was right."

Caroline shook her head. "I dunno know what's going on here, but whenever we get a minute, you've got to tell me how tossing dad overboard saved him. And who's this Charlie?"

"I'll tell you everything, I promise." Jackie got to her knees and gazed across the water. "So how'd you—"

Caroline interrupted, "I dunno. I freaked when you jumped, and just about broke my neck getting down here. If we all make it off this thing alive, I'm going to come back some day and burn that damn rope ladder." She winced and showed Jackie the friction burns on her palms. "I was in the boat for just a few seconds when I saw this big bunch of bubbles come up. I didn't know if you or dad or both were dead. Then I saw you, or at least I thought it was you. It was just a blob at first, maybe twenty feet below, but then I realized it was you trying to swim. My mind went bananas. I couldn't think. You were really fighting, but I couldn't see him. I didn't know you were pulling up daddy too."

Jackie squeezed her sore left hand. "How'd you get us out? I didn't even see you. I was close, then it all went haywire, and something mashed my hand."

"That was me. You know I can't swim, but I'd made up my mind that I was going in after you. I'd gotten as far as the first step off the back of the boat when I saw your hand." Caroline grabbed both sides of her face and shook her head, "God, Jackie, I thought you were dead. Your mouth was open, and water was just pouring in. And your eyes! Geeze, your eyes opened twice their normal size, and the whites and all were glowing this bright snot-colored green." Caroline finally took a breath. "I pulled with everything I had and you came up, still holding daddy's wrist. I had to pry your hand off."

Caroline gave Jackie another big hug. It felt good, but there was no time to enjoy it. They had to act, and act fast. Hoyt Bennett was alive, but those two slugs still had to come out.

Chapter 42

Even in their shaken state, they both agreed that the Coast Guard was the only way. It was just breaking day, and by now, if McClendon followed through with their staged plans, there was probably more than one Jayhawk helicopter searching for missing bodies within sight of the beach. Surely a mayday report of gunshot wounds would turn one their way.

Jackie held her grandfather's hand and watched Caroline awkwardly make her way up the rope ladder. A tear rolled down her cheek, the first of many that were about to come as the dam was beginning to break. Before she fell apart, Hoyt squeezed her hand. Instantly composed, she looked at him through blurry eyes.

"Hey, granddaddy. Mom is trying to get the Coast Guard on the radio. Hold on and help will be here soon."

It was a gurgle, more than words, but Jackie leaned and listened. "I don't know what's in the water out here, but I feel fit as a fiddle."

"Shhh, don't talk now."

"How did you get me in the water? Damn, that hurt. It felt like somebody was sticking white hot fire pokers into those holes."

"Don't ask, and yeah, that hot poker is what I felt with my burn and with that cut. It hurt the worst when it was coming back together."

"This place ain't normal." He was talking better and actually tried to sit up on his elbows. It was too much for him though, and he winced, lying back against the fiberglass. "There's a lot of green down there. The report—the elements."

Jackie's own pain grew watching her grandfather wince, struggling to move. She gently squeezed his hand.

Hoyt coughed, then sucked in a big breath. "The generator powers the radio. Did you—"

"I told her."

"Good." Hoyt looked relieved, but his stare never left Jackie's face. "You know, there's not too many men that could've done what you did. I knew you had some grit in there somewhere. The barracuda, then Mason—" The old man laughed a little and his blue eyes shined. "You and your mother. Takes a lot to get you there, but when you finally do get mad, look out."

"Shhh. You don't need to be—"

"Now don't get bossy. I might have a couple of bullets in me, but I can still whoop you." He coughed again, and a thin ribbon of blood dribbled down his chin.

"You're still hurt, granddad. The water didn't fix you all the way."

"I'll make it. I've got a mean streak too. Where'd you think you and your ma got it from?"

Over the splash of the waves and the wind, Jackie heard yelling from above. It was Caroline.

"Oh no!" Jackie said out loud.

"What's wrong? Generator won't start?"

"She said the power cord to the radio has been cut."

The old man shook his head, "Damn you, Mason."

"Now what do we do?" Jackie's voice trailed off like the last gasps of a deflating balloon.

Hoyt pointed towards the center console. "The keys are in the switch. Check the boat's radio. And while you're at it, see how much fuel we have. Maybe he didn't think to dump the tanks, too."

Jackie made a face. "We can't get you back in this."

"We got out here in it, didn't we?"

"Yeah, but . . . but . . ."

"Quit butting, and start cranking."

Blood was now flowing across his lower lip, making a pink stain on the front of his shirt.

Jackie thought for a moment and said, "What if we put you back in the water? And then mom and I can work on the radio."

"That might work, but I don't think I'm ready to get back in just yet."

Jackie looked at him funny.

"Remember when I told you I'd only seen a couple of sharks out here? Well, I ain't real sure, but I came to while we were coming up. Looked like something big was swimming under us. Everything was kinda fuzzy though. Hell, it cudda just been a dream."

Jackie remembered the large fin she thought she saw. It was big, perhaps three feet from top to bottom. Jackie leaned and peered into the water. "A shark?"

"Maybe." He coughed and spit more blood. "Forget about it. The boat's radio will go twenty miles. We are a bit further than that, but you can try."

Jackie wiped the blood from his chin, then made her way to the controls. She turned the key and everything on the console instrument panel lit up. Quick eyes covered them, mentally checking each display, but below the GPS housing she saw something wrong. The power cord had been sliced almost in two between the unit and where it disappeared into a rubber grommet-covered hole in the console. The partly severed twist of bare copper wires shined like new pennies. She tapped the screen lightly, and the lights flickered on. She looked again at the fuel gauge.

"Over half a tank, granddad."

"That'll be more than enough."

"Can mom get us back?"

His voice was weaker, "She's never touched a boat's wheel, let alone run the engines."

But who's gonna—"

"You are, and don't give me any lip about it. I'm too tired and I hurt too much to argue with some shirt-tailed kid. You've come this far, no need to get shy now. Get us going, and use the boat's radio.

If you don't get an answer, give it a few minutes and try again. Everyone who's wet a line offshore knows where this place is. Just tell them you're coming straight at Wilmington from the Frying Pan. Those Jayhawkers will find us."

Chapter 43

While Jackie worked the radio, Caroline situated Hoyt on a mattress she'd brought down from one of the bedrooms. Moving slowly, she wrapped him snugly in a blanket and put a couple of pillows under his head. Jackie almost cried, watching her mother tenderly manipulating her grandfather's wounded body. She tried the radio again, but there was no answer.

Hoyt whispered something in Caroline's ear, and she turned to Jackie and said, "Daddy said just get us going, and keep trying the radio. While we're running we'll be getting closer to the coast."

Jackie swallowed hard, turned the key, and both engines whined, coughed, then died. She tried it again, and after a moment of indecision, both 225's roared to life then began their slow-roll purr, idling like two poised cats ready to spring.

Caroline loosened the rope on the bow cleat, and Jackie untied the one on the transom, then gently slid the boat in reverse. They were halfway clear when a wave rocked the boat, pushing them into the piling. The boat jerked and fiberglass sang, as the metal deeply gouged the outer hull.

The old man chuckled. "That's coming out of your paycheck, beach girl."

Free of the platform, Jackie turned west and pushed the dual throttle controls a quarter, then halfway down. The boat responded, pitching the bow upward, before leveling off at a decent speed. They both glanced at the larger boat anchored just off the rig as they went by. Jackie thought for a moment about seeing if it had a better radio, but she just pushed the throttles on the Grady White full forward. Fans of water shot from either side of the bow, sending a mist over them. The GPS began tracking their movement and the two dots on the screen began to separate.

Three minutes passed, and behind them, the horizon was blossoming a bright orange. Jackie tried the radio again. Still no answer. She hung the mic on the clip and double checked the GPS, running through the saved waypoints.

Caroline stepped beside her. "Guess he just had a little too much excitement. Pulse and breathing are good, he's just seems to be sleeping." She looked at the controls, then back to her daughter. Her worried face could have written volumes. "I heard you calling. Anyone answer?"

Jackie's eyes squinted against the wind. "Not yet, but we're still a long way out." She pointed to the GPS screen. Two dark spots were there, and one was slowly but steadily separating itself from the stationary one. She pointed at the one in the center of the screen. "This is us. The other one is the tower. All we have to do is head west and we'll run into land somewhere, but I know there's a Wilmington marina waypoint loaded on it somewhere. Plug that in, and we'll ride right to the dock."

While her fingers manipulated the buttons, the boat rose and fell hard over a larger than average wave, sending Jackie's hand hard forward. The unit caught all of her momentum, and the power cord tore completely free, finishing the job Mason LaRue started. The screen flickered, then went hopelessly blank. Jackie sucked in a deep breath as she unsuccessfully tried to catch the severed end before it fell through the grommet down into the console.

Caroline froze. "That was bad, right?" She cradled her head in her hands and screamed, "Damn it! What else can go wrong?"

Over their shoulders, the light station seemed to be a miniature replica of itself floating on the water. The sky above the horizon was a burning fire.

Caroline desperately said, "I know if we keep the sun at our back, we'll be heading more or less west. But we need to be aimed right at Wilmington. We don't have any tools here. Nothing to try to splice the cord back together." She pointed at the light station in the distance. "Let's turn around. I'm sure we can find something on it that will help."

Jackie closed her eyes and lowered her head. When they opened, the answer was right under her nose, staring back at her. The compass! The antiquated, almost forgotten staple of navigation was rocking gently in its fluid-filled globe.

"We don't need to go back," Jackie said tapping the compass with her finger. "Granddad showed me what to do. I can get us back." She recalled how unsteady the compass was in the rough seas on the way out there. Now, in the flatter water, it barely moved at all.

"How are we going—"

"The old compass. It'll get us home." Jackie thought for a moment, then asked, "What's the opposite of one thirty-seven?"

"What?"

Jackie rephrased the question. "I mean what's one thirty-seven plus one-eighty?"

Caroline ran the numbers. "Let's see, one thirty plus one eighty is . . . plus seven. Three-seventeen, why?"

Jackie hadn't turned the wheel since the GPS went down. She pointed at the white line in the compass' housing, "Its reading three-twenty. Pretty close to three-seventeen, huh?"

Caroline seemed to double check the math in her head. "You think you can get us in this way?"

Jackie nodded and picked up the mic again. "mayday, mayday. US Coast Guard, I've got a mayday on the Frying Pan Light Station."

There was a blast of squelch, then nothing. She tried the radio again. This time, a voice came in and out of the static. "We . . . you Frying . . . Station . . . at's your emergen—"

The broken words were music to her ears, and then she felt the warmness of the sun's rays on her back. Behind them, the light station was gone, swallowed by the horizon, and due east, the sun was climbing out of the sea. Jackie LaRue hooked a lock of strawberry-blond hair behind her ear and smiled. It was the fifth day in a row she'd seen the sunrise.